WELCOME TO ISAAC'S UNIVERSE— A BREATHTAKING FUTURE, REMARKABLE . . . AND POSSIBLE!

Incomprehensible dangers on a shifting world of ice and water forge unbreakable bonds between three vastly different races in Hal Clement's:
PHASES IN CHAOS

A woman teaches a winged creature to fly—and, in turn, learns the fine art of invective in Janet Kagan's:
WINGING IT

On a planet where emotions are visible, religion and entertainment are one in Lawrence Watt-Evan's:
KEEP THE FAITH

An outlaw destroys a holy city—and pays a terrible price in Allen Steele's:
MECCA

A daring rescue mission on a wilderness planet calls forth long-neglected survival skills in Poul Anderson's:
WOODCRAFT

Other Avon Books edited by
Martin H. Greenberg

Isaac's Universe Volume One:
The Diplomacy Guild

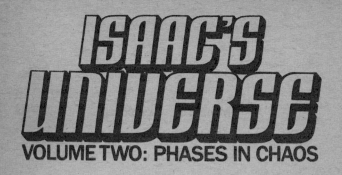

ISAAC'S UNIVERSE

VOLUME TWO: PHASES IN CHAOS

EDITED BY
MARTIN H. GREENBERG

WITH AN INTRODUCTION BY ISAAC ASIMOV

AVON BOOKS ◣ NEW YORK

ISAAC'S UNIVERSE: PHASES IN CHAOS (Vol. 2) is an original publication of Avon Books. This work has never before appeared in book form. This is a work of fiction. Any similarity to actual persons or events is purely coincidental.

AVON BOOKS
A division of
The Hearst Corporation
1350 Avenue of the Americas
New York, New York 10019

Cover illustration by Martin Andrews
Published by arrangement with the editor
Library of Congress Catalog Card Number: 91-91771
ISBN: 0-380-75752-4

First Avon Books Printing: July 1991

AVON TRADEMARK REG. U.S. PAT. OFF. AND IN OTHER COUNTRIES, MARCA REGISTRADA, HECHO EN U.S.A.

Printed in the U.S.A.

RA   10 9 8 7 6 5 4 3 2 1

To Isaac, with thanks

Contents

Introduction

CONCERNING TOLKIEN

ISAAC ASIMOV

IN MY INTRODUCTION TO THE FIRST VOLUME IN this series, I mentioned briefly that in inventing a multi-intelligence universe to serve as a background for these stories, I was influenced by E. E. Smith's stories of the *Galactic Patrol*.

And so I was—but in thinking about the matter since then, I realized that there was a second influence, much stronger than that first one. Why, I thought, did *Galactic Patrol* spring to mind and not *The Lord of the Rings*.

Actually, there's no mystery to it. *Galactic Patrol* was science fiction while *The Lord of the Rings* was fantasy—and when I was thinking up the background to *Isaac's Universe*, I was in a science fiction mode of thought.

So now let me break away from the bonds of sf and think about *The Lord of the Rings*.

The author of *The Lord of the Rings* was John Ronald Reuel Tolkien (1892-1973) who wrote as J. R. R. Tolkien. He was born in South Africa but lived in Great Britain as an Oxford don whose specialty was Anglo-Saxon.

In 1937, he published a children's story called *The Hobbit*. It was not, in my opinion, entirely successful. Tolkien was still feeling his way. In *The Hobbit*, he tended to write down to his readers with a kind of self-conscious coyness.

This, however, grew less marked as the story went on and Tolkien himself was caught up in it. The hero was Bilbo Baggins, the hobbit of the title, a humanoid creature about half the size of a man. The story involves the quest of a group of dwarfs to regain a treasure that once belonged to them but is now guarded by a malevolent dragon. Baggins is sent to accompany them by Gandalf (a wizard who makes his first appearance as a kind of conjurer).

Baggins goes along very much against his will, for he is scared to death. However, as the story proceeds, he grows more heroic (in a very convincing way) and by the closing scenes, he is dominant—with far more brains, more initiative, and more heroism than the other characters in the story.

In the 1950s, Tolkien decided to elaborate on *The Hobbit* and write a long, three-volume continuation designed for adults rather than for children. Bilbo makes his appearance at the start and there is much the same atmosphere as in *The Hobbit*, but he quickly passes on a new task to his nephew, Frodo, who is the hero of *The Lord of the Rings*, and with that the atmosphere changes, deepens, and becomes wholly absorbing.

The center of action is a ring, which Bilbo had come upon accidentally in the course of *The Hobbit* and which now turns out to be the key to universal power.

The story becomes a saga of the fight between good and evil. Good is represented by Frodo and his friends, and by his mentor, Gandalf, who is now portrayed as nearly all-powerful, and even, eventually, as a nearly Christ-like figure. Evil is represented by the Satan figure, Sauron, who needs only the ring to establish his already fearsomely great power permanently and absolutely. It is the task of our heroes, and of Frodo, in particular, to see that the ring is destroyed and to undertake an appallingly dangerous trek for that purpose.

The forces of good win out, but the difficulties are so great and the writing is so skillful that, even after repeated readings, the suspense holds. (I have read *The Lord of the Rings* five times.)

One wonders what was in Tolkien's mind. Actually, I don't like to try to guess the thoughts and motivations in an author's mind. I know, from personal experience, that clever analysts can find a great deal more in a novel than the author ever realized he had put in. (Yes, I have been victimized in this fashion, but I also know that despite my vehement denials that I meant this or that—I cannot entirely account for the workings of my unconscious mind.)

In the same way, Tolkien is reported to have denied any application of his saga to the events of the day or any tortured symbolism of various items in the novels— but I don't believe him.

To me, it seems obvious that Tolkien, between the writing of *The Hobbit* and *The Lord of the Rings*, lived through that dramatic and heart-stopping period in which Adolf Hitler and his Germans took over the control of the European continent in the space of ten months, and Great Britain found itself facing an overwhelming enemy without allies of its own.

If that wasn't Frodo versus Sauron, what was?—And Frodo won.

Another thing. What was this ring of power that all were fighting for? It was an evil ring which took possession of its owner and bent him, all unwittingly and all involuntarily, toward evil. Even Frodo, in the end, was affected and almost failed to carry out his mission. Obviously, the ring was something one feared but perversely wanted; something that once one had one could not let go.

What does that symbolize?

The answer came to me (and an obvious answer, too, once I had it) through a remark made by my dear wife, Janet.

Sauron rules over a region called Mordor, a blasted land in which nothing grows, a land destroyed by Sauron's evil, and one which Frodo must enter to complete his task. The description of Mordor is of a horrifying place.

Well, one day, Janet and I were driving along the New Jersey Turnpike, and we passed a section given over to oil refineries. It was a blasted region in which nothing was growing and which was filled with ugly, pipelike structures, which refineries must have. Waste oil was burning at the top of tall chimneys and the smell of petroleum products filled the air.

Janet looked at the prospect with troubled eyes and said, "There's Mordor."

And, of course, it was. And that was what had to be in Tolkien's mind. The ring was industrial technology, which uprooted the green land and replaced it with ugly structures under a pall of chemical pollution.

But technology meant power, and though it destroyed the environment and would eventually destroy the Earth, no one who had developed it dared give it up or even wanted to. There is no question, for instance, that America's automobiles pollute and filthify the atmosphere, and kill uncounted people with respiratory ailments. Yet is it conceivable that Americans would give up their automobiles, or even curtail their use somewhat? No, the ring of technology holds them in its grip and they won't give it up even if they are gasping for breath and dying.

(Mind you, I don't entirely agree with Tolkien's view of technology. I am not an Oxford don used to the calm pleasures of an upper-class Englishman in a preindustrial day. I know very well that the mass of humanity—including me and mine—derives what comfort they now have from the advance of technology and I do not want to abandon it so that upper-class Englishmen can substitute servants for machines. I don't want to be a servant. While I recognize the dangers of technology, I want those dangers corrected while keeping the benefits.)

Now comes the key question: What has all this to do with *Isaac's Universe*?

The Lord of the Rings is set on a mythological Earth, in which the very geography is unrecognizable. Human beings exist and there is a strong suggestion that they are in the process of taking over and that pretty soon "Middle Earth" (Tolkien's world) will become the Earth we live on.

In addition to human beings, however, there are a wide variety of other creatures. There are the elves, who are more beautiful and intelligent than human beings, and who are essentially immortal. They are creatures of the pleasant forests and may, for Tolkien, have represented the British preindustrial upper classes.

There were also dwarfs, strong and long-lived; ents who are virtual personifications of the forest; wizards like Gandalf, and, of course, hobbits, who clearly represent the tame farmers of preindustrial times.

On the side of evil are the orcs, who were called goblins in *The Hobbit* and who, to me anyway, are representative of the new industrial workers as seen by the disapproving upper-class eyes of Tolkien. In *The Hobbit* he has trolls who speak pure London cockney, but he abandoned that quickly as too broad a representation.

There are also individual creatures that seem to exist

all by themselves. On the side of good is Tom Bombadil, who represents nature; on the side of evil is the monstrous spider, Shelob, who perhaps represents the overpowering multinational conglomerates that now dominate Earth's economy.

There are superwolves on the side of evil, supereagles and a superbear on the side of good.

Most of all there is Gollum, who is, apparently, a hobbit perverted by the long possession of the ring, and who is the most ambiguous creature in the story. Within him is the constant battle between good and evil; and although the weakest and most helpless character in the saga, he manages, in some ways, to achieve the most. It is he, in fact, who, without meaning to, brings the tale to its satisfactory conclusion. I have always sympathized with Gollum and considered him more sinned against than sinning.

This rich mix of different types of intelligent creatures lends unimaginable strength and variety to *The Lord of the Rings* and it had to be in my mind when I thought up a universe with different types of intelligent creatures in it.

MECCA

ALLEN STEELE

TRANSCRIPT: TESTIMONY OF ARNE BEYNES; first officer, EIT *Capital Explorer,* as interrogated by Josep Colyns, special investigator, Diplomacy Guild. *(NOTE: this document is classified* Secret Alpha-Prime. Release is restricted only to members of the Diplomacy Guild with appropriate security clearance. Unauthorized disclosure is strictly prohibited.)

BEGIN TRANSCRIPT

COLYNS: What is your name, please?

BEYNES: You know that already.

COLYNS: This is for the official record.

BEYNES: Yeah? Then officially record this. *[Obscene gesture].*

COLYNS: Mr. Beynes . . .

BEYNES: Oh, so you do know my name, after all. . . .

COLYNS: Mr. Beynes, you should not have to be reminded of the gravity of your situation. You are the only survivor of the Erthuma Free Trader *Capital Explorer.* As such, you are the sole Erthuma witness to the only hostile incident to have occurred between Erthumoi and Locrians since there has been contact between the two races. According to Locrian emissaries, you are also responsible for this breach of the peace. You—

BEYNES: And you trust the word of the bugs more than

1

you do Erthumoi? You've got a problem, my friend. . . .

COLYNS: This is not a matter of whom we trust, Mr. Beynes, nor am I your friend. For the time being, we're trying to assimilate all the pertinent facts. That is the entire purpose of this interview. We need your cooperation to—

BEYNES: Assimilate *this!* The Locrians destroyed my ship! They destroyed the *Capital Explorer* and deliberately marooned me and four others on that *[obscenity deleted]* planet for—

COLYNS: There is also the matter of an important provision of the Erthma–Locrian trade agreements being broken. The *Capital Explorer* should not have been in the Epsilon Indi system, Mr. Beynes, regardless of everything else that has happened. Furthermore, the Locrians have specifically requested, and have been granted, exclusive landing privileges on Epsilon Indi II, the second planet of the system. Both of these protocols were ignored by you and your crew—

BEYNES: Eleven men dead, Colyns! Seven of them were lucky . . . they were killed as soon as the Locrians found us, Captain Francisco among them! The other four didn't get to die until much later! Who gives a *[obscenity deleted]* about your treaties and protocols? They killed my crew!

COLYNS: Just tell me what happened, please. We need to hear your side of the story before the guild can determine who was responsible.

BEYNES: Get lost. Where was the guild when we were dying out there?

COLYNS: The Diplomacy Guild was completely unaware of your situation on Epsilon Indi II. If we had known, we would have intervened on your behalf. But since you had not notified the Spacers Guild of your true destination when you left Wolf 630-3, they listed the

Capital Explorer as missing, presumed lost or destroyed. It was not until the Locrians returned you to Erthumoi space that we—

BEYNES: And that gets you off the hook, doesn't it. Get out of here, Colyns. I'm not talking to you.

COLYNS: As I said before, Mr. Beynes, there has been a serious rift in the peace between the Locrians and Erthumoi. What happened to the *Capital Explorer* is of vital concern to us, since it potentially compromises every treaty established among the Six Races. Now, we can extract the truth from you without your conscious cooperation, but these are processes which will not only take time, but also may be painful to you. In the end, they may eventually lead to the loss of some of your cerebral functions. But as I said, this is of upmost importance to us. If the alternative is war between the Locrians and Erthumoi, I will have no hesitation in suggesting that your mind should be sifted, even if that leaves you an imbecile. I would prefer to have your cooperation, though, if only for the reason that brain-sifting can be unreliable. Have I made myself perfectly clear to you, Mr. Beynes?

BEYNES: Yes.

COLYNS: Very well. Let's start at the beginning. Tell me how you found out about the Epsilon Indi II—

BEYNES: Mecca.

COLYNS: Pardon me?

BEYNES: Mecca. We stopped calling the planet Epsilon Indi II even before we got there. We called it Mecca. . . .

Wolf 630-3 was listed on Erthuma navigation charts as New France, but known by its settlers simply as Wolf; the latter name was far more appropriate. The third planet of the M-class star was cold, windswept, and largely barren except for an equatorial temperate zone where, at high noon on a midsummer day, the temperature sometimes soared as high as eighty degrees Fahrenheit. This was just enough to support the forests that renewed Wolf's oxygen-nitrogen atmosphere, but not much else; the rest of the planet was locked in a perpetual ice age, its northern continents glaciated, its southern regions mostly barren tundra. Wolf was an unkind world; it was habitable by Erthumoi, but only by a slim margin. People went there to make money, not to enjoy the climate or the scenery.

The settlement of Hellsgate probably had another name as well, but whatever it had once been called, that too was lost to all but the official record. Wolf's only two industries—mining and shipbuilding—were centered in Hellsgate. Raw materials mined in the southern tundra made their way to Hellsgate, where they were refined and processed and eventually became the hulls of starships: heavy freighters, mainly, although also occasionally an exploration ship or a trader came out of the shipyards. Hellsgate was not the sort of place which bred poets or philosophers or politicians. Its men and women had calloused hands and heavy, scarred faces, and their lives were measured either by a risky sort of longevity—how long they lived until some industrial accident crushed the life from their bodies—or by how long it took for them to amass enough credits to escape from Wolf.

Very often, though, the inhabitants of Wolf fell into a limbo between those extremes. It was in one of Hellsgate's many slums surrounding the shipyards that *Capital Explorer*'s first officer Arne Beynes found one of these cases, a blind man named Sedric.

"You said you had a bottle for me," Sedric said as he shoved open the door of his shack. It was a demand rather than a question. The old man felt his way around the wire-spool table in the middle of his one-room sheet-metal hovel while Beynes stood in the doorway, trying to see through the gloom.

The hovel smelled of grime and cheap booze and feces. If there was another chair in there besides the one which Sedric claimed, Beynes was reluctant to sit in it. "If you want a light," Sedric added, "you're going to have to find it yourself. Don't have much use for the things myself." He laughed as if that was the best joke in the galaxy; it brought up another wad of phlegm from his lungs, which Sedric hacked up and spat in the nearest available direction. It seemed to Beynes as if the way they had taken from the bar where he had found Sedric had been marked by the old duffer's cobs.

In the weak light cast through the open door from the sign above a skin theater across the road, Beynes spotted a pull cord hanging from the low ceiling. He grabbed it and yanked; a weak glow sprang from a bare, seldom-used bulb in the ceiling. Sedric's home looked even more disgusting in the light than it did in darkness: a bare mattress, a broken cabinet containing cans of bad food, a battered com terminal with a bashed-in monitor screen, a sink filled with rotting dishes and—incongruously enough—an ancient poster-print of a Deschenes painting stapled to the half-open bathroom door. Next to the table was a stool that looked safe enough to sit upon, though.

Sedric's head jerked a little as Beynes moved the stool and sat down. "Okay, you found the light and the other chair," he rasped. "Now where's the bottle?"

"Just wait a minute, all right?" Beynes unzipped his coat, reached into the inside pocket, and pulled out the fifth of cheap whiskey he had bought, on Sedric's insistence, before they had left the Wolf's Tooth. Beynes twisted open the seal and shoved it across the table into the blind man's filthy grasp. "Okay. Here. . . ."

"Thanks. You're a pal." As Sedric rocked his head back and drank with a greed that went far beyond thirst, Beynes checked his watch. He still had twelve standard hours left until the *Capital Explorer* was scheduled to lift from Wolf, following its refit in the shipyards, but the first officer didn't want to spend a minute more than was necessary in Sedric's home. He wondered what the hell he was doing here in the first place, although he already knew the answer to that: He and the crew were desperate for a profitable operation, especially since the debacle with the Crotonites. If we weren't on the verge of bankruptcy, Beynes thought, I wouldn't be bothering to check this out. . . .

On the other hand, this was a blind, alcoholic old geezer he had met in a burnt-out bar on a low-rent planet. It was entirely probable that the story Sedric had laid upon him in the Wolf's Tooth was a fabrication intended to lure Beynes into buying him another bottle of hooch—or worse. Eyeing the door behind him, Beynes gently slid back the hem of his coat to expose the grip of his blaster. Sedric himself couldn't take him on even if his eyes were still good, but there was no telling whether the old guy hadn't worked out a deal with one of his neighbors. . . .

"Take it easy, Arne," Sedric murmured, putting down the whiskey bottle. Irritatingly, he pronounced his first name as *Arn-nee*. "Relax. Take your hand off the gun. I'm on the straight level with you here."

He must have heard my hand moving my coat, Beynes thought. It was remarkable how much blind men could pick up from even the slightest audible clues. "Let's get to business, okay?" he said. "You said you knew something about the extragalactics."

"Maybe I do. . . ." Booze still dribbling down the corner of his mouth onto his crusty, unshaven chin, Sedric cocked his head back and forth. His eyes—dead white as fish skin, walleyed and eternally gazing in two separate directions at once—seemed at once to be completely vacant and holding mysteries only blind men can see. He shrugged. "And maybe I'm just a weird old drunk leading you down the primrose path."

Laugh. Hack. Spit. Beynes was getting fed up with this stuff very fast. He took the blaster out of its holster and carefully laid it on the battered tabletop. "And maybe I should just take your head off," he said, knowing that Sedric would interpret every sound he had just made. "One more weird old drunk found in the ghetto with a stump for a neck . . . who's going to give a damn?"

Sedric surprised him. He only grinned. "Nobody. But you won't find any ex-gees if you shoot my head off neither." The gap-toothed grin faded. "Straight info, Mr. Beynes, like I told you. Guaranteed to lead you and your shipmates to a planet where the ex-gees set down once. And . . ."

He knocked his fist against the tabletop. "It's right here in the local arm. You won't have to hyperjump to another part of the galaxy for this one. Hell, you can even see Sol while you're standing on it, if you look in the right direction."

Beynes stared at him. "You're crazier than you look. If it's that close to Old Earth . . ."

"Why didn't someone find it before?" More laughter and phlegm. "Let's just say the exploration teams and the Diplomacy Guild haven't been comparing notes as thoroughly as they should. Everyone overlooked this place, Arne. Right under their noses, and they let it go. Stupid jerks . . ."

Sedric shook his head and picked up the whiskey bottle again. "Practically just around the bend. Your ship can make it there within a day or two." He took another gulp of whiskey, sighed, and set the bottle back on the table. "But I'll let you know one thing for free. You'll have to break some laws to get to it. It's hands off to Erthumoi, and that's because it's someone else's territory. Okay? That's fair enough to tell you that before we've even made a deal."

Beynes didn't understand. "It belongs to one of the other five?" Sedric nodded. "Then they know about it already." Sedric shook his head. "But if they have a claim on it, then they must—"

"No, they don't," Sedric said with convincing finality. The . . . uh, the race we're talking about . . . they don't know themselves what they've got, and they don't visit this place often enough to find out for themselves. So it's there for the taking, and I shouldn't have to remind you what's being paid for info leading to the ex-gees these days."

He crossed his arms across his shrunken chest and leaned back in his chair. "That's all you get to know for free, First Mate." Despite his drunkenness, Sedric seemed to have taken on a hue of absolute credibility. "The rest comes only when you put the money on the table."

Beynes began to inch his right hand toward his gun. "Don't think about it," Sedric added. "Like I said, you won't know nothing if my brain's been blown to atoms."

Gritting his teeth in frustration, Beynes inched his hand away from the blaster. "How much?"

Sedric sucked in his breath. "Fifty thousand. On the table." He smacked a hand on the top of the spool. "Cash. And don't tell me you have to go back to your ship to get it. First mates always carry that much in order to bail out crew members who get in trouble during shore leave."

"You're crazy." Beynes immediately slid back the stool and stood up.

"Don't play with me, boy," Sedric hissed. "Fifty thousand or nothing. I'm sick of living in this dump, and I've been waiting for an opportunity like this for a long time now. Fifty gets you the system, the planet,

everything you need to know to make a major find."
He hesitated. "Three choices, Mr. Beynes. Kill me,
walk out of my house, or put fifty on the table and we
start talking. Two ways leave you empty-handed . . .
the third makes you rich."

Beynes stopped. His hand hovered above his blaster.
"If the info's that valuable," he asked, "why haven't
you used it before?"

The old blind man smiled. "I'll tell you when you
put the money on the table." He shrugged. "You
haven't picked up your gun yet, so you've got nothing
to lose," he said gently. "Put your money on the table,
Arne, and you get the rest."

Arne Beynes slowly sat down on the stool again.
He reached into another inside pocket of his coat,
pulled out his wallet, and counted out ten high-
denomination notes onto the table. As each note
landed on the table, Sedric picked it up, gently
rubbed it between his fingertips, measuring the
width of the paper and the distinctive notches in
the corners. Once the money was counted, Sedric
folded it all together and shoved it into a pocket
of his filthy trousers.

"The star system you want is Epsilon Indi," he
began. "The planet is Epsilon Indi II—"

"What's its name?" Beynes asked.

"It doesn't have a name," Sedric replied. "The
Locrians won't give it one. If you want to call it something, call it Mecca."

COLYNS: How did Sedric know about Mecca?
BEYNES: I don't know. He wouldn't tell me everything
. . . I guess as insurance that I wouldn't kill him . . .
but it's pretty easy to figure. Stuff gets around a place
like Hellsgate, where a lot of ships tend to come and
go. Stories get handed down from crew to crew, especially in joints like the Wolf's Tooth. It's garbage most

of the time, but this guy seemed to have a handle on things. I guess he heard rumors about ex-gee artifacts in the Epsilon Indi system, did some checking until he put things together, then waited until he found someone who was willing to meet his price.

COLYNS: Or someone who was willing to take the risk, you mean. It's not a secret that the Locrians had made a claim to Epsilon Indi II. When the guild formed our trade agreements with them, they were very explicit about it, since that star system is located only eleven light-years from Old Earth. Because there wasn't much in that system which interested Erthumoi—

BEYNES: The Diplomacy Guild was only too happy to give them what they wanted. I know that.

COLYNS: Then you should also know why the Locrians were so insistent. That planet has considerable spiritual significance to one of the major Locrian religions, the Far Travelers. They consider it to be a sacred world, a holy place from which all wisdom and knowledge spring forth. During the ninth month of each of the planet's years, members of the Far Travelers make a hegira, a pilgrimage, to Epsilon Indi II, where they meditate and worship. For that reason, the Locrians wanted the planet to remain untouched by Erthumoi.

BEYNES: Sure. That's why my source called it Mecca. Something to do with one of the Old Earth religions, I guess. But do you know why the Locrians consider Epsilon Indi II to be a sacred world?

COLYNS: The Far Travelers don't discuss their beliefs with anyone, rarely even other Locrians, from what we know of them. Even their name for the planet is unknown except amongst themselves. Until the *Capital Explorer* went there, no Erthumoi had ever set foot on Epsilon Indi II. But you say you had heard of extragalactic artifacts there. . . .

BEYNES: That's why we went, sure.

COLYNS: But planetfall by Erthumoi, or by any of the

other Six Races besides members of the Far Travelers
on Epsilon Indi II is strictly prohibited by galactic law.
I don't see how you could have possibly thought you
could get away with it, or what you could gain by—
BEYNES: Come on, Colyns. You should know better
than that. There's a high reward for any artifacts that
might lead Erthumoi to the ex-gees. We were business
people, first and foremost. If we managed to find something on Mecca worth salvaging, we could have all
been rich. And nobody would have had to know exactly
where the artifacts had come from, either. We could
have claimed that the discovery had been made on any
planet or moon in one of any number of neighboring
systems. And since the Far Travelers were supposed to
visit the Epsilon Indi system only once during each
sidereal calender, the chances of the Locrians dis-
covering that we had been there were almost null. At
least until we had found what we wanted and made our
getaway, that is.
COLYNS: So you thought it was the perfect crime.
BEYNES: I wouldn't call it a crime, no. It was more
like a business opportunity.

Captain Francisco was drunk by the time the *Capital
Explorer* reached Mecca; this was nothing unusual,
even if it was insulting to the bridge crew. As soon as
the free trader came out of hyperspace at Epsilon Indi's
heliopause on the outer fringes of the five-world system, the captain had put his first officer in charge of
the bridge, gone down to his cabin, and opened his first
bottle of wine as the ship moved down-system.
   Eight hours later, when helmsman Ahmad reported
that standard orbit had been achieved around Epsilon
Indi II, Francisco was still conscious but hopelessly
inebriated. He staggered back to the bridge, demanded
Beynes get out of his damn chair, then proceeded to
order the dropship to be readied and for a six-person

landing party to be convened. The irony of the situation was not lost on Beynes; the *Capital Explorer* had come to Epsilon Indi II on a lead given by one wet brain, and it was making planetfall under the guidance of another.

"If we make enough from the salvage," he later murmured to D'Lambert as they stood in the dropship bay watching the excavation robots being loaded into the lander's cargo hold, "we should consider buying up Francisco's shares."

The science officer smiled as he gently stroked his beard. "Watch your mouth, Arne," he said softly. "You keep talking like that and it could begin to sound like mutiny."

"Mutiny?" Beynes grinned and shook his head. "I prefer to think of it as renegotiation of our contracts."

As a free trader, the *Capital Explorer* was owned and operated by its own crewmen. Once the ship's overhead costs were met, the profits from its ventures were split according to the number of shares each crewman owned in the ship. Francisco was the *Capital Explorer's* captain not so much out of experience as by the fact that he owned the most shares. But Beynes and D'Lambert between them owned just as many shares as Francisco. Not only that, but Beynes had logged as much time in hyperspace as Francisco—and, unlike the captain, the first officer's sense of command was not lost in a bottle. If this trip was profitable enough, they could probably buy up Captain Francisco's shares. And the way things had been going recently for the *Capital Explorer,* Francisco was overdue for a long, happy retirement . . . probably comatose on the floor of some spaceport beer joint. There wasn't much difference between Francisco and Sedric, come to think of it.

D'Lambert eyed the captain with disdain. Potbellied and unshaven, he was swaggering around the bay, shouting redundant orders to the crewmen who were preparing the dropship for flight. "Not that it isn't a bad idea, whatever you want to call it," he added with dour humor. "Of course, if you think the captain's ripped now, just wait till we get planetside."

"Hmm?" Beynes glanced at the science officer. "What do you mean?"

"The atmosphere."

"What about it? I thought you said it was oxygen-nitrogen."

"It is," D'Lambert said. "But the average pressure is only sixty-nine torr. That's kind of thin for Erthumoi." He nodded toward the last of the excavation robots as it lumbered up the ramp into the dropship. "That's why I recommended that we bring down the 'bots. We're all going to be a little light-headed down there, and manual labor will be hard enough as it is."

Beynes grunted. "But I guess the atmosphere is all right for the Locrians."

Yet D'Lambert shook his head. "No, it isn't," he replied. "That is what's funny about the place. The atmosphere might be a little thin for us, but it's still too dense for the Locrians. Neon content is just a bit scarce for their liking too. Oh, sure, Locrians *could* live there without breathing apparatus . . . but they'd be in a daze most of the time." He shrugged. "I don't get it."

It *was* strange. Epsilon Indi II orbited a K5-class orange dwarf, just like the Locrian's native star, but it was almost fifty thousand light-years from the Locrian home world in the Cygnus arm of the galaxy. The Far Travelers had come a long way to settle a planet that was just on the fringe of habitability for their race. Yet D'Lambert's scan of the planet's barren surface had found an indistinct cluster of objects near the planet's equator that were undoubtedly artificial. There were no life readings from the scan—without a doubt, the settlement was abandoned—yet it appeared as if Locrians had lived on this desert planet at one time. But why *here*, of all places? It didn't make any—

The communicator on his belt buzzed, interrupting his train of thought. Beynes unclipped it and held it to his face. "First officer," he said.

"Arne, this is Ahmad." The helmsman voice sounded distraught. "We've got a problem."

As Ahmad spoke, Beynes noticed that Captain Francisco, who was standing not far away, had looked up at the sound of his first officer's communicator buzzing. There was a look of suspicion on his face, and already the captain was beginning to lurch toward Beynes and D'Lambert. Terrific, Beynes thought. The helmsman had undoubtedly notified the first officer because he knew that the captain was too crocked to responsibly handle any problems; despite his discretion, though, Francisco wanted to hone in on the act. No way it could be helped, though . . .

"Give it to me straight," Beynes said, as D'Lambert stepped a little closer to overhear what was being said.

"Sensors just located a Locrian satellite in low orbit," Ahmad reported. "We didn't pick it up earlier because it was over the far side of the planet from our orbital position, but we caught up to it as we came over the limb. As soon as we spotted it, the com officer told me that it transmitted a hyperspace signal on a Locrian frequency. Bad news, Arne. I think it's a sentinel."

"Damn!" Beynes hissed. If the Locrian satellite was an automatic sentry, then the Locrians were probably finding out just now that an unidentified vessel was making an illegal visit to their territory. He shot a look at D'Lambert; the science officer silently shook his head. They were in trouble.

"Okay, Ahmad," Beynes said. "We're going to scrub the drop. I want you to ready the engines for a quick getaway and reprogram the computers for hyperjump into the nearest available system within a parsec. If we—"

All at once, the communicator was snatched out of Beynes's hand. "Belay that order, helm!" Francisco rasped, roughly shoving his first officer out of the way. "What's going on up there?"

The captain blearily listened as Ahmad repeated himself. "Who the hell says you can sh— I mean scrub the drop?" he slurred. "You don't take your orders from Number One, Mishtuh Ahmad, you ged'dem from me! Now destroy that bug satellite an' ged ready to send th' dropship!"

"Captain—" Beynes began.

"And you shaddup!" Francisco shouted, jabbing a forefinger at Beynes's face. The first officer stepped back, repelled as much by the rancid smell of wine on Francisco's breath as by his anger. "Yer not the cap'n, Beynes! *I'm* the cap'n!"

D'Lambert hesitantly took a step forward. "Captain Francisco," he said diplomatically, "if the Locrians know we're here, they'll undoubtedly come to investigate. We don't want to be anywhere near—"

"We'll be outta here long before they geddere." Francisco drunkenly swept his right arm in the general direction of some imaginary place of refuge, his left hand still holding Beynes's communicator to his face. "We got *hours* 'fore they get here! Now destroy that satellite, helm! We're proceeding with the drop! Cap'n out!"

Francisco shoved the communicator into Beynes's chest. "Don't get cute wi' me again, Beynes," he growled as Beynes fumbled for the handset. "Next time you try somethin' like this, it's mutiny, and I'll be only too happy t'haul you inna the airlock and push th' button. Y'got that?"

"Yes, sir, Captain," Beynes said stiffly.

"Futh'more—" Francisco belched and went on.

"Furthermore, I wonchu inna landing party with me. You too, D'Lambert, because I wan' you . . ."

He searched his fogged brain for the correct word. "Your *expertise*," he finished. Then he glared at Beynes. "An' because I don't trust you with my ship. Y'unnerstand?"

Beynes said nothing. D'Lambert was also silent. Captain Francisco staggered back a couple of steps, sucking in his gut and gloating like a barroom thug who had just bullied a smaller man into buying a round for the whole house. "Carry on, men," he said haughtily, then began to swagger back to the waiting dropship.

Beynes slowly let out his breath and shot a look at D'Lambert. The science officer slowly shook his head. "Whatever the ex-gees left down there," D'Lambert whispered, "I only hope that they put it in plain sight."

COLYNS: You're saying that, during this incident, Captain Francisco was drunk and behaving rashly.

BEYNES: Colyns, the captain was always drunk and behaving rashly. That's one of the reasons why we were willing to risk going to Mecca in the first place. The *Capital Explorer* was losing money because of him. Once we got screwed in a deal with the Crotonites because Francisco was stoned when he was at the negotiating table with them. I mean, it's hard enough to get a fair deal with them even when you're cold sober, and he went into a trade negotiation with them after drinking for six hours straight. A couple of more trips like that, and we would have been bankrupt.

COLYNS: It sounds to me like you're trying to pass the blame onto a dead man.

BEYNES: That's because I'm not the only one to blame! I tried to get us out of the system when Ahmad discovered the orbital sentry!

COLYNS: But you were the one who recommended the voyage to Epsilon Indi II—

BEYNES: To make up for everything we had lost because of Francisco. I'm telling you, we were that close to having to put the *Explorer* up for auction. If we could have found ex-gee artifacts worth selling . . .

COLYNS: And what did you find on the planet?

BEYNES: Not what we were expecting.

The relentless glare of the orange sun caused the thin air of Mecca to shimmer above the hard rock and sand of its flat landscape. The world was one large desert, simultaneously banal and hostile. Beynes unknotted the bandana from around his neck and passed it across his face, sponging up the sweat once again. He peered at the grimy rag before he carelessly pulled it around his neck again; he couldn't wait to get back to the *Capital Explorer*, if only to take a shower. Epsilon Indi II was a dead whore of a planet . . . a dead whore with nothing in her purse worth stealing.

No: wrong simile. A landfill—that was a far more accurate description. The ex-gees left a complete city on the moon of that planet in the W49 nebula, the one found not long ago by the *Achilles* which had awakened the Six Races to the existence of the extragalactics. Here on Epsilon Indi II, though, there was only an open pit filled with bits of metal and glass debris, waste that even the ex-gees couldn't recycle. From not far off, near *Capital Explorer*'s dropship, Beynes could hear the rumble of the excavation robots as they scooped up dirt from the bottom of the pit, searching through the pit for anything of consequence. Most of the landing team were standing at the lip of the pit, idly watching the robots, perhaps still hoping that the machines would uncover something worth salvaging beneath the layers of rubbish.

Little chance of that, however. Beynes could still

hear D'Lambert's words, after the science officer had wheezed his way out of the craterlike pit near the landing site to pronounce his verdict on their find. *The extragalactics might have landed here once*, he had said, *but if they did, it was only to dump their trash. An archeologist might find something interesting in all this junk, but there's nothing here we can take to the bank. Sorry, Arne, but that old drunk on Wolf sold you a red herring.* Then he had returned to the bottom of the pit to rummage through the debris some more, in the futile hope that he could still unearth something which the robots might miss. Beynes had communicated with him only ten minutes ago, and D'Lambert had only treated him to an earful of obscenities.

The ex-gees had left behind a trash pit . . . but the Locrians had left something much more interesting. Beynes turned to gaze again at the city located a couple of hundred meters away. The word "city" seemed inappropriate for the cluster of high, domelike mounds which lay not far from the pit. D'Lambert had been the first to make sense of the earthworks; he compared them to the domes that termites on Old Earth constructed from the soil in the Australian outback. Since the Locrians were, in the most general sense, highly evolved insects, it would make sense that they were responsible for the domes.

The city—village, colony, sand castles, termite domes, whatever the hell you wanted to call it—seemed to glisten in the sunlight; despite its rudeness, it seemed to have a stark, weird majesty of its own. Beynes and D'Lambert had ventured within twenty meters of the settlement, as far as they dared to go without leaving footprints which could not be easily raked over before the dropship left. Even from that cautious distance, they could see doorways and windows within the fragile-looking domes, all just the right size for Locrians. More importantly, though, it seemed as if the Locrians had used material from the ex-gee landfill to strengthen the walls: there were shards of glass and metal and polycarbon alloys in the domes, all of which matched the alien trash in the landfills. It was probably the only use that could ever be derived from the junk left in the pit. D'Lambert compared this to Erthuma artifacts which were sometimes found lining the nests of non-sapient creatures; similarly, the Far Travelers had undoubtedly plundered the landfill to build their settlement.

But why such primitive dwellings for a starfaring race? Had the Locrians forgotten how to construct better shelter for themselves while they were here? Or was this just their way of going native? Maybe this is where the bugs head when they want to go wilderness camping. . . .

The air's getting to me, Beynes thought, shaking his head. He was getting light-headed already. D'Lambert had warned him about this. He checked the chronometer on his wrist. Still a couple of hours left within the safety margin between the launch time of the dropship and the ETA of the first Locrian starship. However, Ahmad had reported only a few minutes earlier from the *Capital Explorer* that the ship's long-range sensors had detected nothing on the fringes of the system. No hyperspace disturbances, no vessels of either Locrian or Erthuma registry; there was nothing else in the system since the Locrian satellite had been torpedoed. You should be grateful, Beynes told himself. Even if nothing on this dustball will pay our bills, at least we'll still get out of here without—

His communicator buzzed. Beynes unsnapped it from his belt and held it to his face, but even before he could speak, Francisco's voice grated through the earpiece: "What have you got for me, Beynes?"

You mean like a long-lost bottle of ex-gee booze? Beynes sighed as deeply as he could in the sparse atmosphere—that unconscious gesture was enough to make him a little more giddy—but he held his tongue. Francisco had been out on Mecca's surface for only a few minutes before he had retreated to the dropship. The slob was undoubtedly "supervising" the operation from the lander's flight deck, nursing a wicked hangover and counting the hours until he was safely back in his quarters on the *Capital Explorer*, cuddling up with another drink against his not-unfounded paranoia about mutiny. "Nothing yet, Captain," he said steadily. "It's a trash pit, just as the science officer theorized earlier. I don't think we're going to—"

"I don't care what you think," Francisco interrupted. "What about the Locrian city? Anything in there worth getting?"

Beynes brow furrowed. "Captain, I don't think . . . I don't believe we should be messing with the Locrian settlement. We're already on shaky ground just by landing here. Going into the city could be dangerous, even if there was anything in there we could salvage. From the looks of it, I don't think—"

"And I just told you that I don't give a damn what you think or believe, Beynes!" Francisco shouted. "Your opinion is worthless to me! We didn't come halfway across the local arm just for you to be concerned about some abandoned bug digs. Now I want you to get D'Lambert and a couple of men and—"

All of a sudden, Francisco's voice was interrupted by a high-pitched triple beep. It took Beynes a half instant to recognize it as the signal for an emergency comlink override; as the listless fog in his head evaporated, Ahmad's voice came over the communicator. "Landing party, this is the *Explorer!*" the helmsman yelled. "Priority alpha-three-two emergency!"

Alpha-three-two was a rarely used Erthuma code: It meant that a starship was under possible attack in space. Beynes didn't wait for Francisco to remember his responsibilities or even to make the appropriate encoded reply. "Ahmad, this is Beynes! Report on conditions!"

"Locrian vessel has just come out of hyperspace above planet surface! Same orbit, range four hundred kilometers and closing! Repeat, we've got a Locrian vessel near us!"

Beynes froze. A Locrian ship coming out of hyperspace this close to a planet? That was a near-suicidal maneuver a ship's commander would only risk if . . . *no!* "Hail friendly!" he shouted. "Ahmad, hail friendly!"

Pause. In the background, he could hear emergency alarms and indistinct voices shouting across the bridge of the orbiting trader. "No reply to friendly hails on standard channels, Arne! Range two hundred kilometers and closing—!"

Suddenly, Francisco's voice broke across the comlink. "Helm, arm and fire weapons!" he screamed. "Repeat, arm all weapons and fire!"

"No!" Beynes shouted into the communicator, instinctively glancing up at the hazy blue sky above the city. "Belay last order, Ahmad! Repeat, don't—!"

There was a sudden, harsh *sqqqaaaawwnnkkkk!* over the comlink: the unmistakable sound of an electromagnetic pulse caused by a nuclear explosion. An instant later a miniature supernova flared in the sky above the western horizon.

"Ahmad!" Beynes shouted. "*Capital Explorer,* this is Beynes, please respond! *Ahmad . . . !*"

Static fuzz had permanently replaced Ahmad's panic-stricken voice. Beynes watched, breathless and open-mouthed, as thin white streaks began to plummet across the highest reaches of Mecca's stratosphere. Through the roaring in his ears, he could hear the horrified screams of the rest of the landing party gathered near the ex-gee trash pit. Beynes wanted to scream himself, but his breath seemed to have been sucked out of his lungs as he watched the remains of his ship disintegrate in Mecca's upper atmosphere. The Locrians, the Locrians, the Locrians had just . . .

"Clear ship!" he abruptly heard Francisco yell through the communicator.

Clear ship . . . ? As often as Beynes had heard this command, it still took him a moment to realize just what Francisco meant. Even then, Beynes wasn't certain. He lifted the communicator to his numbed face again. "Captain, I don't—"

There was a sudden roar from behind him, an overwhelming nuclear-fusion pulse which was louder than the blood in his ears. A sirocco swept around him, dust kicked up by the hot blast of an artificial wind, and a miniature earthquake trembled beneath his boots. Even before Beynes could turn around, he recognized the sound of the dropship's engines being quick-started. Sand stung his face, forcing him to his knees, as he clenched the communicator to his mouth and shouted, "Francisco—!"

"Ship up!" the captain shouted.

"Francisco!" Beynes screamed. Through the sandstorm, he could see the massive shape of the dropship ponderously rising on white-hot pillars of exhaust from its thrusters. The vessel ascended twenty meters, thirty, fifty, its landing gear still carelessly extended; the captain was abandoning them, leaving them in this hellhole, making his own escape from the wrath of the Locrians. . . .

"Francisco," he howled, "you *bastard . . . !*"

Then the spacecraft seemed to list to starboard and pitch forward, as drunkenly as Beynes had seen Francisco himself lurch through the corridors of the *Capital Explorer,* losing altitude but picking up velocity as the captain fought the controls. Already Beynes knew what was wrong. Pages of flight instruction manuals seemed to sweep past his mind's eye, warnings of what could go wrong . . . *you don't take off like that; you haven't got enough power; you can't* . . . as he threw himself flat upon the ground.

The last thing Beynes saw—just before he covered his head with his arms, as he dimly heard Francisco's last desperate, infuriated screams through the communicator still clutched in his hand—was the final glimpse of the dropship hurtling straight toward the lost city of the Locrians. Then there was the ear-shattering explosion and the fireball. . . .

COLYNS: Why did the dropship crash?

BEYNES: I figure that Francisco didn't prime the engines correctly for lift-off. I mean, you can't just hop in a ship, push a few buttons, and off you go. You can make a quick-start launch of a dropship by skipping a few details, but if you don't do everything exactly right, the fusion reactors will simply shut themselves down to prevent an implosion. The engines won't sustain thrust for escape velocity and . . . y'know, down you go.

COLYNS: So you think the destruction of the Locrain settlement was an accident?

BEYNES: Do I think . . . haven't you been listening to me? I saw what happened, Colyns. The dropship plowed right into the city. We were just lucky that the reactors had already been scrammed by the computers or there would have been a five-klick crater where we were standing.

COLYNS: I'm simply trying to get all the facts straight for the official record, Mr. Beynes—

BEYNES: Then get this straight, Colyns . . . whatever else we meant to do on Mecca, destroying the Locrian settlement was not one of them. D'Lambert and I went out of our way to keep out of the city, even after Francisco demanded that we start looting the place. The last thing we ever intended to do was even get near the city. It was an accident, I'm telling you! Francisco did it!

COLYNS: I understand, Mr. Beynes. Your assertion is part of the record. Now, please tell me what happened when the Locrians arrived. Were there any hostile acts by you or any of the survivors of your landing party?

BEYNES: No, there weren't. But not that we didn't want to. . . .

When they spotted the Locrian lander entering the atmosphere, almost everyone wanted to barricade themselves within the rubble of the city and take out as many of the bugs as they could. The destruction of the *Capital Explorer,* the sudden deaths of their crewmates, Francisco's death: All were still fresh in their minds. They wanted revenge, pure and simple, regardless of who might be at fault.

But only three members of the landing party were armed with blasters, and although it was suggested that the robots be jury-rigged to ram the Locrian lander once it made touchdown, it was quickly pointed out by D'Lambert that the machines were strictly designed for mining operations, not war maneuvers. Any plans for attacking the Locrians, therefore, were predestined for failure . . . and once the huge Locrian vessel landed and the aliens began to emerge from its hatches, their sheer numbers made it apparent that the surviving Erthumoi were outnumbered by at least six to one.

It therefore came to pass that, within an hour of the dropship's crash in the city, the five surviving crewmen of the *Capital Explorer* found themselves surrounded by twenty-two armed Locrians. The tall insectile aliens towered around them, their exotic-looking weapons held steady in their four spindly arms. Their guns were not pointed directly at any of the Erthumoi, yet they were not completely turned away either. Despite the

compatible environment, the guards all wore bubble-
helmeted breathing gear, obviously to keep themselves
from becoming delirious in the too rich atmosphere.
Through the helmets, Beynes could hear them speaking
to one another, an arcane chittering which caused their
mandibles to twitch rapidly. If a universal translator
was available, he might have been able to understand
what they said, but their translators had all been in the
dropship when it had crashed: One more curse to add
to Captain Francisco's unbeloved memory.

Yet it wasn't the guards who most attracted the first
officer's attention. It was the behavior of a second,
smaller group of Locrians which had come down the
lander's ramp behind the armed force. Eight Locrians,
all of them wearing long red cloaks; the hoods were
thrown back because they apparently didn't fit over
their helmets. They followed the guards to the small
group of nervous Erthumoi and stood together behind
the ring of armed Locrians, silently waiting until all of
the landing party had been surrounded.

"Far Travelers," D'Lambert murmured to Beynes.
"That must be what the robes—"

"Silence, please." The filtered, translated voice
came from one of the red-robed Locrians, standing in
the middle of the group. He wore a translator on his
narrow, carapaced chest. Beynes knew that Locrians
could speak the Erthumoi standard language, but that
was only on diplomatic occasions; this one apparently
wanted to distance himself, if only subtly. "You will
not speak until you are directly addressed," the Locrian
continued. "Disarm yourselves immediately."

There was no overt threat in that demand, but when
confronted by almost two dozen Locrian weapons, the
implication was nonetheless final. D'Lambert and
another crewman carefully unholstered their blasters
and gently tossed them at the feet of the Locrians stand-

ing nearest to them. Beynes was more hesitant in ridding himself of his only means of protection.

"I'm First Officer Arne Beynes of the EIT free trader *Capital Explorer* . . ." he began.

The Locrian closest to him took a single step forward, the weapon in its hands swiftly training upon Beynes's face. "Be silent and disarm yourself, First Officer Arne Beynes," the Far Traveler demanded.

Beynes took a deep breath of the thin air, then obediently unbuckled his blaster and tossed it, belt and all, past the Locrian guard who had advanced upon him. The Locrian stepped back into the circle again, its weapon once more returning to a ready position. A couple of Locrians chittered at each other; one of the aliens hastily scuttled around the circle, confiscating the Erthuma sidearms. Beynes realized that he and his crew mates were now completely at the mercy of the Far Travelers and their escorts. A sickening sense of helplessness clawed into his guts.

"Who are you?" he said. "What do you intend to do with us?"

There was a brief moment of hesitation from the Far Traveler who had spoken. "I have been designated Speaker-to-Erthumoi," it said at last. "Your fate will be decided shortly by myself and my breathren. That is all. Be silent now."

This was too much for him to endure. "Silent, hell!" Beynes snapped. "You've destroyed my vessel, you green bug-eyed—!"

The Locrian guard near him lowered his weapon and fired; five centimeters of rock and sand were vaporized between Beynes's feet. The first officer jumped back, staring at the guard who had just fired. "Your guy just shot at me!" he yelled.

"If he had meant to fire at you," Speaker-to-Erthumoi responded, "you would be one with the universe now. Your ship was destroyed because it was preparing to fire upon us. We monitored your communications and know this is true. We regret this fatal action, yet we were forced to protect ourselves.''

''That was a mistake!'' D'Lambert protested. ''We didn't . . .''

Another Locrian leveled the maw of his weapon at the science officer. Beynes grabbed his arm to shut him up. ''Be silent,'' Speaker-to-Erthumoi commanded. ''Nonetheless, you are guilty of trespass and the destruction of holy ground. Your penance will soon be decided upon.''

Again, Speaker-to-Erthumoi seemed to hesitate. Then, from underneath his long robe, he extracted a flat case which Beynes recognized as a multilanguage book. The Far Traveler opened its clamshell lid, touched a couple of studs, then closed it and tossed it through the circle of guards into the blackened hole in the soil left by the Locrian disintegrator. ''If it helps you to understand,'' it said, ''you shall read this.''

There was a little more untranslated chittering, this time between the Far Travelers and their escorts, then the eight robed Locrians turned and began to walk away.

As a group, the acolytes went directly toward the destroyed city where a black pillar of smoke still rose from the scorched wreckage of the dropship where it lay on top of the crushed, caved-in domes. The hulk looked like a massive child's toy that had been carelessly dropped upon a cluster of anthills; for the first time in the past hour, Beynes began to look at the destruction through the huge, multifaceted eyes of the Locrians. He wanted to call out to Speaker-to-Erthumoi, to insist that it wasn't *his* fault, that *he* hadn't been responsible for the irreparable damage done to their city. . . .

Yet it was not just the threat of the guard's weapons

that choked his words in his throat. Beynes glanced at D'Lambert. The science officer met his gaze for a moment, then he stoically looked away to watch the Far Travelers. Perhaps the same dark thoughts had occurred to him.

The Locrian disciples stopped just outside the ruins of their city. As one, they slowly kneeled in front of their shattered domes in a semicircle that seemed to mirror the positions of the guards around the Erthumoi. Then, to Beynes's astonishment, they unfastened their helmets and removed them from their heads. Very few members of any of the Six Races had ever seen one another without breathing apparatus of one kind or another. For the briefest of moments, the heads of the eight Locrians were as bare as those of the Erthumoi standing nearby. Then they raised the hoods of their cloaks to cover their elongated skulls, and the Far Travelers were still.

Still, but not mute. Even from the distance, Beynes could barely hear them conversing with one another, their alien language carried to him by the hot breeze which ruffled their robes. The guards around the Erthuma landing party remained silent, watching the Erthumoi through their helmeted eyes.

Beynes remembered the book that Speaker-to-Erthumoi had tossed at his feet. Kneeling down, he carefully picked it up, wiped away the sand, and unfolded the cover. The book had been programmed for Erthuma. He sat down and switched it on, and as the rest of his crewmen kneeled and sat around him—carefully maintaining their silence but reading over his shoulder—Beynes began to page through the hypertext.

Unnoticed, the shadows around them started to lengthen as Epsilon Indi began to set below the western horizon beyond the demolished city, and Mecca's cold night began.

* * *

COLYNS: And you say this book you were given by Speaker-to-Erthumoi . . . it was the history of the Locrians?

BEYNES: No, no . . . it was the history of the Far Travelers, though maybe "history" isn't the right word for it, either. More like their Koran or Torah or Holy Bible, however you want to phrase it. . . .

COLYNS: Their scriptures . . .

BEYNES: Sort of like that, but I can't imagine an Erthuma throwing a Torah or a Koran in the dust at the feet of an unbeliever. Maybe it was just a book, Colyns. At any rate, it told me—it told us—about the Far Travelers, about what Mecca meant to them.

COLYNS: So what did the book say about—?

BEYNES: Will you just shut up and listen to me? Your recorder's getting all this, so stop with the questions already. Look . . . the Far Travelers didn't start as a religion. They were . . . I guess you could say that they were political dissidents, although maybe that's not an accurate description either. They were a group that didn't believe in the majority opinion on the Locrian homeworld—

COLYNS: That sounds unlikely. The Locrians don't have a history of intraspecies warfare.

BEYNES: That's because they used to kick out anyone who didn't agree with the status quo. Remember, this is a species that developed the technology for starflight over three hundred thousand years ago. They were able to exile their dissidents to interstellar space when Erthumoi were still burning witches. That's how the Far Travelers got started. They were given . . . well, for lack of better terms, a starship and a set of directions and orders to get lost. The directions they were given led them to a K5-class star on the other side of the galaxy, one that their probes had already determined contained a planet capable of supporting Locrian life.

COLYNS: Epsilon Indi?

BEYNES: Uh-huh. And the planet was Mecca . . . what we call Mecca, at any rate. The book carefully deleted their name for it from Erthuma language. I guess the Locrian name for it is considered sacred in itself.

COLYNS: I see. And how long ago was this?

BEYNES: I don't know. The book wasn't specific on that point . . . more evasion, like their name for the planet. My guess, though, is that it happened just before Erthumoi discovered how to make the hyper-jump. But I do know that the Locrian ship was designed for one-way travel . . . again, this was how the Locrians got rid of their radicals . . . so once the Far Travelers arrived at Mecca, they couldn't leave again. For some reason or another, that ship crashed on Mecca, so they could salvage little of anything from the wreckage. They had to make do with what they had. And, to really make things more pleasant, the planet wasn't entirely habitable because its atmosphere was a little too oxygenated for them. But they were shipwrecked with no way home, so they had to get along with what they had.

COLYNS: And the extragalactics . . . ?

BEYNES: The ex-gees had already visited Epsilon Indi II long before the Locrians arrived. D'Lambert was right. It was just a dumping ground for them, a place to leave their trash. But the Locrians found their trash heap and, since they were running short of raw materials, used the junk to help build their city. But the important part of this whole thing is the fact that the oxygen content of Mecca's atmosphere ran a bit high for them. They tended to . . . well, the book says that they had holy visions, revelations about the uniformity of the universe and so forth and so on; but it doesn't take an exobiologist to figure out that they got mass hypoxia. They hallucinated like crazy.

COLYNS: Mass hypoxia? A whole colony perpetually drunk on . . . ?

BEYNES: Drunk, hallucinating, receiving divine revelations . . . maybe it's all the same thing. I mean, we got into this whole mess because of a couple of Erthuma drunks, so what's a few more? Anyway, whatever political quarrel the Locrian exiles had with the home world became absorbed into this religion that was developed on Mecca.

COLYNS: And the city . . .

BEYNES: The city was where everything happened for them, where their whole system of beliefs was developed. They managed to survive there, but just barely. The book said that they lost most of the original crew, and that they had a fifty percent mortality rate among the next two generations that lived there. It claims that only the ones who embraced the religious beliefs of the dominant sect survived, but maybe that's just the way the winners interpreted history. Hell, who knows? Anyway, after so many years another Locrian vessel ventured into the Epsilon Indi system to check up on them, and that's when they found the third generation descendants of the original exiles . . . but now these guys were the Far Travelers.

COLYNS: But they left Mecca . . . I mean, Epsilon Indi II. . . .

BEYNES: Right, because it had been foretold in their mythology that they would one day be rescued by their brethren. There was a lot of "and the heathen shall see the true light" in the book, but my guess is that the Locrians had softened up a little and decided that their race could accommodate more than one system of belief. Anyway, that's how the Far Travelers left Epsilon Indi II. As far as I can tell, they're still a rarity among the Locrians, because only descendants of the original exiles are allowed into the sect, so this is not a religion that seeks converts. But Mecca—or Epsilon Indi II, if you still want to call it that—is considered a holy world, and the majority of Locrians are willing to cede this single planet to the Far Travelers. It may be just a guess on my part, but it could be that this was the only colony of forced exiles that was ever known to survive this kind of ordeal. I suppose that earned a sort of respect for them.

COLYNS: So the city the *Capital Explorer* found . . . ?

BEYNES: The holiest of holies. And we crashed a ship right into it. Wiped it out.

COLYNS: But the Locrians who brought you back didn't say anything about—

BEYNES: Because the city is back the way it was.

COLYNS: But I . . . you just said that you . . . that Francisco crashed the dropship into the settlement and—

BEYNES: Their religion forbids them from killing except in self-defense. That didn't stop them from finding a creative way of making us do penance. . . .

Through Mecca's long night the Far Travelers sat at the periphery of their demolished settlement, seemingly impervious to the chill which had settled upon the desert after the sun went down, while the Erthumoi huddled together for warmth, their silence enforced by the tireless Locrian guards. The survivors of the *Capital Explorer*'s landing party were given water; on occasion an individual was allowed to walk outside the circle a short distance to relieve himself, but they were denied food or even whispered conversation among themselves. One by one, the Erthumoi fell asleep, curled around each other and shivering in the dark, cold night.

All except Beynes, who held his own sleepless vigil. As the night wore on, he watched the Far Travelers, wondering what visions were being seen by their great eyes, what was being discussed in their alien tongue. Only one thing was certain to him: When morning came, he and his crew mates would be summarily executed. He now understood the serious degree of their trespass upon this world, the enormity of their sacrilege in destroying the holy city. Indeed, he felt a sort of shame which he had never experienced before. Blind Sedric had told him that he would be able to see Sol from Mecca; as Beynes searched the starry sky, trying to decided which point of light represented the home system of Old Earth, he found himself recalling long-forgotten history lessons from his school years. As a consequence of his own greed, an ancient birthright had been pulverized, a relic of a forgotten culture destroyed as mindlessly as the nose of the Sphinx in ancient Egypt on Old Earth had been shot off by a trigger-happy soldier.

For this transgression, Beynes was sure, he and his men would die. Despite what he had read in the Locrian book, he could think of no other punishment that would befit their blasphemy.

When Epsilon Indi rose above the eastern horizon, the Far Travelers stirred once again from their long meditation. Disdaining their helmets, the acolytes turned and slowly walked back to the captive Erthumoi, who had already been awakened by the dawn's first light. As the other Far Travelers waited outside the circle of guards, Speaker-to-Erthumoi stepped into the circle and strode directly to Beynes.

As the first officer watched, Speaker-to-Erthumoi folded back the hood of his cloak. Then, unexpectedly, the scaly exterior of the Locrian's single eye peeled back, exposing the orb to Beynes. It was an uncomfortable sight; Beynes felt himself squirming inside, and he fought the impulse to look away. He knew, of course, that the Locrians were most vulnerable when their eyes were exposed. If he had wished, he could have killed Speaker-to-Erthumoi with a single strike of his fist to its face. But Beynes intuitively knew that he would be dead even before he raised his hand. Instead, he kept stock-still and forced himself to look straight back at that hideous eye.

After a time, Speaker-to-Erthumoi spoke. "We have decided upon your penance," it said. "You will not die, despite what you believe, First Officer Arne Beynes. We do not kill except when we are forced to take lives to preserve our own."

Beynes was shaken, although he should have been relieved. It seemed as if the Locrian had been able to see straight into his soul. Forgetting the command not to speak, he asked, "Then what will happen to us?"

"In time," Speaker-to-Erthumoi continued, "you and your companions will be returned to your own people, with an explanation of what has transpired on this world. Although your crime is serious, so is the fact that we destroyed your vessel and the Erthumoi aboard. Yet this is an isolated event, and it will serve neither Erthumoi nor Locrians if it is allowed to escalate into war between our races. We have drawn enough blood from each other."

The Far Traveler paused. "Provided, of course, that penance is done."

Beynes took a deep breath which seemed to rattle in his chest. "What sort of penance, Speaker-to-Erthumoi?"

"You have read our history," the Locrian said. It was not a question. Speaker-to-Erthumoi held out a limb, and Beynes handed back the book he had been given the evening before. The Far Traveler returned it to the inner pocket of its cloak. "Therefore, you know now how this city was constructed, and why. The Far Travelers have made pilgrimages to this site for hundreds of standard years. It is a keystone of our faith that this place remains intact because of the sacrifices that were made. As it was, it must continue to be, even if the holy labor must be repeated by Erthumoi."

Beynes was confused. "I don't understand—" he began.

"No," Speaker-to-Erthumoi replied, "but eventually you shall, when you have made these sacrifices yourselves."

And it was then that Beynes realized exactly what penance the Far Travelers had decided upon.

COLYNS: You . . . rebuilt the Locrian city?

BEYNES: The five of us were marooned on Mecca to rebuild the city. The Locrians gave us our lives . . . but in return, they claimed our labor. We were given adequate food and water to sustain us, plus whatever we could salvage from the wreckage of the dropship. But they destroyed our robots so that we couldn't use them and took away any tools that might have helped us rebuild the city, and all our communicators were taken away so that we couldn't make a beacon. Just as the Far Travelers themselves had to do when they were shipwrecked on Mecca, we had to remake the city with our bare hands, if only to provide ourselves with basic shelter.

COLYNS: And the Locrians . . . did they ever check on your progress?

BEYNES: During the ninth month of each sidereal year, a group of Far Travelers made their hegira to Mecca. When they came, they brought us food, water, medical supplies, whatever we needed . . . except tools or freedom. Each time they came, we had rebuilt a little more of their city, and each time those of us who were still alive thought that they would finally exhibit mercy. We begged, man, we pleaded . . . but the only mercy we found was in death itself.

COLYNS: Your crew . . .

BEYNES: Died. One by one, over the next seven years, rebuilding that damn city of theirs. It was slow death. It would have been even if we had been given proper tools. The thin atmosphere meant that we tired easily, so it never seemed as if we had the strength to go on. Most of the time it felt as if we were drunk, and it was from nothing more than the air itself. That and the heat . . . or the cold of winter. I don't know which was worse. It took more than a year just to get the dropship wreckage out of the ruins and drag it all to the landfill. Some of it we could use to make the domes, but mostly we used dirt and sweat. Sweat, spit, piss, blood . . . whatever we could use to make the dirt hold together. . . .

COLYNS: I don't—

BEYNES: We used our own spit and piss to cement the walls together, and when one of us died, his blood was drained and used to make the domes. . . .

COLYNS: I . . . I . . .

BEYNES: Their blood, Colyns! Human blood went into those walls! Even when they died they weren't free from their penance! One time we ran short of food, so we had to—

COLYNS: I see . . . and . . . and you were the last to survive?

BEYNES : D'Lambert, my best friend, my only friend . . . he died in the sixth year. Everyone else was dead by then. After that, I was alone. . . .

COLYNS: I'm sorry. Did he . . . I mean, was he . . . ?

BEYNES: As if I had a choice? For a time after that I went mad. I contemplated suicide, but I couldn't bring myself to take that way out. I had to finish what I had started. I owed it to—

COLYNS: Of course . . . I see. . . . And in the seventh year . . . ?

BEYNES: I finished the city myself in the seventh year. When the Far Travelers came back in the ninth month of that year, they kept their promise. I was returned to Erthuma space . . . and you know the rest.

COLYNS: I see. This is . . . interesting.

BEYNES: Interesting? *[Obscenity deleted.]* Eleven people died because of the Locrians, and all you can say is "interesting"? Look at my hands, Colyns! Look what has happened to my hands . . . !

COLYNS: Mr. Beynes, your hands are fine.

BEYNES: *[Obscenity deleted.]* What about the Locrians? How do they answer for all this?

COLYNS: I'm sorry for all that has happened to you, Mr. Beynes, but if you think Erthumoi are going to declare war against the Locrians simply because eleven people died, you are sadly mistaken. The peace which exists between the Six Races is far too valuable for it to be disturbed by a dead bunch of pirates. In fact, this incident will never become public knowledge . . . and you will disappear.

BEYNES: Disappear? You *[obscenity deleted]*, even the Locrians wouldn't kill me! Why should Erthumoi—

COLYNS: You misunderstand me. I didn't say that you would be killed. You will simply disappear. There are many places in the galaxy where you can be safely hidden. You will live out the rest of your life in comfort, because there's nothing that we can do to you that is worse than the punishment you've already received. . . .

BEYNES: My hands . . .

COLYNS: Your hands will be taken care of, Mr. Beynes. I promise. But you will not be allowed to come in contact with anyone. Your story will die when you die . . . it's only necessary to isolate you until that day comes.

BEYNES: And my crew mates? Ahmad, D'Lambert, Captain Francisco, all the others . . . what about them?

COLYNS: I think you'll still have them to keep you company. This interview is over, but before I leave, Mr. Beynes, tell me something, not for the official record. Who do you think killed them? The Locrians, or you yourself?

BEYNES: Mecca. . . .

COLYNS: I see. . . . I have to go now, Mr. Beynes.

BEYNES: Mecca. . . . I think even the Locrians call it Mecca.

END TRANSCRIPT

THIRTY PIECES

HARRY TURTLEDOVE

THE HIDDEN FOLK ARTIFACT LEAPED UPWARD from the soil of La Se Da, beautiful and incomprehensible as all such artifacts were. Bortha the Naxian slithered over to a bank of instruments. It-she extruded a fringed flipper from its-her long, snakelike body and adjusted a detector. Even adjusted, it still provided no useful information. Bortha sighed, a long, hissing noise.

Beside it-her, Eberhard Richter's shoulders sagged. It-she felt waves of frustration flowing outward from the Erthuma. The empathic sensation was almost strong enough to make its-her scales curl. It-she said, "Don't despair, Eberhard. We may yet find a way to solve its mysteries."

"I doubt it," Richter said, gloomy still. "No one else in the galaxy has, not for as long as we've been trying. Sometimes I wonder why we keep at it."

"Leave if you care to, galactics," said Jo Ka Le, the leader of the La Se Dan scientific team that was working with the off-worlders to try to figure out what, if anything, this relic of the Hidden Folk had once been good for. Like Bortha and Richter, he used Standard English; of the starfaring races, Erthumoi visited La Se Da most often. He continued, "We shall persevere, and one day we shall triumph over our ignorance."

Jo Ka Le's emotional output was full of determination. Bortha had to make a distinct effort to notice the individual contribution the La Se Dan scientist made; on La Se Da, determination was an ever-present underlay, like the microwave radiation that still echoed through the universe from the ancient shout of the big bang.

Bortha swung one golden eye toward Jo Ka Le. Itshe found the La Se Dan extraordinarily ugly. He looked more like an Erthuma than like any other galactic race, which from a Naxian's point of view was a bad start. To the sinuous Naxians, Erthumoi looked like poorly articulated puppets. To make the matter worse, though, Jo Ka Le had fur all over his body, not just on his head. The very idea made Bortha itch. So did the shade of the fur, a peculiarly bilious green. Jo Ka Le was shorter than the average Erthuma, too, but wider and more massive.

But however ugly Bortha found the La Se Dans, itshe had to respect them. No wonder the folk of La Se Da constantly projected that air of implacable determination. They had a lot to be determined about. A few hundred years before, they'd done their best to destroy themselves, smashing up their planet in a thermonuclear war with the usual chemical and biological supplements.

Intelligent races sometimes did commit suicide; dead worlds were scattered all through the galaxy. When races tried suicide but failed, they usually abandoned high technology thereafter, as if afraid to give themselves a second chance at ruin.

The La Se Dans were different. They were intent on regaining all the knowledge and skills they'd ever had, and more—thus the planetary mood of determination that constantly impinged on Bortha's sensorium. The arrival of the star travelers to study the enigmatic structures the Hidden Folk had left behind on La Se Da only added another goal to the locals' fanatic reacquisition of technology—they were intent on becoming the seventh race with hyperdrive in the galaxy.

Bortha suspected they would succeed, and probably soon. If perseverance counted, they certainly would. The idea was not altogether appealing. One planet full of orderly, disciplined, fierce La Se Dans was bearable, even if they sometimes did give it-her a headache. If they went bad again here, they would only wreck themselves. Loose in the galaxy, who could say how much mischief and destruction they might cause?

On the other hand, the galaxy had survived the appearance of the Erthumoi, so it could likely survive anything.

With that in mind, it-she asked Jo Ka Le, "How fares your new physical sciences research facility?"

Now the La Se Dan's emotional radiation changed—to upwelling anger. "It would go better, my visitor from beyond the stars, if any of your races would share with us your bounty of knowledge. Then much we are forced to uncover slowly and laboriously for ourselves would soon become clear, and we could gain the freedom to expand that we so desperately require."

Bortha said, "That has never been the policy of the galactic races. Each of our species appreciates the technology the more because it is truly self-developed. We've earned the right to use it, not depended on the charity of others."

Jo Ka Le's anger rose higher, and grew so intense that it made Bortha's head begin to pound. Although he could not sense that anger, Richter spoke as if to soothe it, saying, "All of our races wonder, however, if La Se Da may not be a special case which deserves this help. Perhaps soon we will be able to furnish you the assistance you need, the more so as you have come so far on your own."

But Jo Ka Le had not been angry at Bortha alone. He said, "We would also proceed more quickly if Vu

Te Mi terrorists did not continually raid my nation's laboratories in an effort to slow us down until they gain control of these technologies and thus come to dominate La Se Da.'' The Naxian felt his anger change to somber satisfaction. "We caught a raiding party of theirs last night. We flayed the hides off the lot of them, a little at a time, and used them to decorate the walls of the neutrino generator. And the bodies we chopped up and fed to the *ha fe qo*.''

Ha fe qo were domestic animals of some sort. At the moment, Bortha did not feel like making the effort to remember what sort. Before it-she came to La Se Da, it-she had never imagined intelligent beings undertaking the destruction of other intelligent beings with such fiendish gusto. The very notion left it-her sickened. It would have been impossible among Naxians, who by their very nature felt opponents' pain as if it were their own.

Jo Ka Le said, "You starfarers of course keep to yourselves much of what you do. Our primary research goal with these Hidden Folk artifacts is to find one that serves as a device for focusing neutrinos. We can generate them in profusion, but only so they radiate in all directions. Given a coherent neutrino beam, we should at last begin to approach our capabilities.''

Bortha said nothing. Not only that, it-she made sure its-her long, thin body gave no clue to what it-she was feeling, not that it was likely Jo Ka Le could have interpreted Naxian body language in any case. Hiding what it-she felt came as hard to it-her as learning a foreign language did to most Erthumoi. Among themselves, Naxians did not—indeed, could not—conceal their emotions. When dealing with races that lacked the empathic faculty, however, such dissembling often proved surprisingly valuable.

This, Bortha judged, was one of those times. Jo Ka Le was perfectly correct—if the La Se Dans did manage to create a coherent neutrino beam, they would be very close to the secret of the hyperdrive. Bortha still wasn't sure it-she was comfortable about the idea of these fierce aliens breaking loose among the stars.

It-she turned its-her empathic sense toward Eberhard Richter. The Erthuma, as far as it-she could tell, sympathized completely with the locals' aspirations. That did not reassure it-her. If anything, it made it-her worry more. Erthumoi and La Se Dans looked pretty much alike (at least to a Naxian's eyes) and had relatively similar emotional response patterns (at least when judged by the very different standards Naxians employed). The two species might make natural allies against the other starfaring races. Even the brash, aggressive Erthumoi had not been able to disrupt the peace that prevailed in the galaxy. But put them together with the ferociously capable and capably ferocious La Se Dans . . .

If, however, Richter was on the point of giving away the store (or rather, the hyperdrive), he gave no sign of it in Bortha's presence. He told Jo Ka Le, "I wouldn't rely on help from Hidden Folk technology, if I were you. We haven't encountered a relic of a neutrino focuser anywhere in the galaxy."

"So you say," Jo Ka Le answered, his voice and his emotions heavy with suspicion.

"So I say," Richter agreed. He did not react to Jo Ka Le's tone. Bortha found that hard to fathom. Even mind-blind creatures like Erthumoi developed hit or miss ways to sense emotions. Admittedly, those functioned less well between species, but Jo Ka Le's feelings were neither complex nor subtle. Whatever else one could say about them, the La Se Dans were honest in their viciousness.

Jo Ka Le muttered something uncomplimentary under his breath. Without so much as a farewell, he turned away from the two representatives of the galactic civilization and strode—strutted, really—to the ground car that waited for him. The driver, who had waited with the vehicle (a manifest waste of time as far as Bortha was concerned, especially in a race that claimed to value efficiency), sprang out to open a door for Jo Ka Le and close it after him once he got in. The driver returned to his post, started up the ground car, and drove away, leaving behind the acrid reek of incompletely burned hydrocarbons and a considerable improvement in the emotional atmosphere.

Bortha turned to Eberhard Richter. Alien though he was, he seemed urbanity personified when compared to the La Se Dans. "Whether or not they find an artifact of the Hidden Folk that acts as they require, they are getting close to developing the hyperdrive for themselves," the Naxian said, a moment later adding, "It worries me."

"I admire them," Richter said; as usual, his Standard English held a slight guttural undertone. Bortha could sense that he meant what he said. He went on, "They remind me of my own people, the *Deutsche*— Germans, you would say in Standard. We have had a long history of fighting wars—often losing wars, for with our strength of purpose we would sometimes confront nearly every other nation on Earth—and regaining our strength again afterwards. The will is powerful among us, as it is among the La Se Dans."

Bortha's body twisted slightly—let Richter make what he could of that. It-she said, "Surely Erthumoi did not display the savagery in which the locals revel." Even Erthumoi could not be that bad, it-she thought.

"Given the technology available at the time of those wars, close enough," Richter said. "It was a good while ago, though."

"I'm glad to hear it," Bortha said, a little faintly. Warfare did not come naturally to Naxians. They traditionally worked to get their way by chicanery rather than violence.

These days, of course, they could kill at distances infinitely greater than their empathic faculty could span. Clashes with other, less sensitive starfarers had taught them that fighting back was sometimes necessary; in recent times, Naxian had even battled Naxian once or twice. All the same, Bortha could no more imagine its-her species acting with the savagery of the La Se Dans—or even Richter's *Deutsche* Erthumoi—than she could contemplate the prospect of stars emitting perfume instead of photons.

It-she said, "It might have been better for everyone's peace of mind if the locals had succeeded in exterminating themselves. Then we would not be facing the imminent prospect of their escape into the galaxy."

"It wouldn't have been better for them," Richter said sharply. "We Erthumoi came within centimeters of destroying ourselves, too; we even used nuclear weapons on each other, though not on the scale the La Se Dans did. I admire them very much for pulling themselves together as well as they have."

Again, he spoke nothing but the truth; Bortha could sense that. It-she twisted her body again. Alien, it-she thought. Richter's species might understand the use of the hyperdrive, but his thought patterns remained as strange to it-her as his revolting physiognomy. How could he admire bloodthirsty savages like these? No, the La Se Dans weren't savages, but folk with a high culture who nonetheless remained bloodthirsty. To Bortha's way of thinking, that was worse.

More harshly than it-she had intended, the Naxian said, "Let me remind you that the galactic races agree the locals' rise to starflight should not be aided."

"I know," Richter said. "Still, I wonder what the Hidden Folk would have done here."

Bortha's tongue flicked out from between its-her

teeth in exasperation. As far as the six present starfaring species could tell, the Hidden Folk had dived into a black hole millions of years before, then pulled its borders in after them, leaving behind only occasional mysterious artifacts like the one beside which the Naxian and Erthuma were camped. All the present starfarers were convinced the Hidden Folk had been both nearly omniscient and nearly omnibenevolent.

As far as Bortha was concerned, however, more than *near* omnibenevolence would be required before anyone went around helping the La Se Dans expand. It-she said, "These people would make even the Hidden Folk nervous."

"The Hidden Folk would manage somehow." Richter's emotional radiation said he was dead sure of that. He went on, "Since they aren't here to guide us, we have to manage for ourselves. I expect we will, one way or another."

Erthumoi, Bortha thought, should not be allowed to run around loose in the galaxy. Standard English possessed a phrase the Naxian had puzzled over for a long time: "muddling through." It translated into Bortha's language as a self-evident contradiction in terms: carrying on without thought, with strong overtones of having no more sense of time-binding than an animal. But in the Erthuma speech, its connotations were all positive. Heedlessness was a strange virtue of which to boast, but one demonstrated again and again in Erthuma history.

"Looking at you people," Bortha said, "I wonder how you managed not to follow the La Se Dans' path through the fire."

"So do I, sometimes," Richter admitted. "I—"

He broke off abruptly, for a brisk crackle of small arms fire started up somewhere not too far away. Bortha and he hurried to the tent they shared; it was proof against heavier weapons than rifles. La Se Da demanded equipment like that.

Several new guns began to fire out on the perimeter the La Se Dans of Fa Na Ye maintained around the Hidden Folk artifact. "I wish they could learn not everyone not of their faction is an enemy," Bortha said.

Richter frowned. Bortha could read Erthuma facial expressions; they were useful when subjects under discussion evoked no strong emotional responses in Erthumoi. Richter said, "Bortha, you've learned Standard English so well, you can be confusing when you speak it." While the Naxian tried to puzzle out whether that was compliment or insult, Richter went on, "I still think you're too hard on these people. All of the starfaring races would sooner treat with their own kind than with others. Wouldn't you rather be here with another Naxian instead of me?"

Since the answer to that was yes, Bortha did not answer. It-she said, "Preference is one thing, slaughter another." Richter grunted. His emotions said Bortha had scored a hit, but the Naxian could sense he had not changed his basic attitude toward the Le Se Dans.

It-she thought about arguing further, but decided not to. Erthumoi were contrary creatures, too apt to go in a direction opposite that in which one hoped to push them. Sometimes it-she thought them even more alien than Crotonites. Maybe it had something to do with their possessing permanent appendages. Naxian psychologists often speculated about that; most of them held that their physical mutability made them more flexible mentally, less intransigent, than other races.

It-she wondered if that meant Richter was likelier to talk it-her around than it-she him. It-she hoped not. The gunfire on the perimeter had stopped, but a wounded La Se Dan screamed on and on and on. Finally one more shot rang out. After it came silence.

* * *

"I do apologize for the racket yesterday," Jo Ka Le said when he joined the galactics the next morning. "Merely a few raiders from Vu Te Mi. We slaughtered them." He radiated satisfaction for all—or at least Bortha—to sense.

"Why did that one scream so long?" Bortha asked.

"To suffer, and to let us enjoy his suffering," Jo Ka Le answered. Cruelty was a La Se Dan vice; hypocrisy was not. But straightforward cruelty remained as cruel as any other sort. Bortha saw nothing admirable in it, and wondered yet again how Richter could feel as he did about these people. For once, its-her empathic sense did it-her little good. It-she knew what the Erthuma felt, but not why he felt it.

"Shall we get on with the day's program?" he said now. "It's your turn today, Jo Ka Le."

"All is in readiness," Jo Ka Le said. Since this new artifact of the Hidden Folk had been unearthed, galactics and La Se Dans had alternated in their efforts to coax meaning from it. The La Se Dan method—typically, Bortha thought—was to try testing it to destruction. The locals had tried to saw chunks off it, had bombarded it with X rays, microwaves, military lasers, corrosive gases—everything short of fusion weapons, and they might have used those had it been farther from one of their urban centers.

They'd learned nothing with their aggressive approach. The starfaring races had more subtle probes available. But as Bortha had to admit, they'd learned no more than the La Se Dans. Most gadgets the Hidden Folk left behind were and remained inscrutable. But the few that could be made to do things, or did them of their own accord, did things so astonishing and so far beyond even the starfarers' technology that all artifacts had to be fully evaluated.

Jo Ka Le said, "Perhaps converged focused particle

beams will give us some notion of the artifact's internal structure.''

"Perhaps," Bortha said. The Naxian didn't believe it, not really, but had to admit to itself-herself that it-she wasn't sure. The power the La Se Dans were going to throw into the particle beams would have pixilated electronics on the surface of their nearer moon. Brute-force approaches to technology had their limits, but they sometimes achieved breakthroughs impossible when experimenters admitted there were such things as limits.

Under Jo Ka Le's direction, the scientific crew of locals spent the morning getting the particle beam equipment set up. About halfway through, something went wrong. Jo Ka Le screamed curses at the unfortunate researcher in whose area the problem lay. Instead of the fury Bortha would have felt at such treatment, the scientist quivered with a fear so all-consuming that it not only removed any chance of his being able to fix things but also gave Bortha an acute case of the shivers.

Never the most patient of beings, Jo Ka Le ignored the researcher's stammered explanations. A final bellow of rage from the La Se Dan scientific chief brought out a pair of armed La Se Dans who took the luckless underling away.

Jo Ka Le turned to the watching galactics. "He came from a labor camp, the worthless son of a mutated mother. Another spell in one will remind him he was let out on condition that he succeed—and will remind the others, as well.''

"Meanwhile, of course, your research is delayed." Bortha was not normally sarcastic, but La Se Da had a way of bringing out the worst in it-her.

In any case, Jo Ka Le was proof against heavier caliber irony than it-she could bring to bear. "Not for long," he answered calmly. "The security forces will pull out someone else—they have lists of males with the necessary expertise.''

Sure enough, the replacement arrived before noon. He proved desperately, fawningly anxious to please Jo Ka Le, and also proved able to get the balky instrument going again, which let him do as he'd aimed.

"You see," Jo Ka Le said to Bortha, "we are now in position to begin, and with a staff truly motivated to succeed.''

"I see," Bortha said, and let it go at that. Passing judgments on the La Se Dan way of doing things was not its-her job. Had it been, Jo Ka Le and every member of his species would have been in serious trouble.

Noisy generators pumped power into the twin particle beams. Glowing ionization tracks marked their passage through the air before they impinged upon the artifact the Hidden Folk had left behind. Artifact, Bortha thought, was just a fancy archaeological term for thing, a name given for the sake of naming, not because it truly described.

"I wonder if this one will show perfect reflectivity, the way so many of them do," Eberhard Richter said.

"Do you know, I rather hope it does," Bortha answered. It-she took malicious pleasure in visualizing Jo Ka Le's fury and discomfiture. Then pleasure faded to be replaced by shame. The complete failure of the La Se Dan experiment, it-she was sure, would not make the scientific chief recall his luckless underling from the labor camp to which he'd been consigned—or, more accurately, reconsigned.

In any case, the artifact proved permeable after all. The La Se Dans standing by their machinery shouted excitedly. Their fur stood on end, so they seemed twice as big as they really were. Jo Ka Le yelled something in his own language, then turned to the galactics and fell back into Standard English: "I am having them tighten the focus on the beams, to improve the resolution on the images we're obtaining."

Richter moved his head up and down, an Erthuma gesture the La Se Dans had learned to understand. Despite itself-herself, Bortha had to admit Jo Ka Le knew what he was doing. Somehow, though, that thought made it-her like him less, not more.

"May we see what you're getting?" it-she asked. On most worlds, that would have been a matter of course. On security-mad La Se Da, uninvited peeking was only too apt to be equated with espionage.

"Come ahead," Jo Ka Le said. Bortha could feel his reluctance, but he didn't dare make it overt. It-she slithered over to the bank of instruments, raised itself-herself up on its-her tail so it-she could look over the shoulders of a couple of La Se Dans.

The screen showed a grainy image, the pattern shifting as the intersection point of the two particle beams moved within the artifact. Beside it, a printer delivered a series of graphs analyzing changes in composition. "Can you make out any trace of a pattern?" Bortha asked.

The La Se Dan who was studying the graphs said, "Looks as ought to be one. Looks deceive. Computer finds none."

Bortha had to work hard to follow his Standard English. When the Naxian did, it-she said, "Can you increase the resolution?"

"System at maximum," the La Se Dan said. "Maybe computer analyze, tell something. Maybe just make mystery one level deeper." Bortha pretended it-she hadn't heard that. Erthumoi were the only starfaring race that used artificial intelligences. The Naxians preferred to do their own thinking.

"Nonsense," Jo Ka Le declared. "One day we shall fully understand these mysteries. Even a generation ago, we would have despaired at the prospect of ever penetrating to the internal structure of one of these objects. Now that we begin to discern it, purpose will surely follow.''

''Not necessarily,'' Bortha said. ''We galactics have been studying the artifacts of the Hidden Folk for centuries, and all we've achieved is frustration.''

''We shall succeed,'' Jo Ka Le said. As usual, he radiated determination. Bortha knew full well that the enigmas surrounding the Hidden Folk did not yield to determination alone. Sooner or later, the La Se Dans would come to the same conclusion. It-she did not care to feel Jo Ka Le's anger when he heard that, so it-she kept quiet.

Eberhard Richter said, ''When your computer analysis is complete, Jo Ka Le, I would like a copy of the raw data so we humans—Erthumoi, you would probably say—can run it through our own machines. Perhaps our different systems will come up with something you've missed.''

''Perhaps they will,'' Jo Ka Le said. ''But if they do, what are the chances you will share the new data with us? You starfarers specialize in taking our hard-won knowledge and giving nothing in return. Before we give you anything, we will have from you information in return. You must learn to treat us as equals, for the day will come when we travel out among the stars to join you.''

''I think I may perhaps have some things in which you'll be interested,'' Richter answered blandly. Bortha looked at him with more than a little alarm. It-she probed his feelings, not just passively letting them wash over it-her but digging deep into them. As it-she'd feared, it-she still found sympathy for the La Se Dans. It-she knew only too well what would interest Jo Ka Le. It-she did not think he had any business getting it.

The La Se Dan also understood. ''So?'' he said. He practically quivered with eagerness; even a mind-blind creature like the Erthuma had to notice it. Jo Ka Le went on, "You know what we want. Will you provide it?"

"In exchange for the important data on the Hidden Folk that you La Se Dans have just discovered, yes, I think I will," Richter said. Bortha was convinced he'd lost his mind. The internal structure of the artifact might be interesting, but it wasn't of any immediate great import. The details of the hyperdrive, however— and Jo Ka Le could be seeking nothing less.

The Naxian probed Richter again, hard. He was anxious now, as well as being sympathetic to the La Se Dans. Had he seen something in the probe of the artifact that Bortha had missed? It-she could find no other explanation for his emotions or his actions. It-she wondered how to stop him from betraying all the galactic races, his own included.

Simple, straightforward murder came to mind. Would it-she have thought the Erthumoi unlikely to investigate the sudden death of one of theirs on a planet important to them, it-she might have tried it, or at least thought about it harder. But it-she could not conceal guilt, not from another Naxian, and the Erthumoi would be certain to have among its-her questioners a Naxian from a world unfriendly to its-her own. Their learning she had slain Richter could touch off a war as bad as the one it-she feared if the La Se Dans gained access to the stars.

That left—what? It-she had no idea. It-she worried at it all day, as if it were a piece of tuber stuck between palatal teeth, but had no better luck with it than she usually did getting tuber free without a tongue pick and a mirror.

That evening, it-she tried to talk Richter out of trading information to the La Se Dans in exchange for their images of the interior of the Hidden Folk artifact. "Now that we know particle beams penetrate the thing, we can get our own data—and probably orders of magnitude finer than anything these planetbound lunks produce. Come on, Erthuma, tell me I'm wrong if you can.''

Eberhard Richter's only answer was a grunt. Instead of talking to it-her, he was busy talking to his computer. The concentration that required shielded him from Bortha's continuous probes. It-she grew desperate enough to try probing the computer. A moment of that was plenty to remind it-her why its-her race had never tried to develop machine-based intelligence. The computer's rigid, emotionless—soulless, tasteless—thought patterns baffled and repelled it-her. It was not alive, nor even decently dead. It was revolting.

Richter did not find it so. Humming tunelessly, he studied the machine's vision screen, ordered a couple of changes, studied again, ordered one change more. He grunted once more; Bortha felt his satisfaction. It chilled it-her. Richter ordered the computer to format the information to meet La Se Dan hardware requirements.

''You are really going to do this?'' Bortha asked as the computer spat out a small, square data card of the sort La Se Dan machines used.

''I am,'' Richter answered. ''I assure you, it is for the best.''

Bortha probed again, as deeply as it-she could. Even if he'd wanted to, the Erthuma could not have concealed himself from it-her. He believed every word of what he'd said. Bortha believed he was out of his mind. How anyone could so misjudge the potential for galaxy-wide danger the La Se Dans represented was beyond it-her. Never had it-she wished more that the empathic sense would let it-her know what someone else was thinking as well as what the being was feeling. Whatever Richter's thought processes were, it-she could not fathom them. Alien, alien . . .

The Erthuma said, "Once Jo Ka Le and I have completed our dealings here, I suggest you and I go back to civilization."

That surprised Bortha a little; it-she had expected Richter to want to stay and help the La Se Dans develop the hyperdrive they would surely try to build with the information he was feeding them. It-she said only, "As you wish."

If Richter could not figure out for himself that it-she would enter a complaint against him not only with his home-world government but also with other Erthumoi and with every other starfaring race, that was his lookout. But if it-she had its-her way, every civilized being from this time forth and on down the eons would curse his name. If it-she could not stop him from turning the La Se Dans loose in the galaxy, it-she would take revenge. To a Naxian, that was almost as important. It-she thought of ways to defame the entire Erthuma species for having made the mistake of hatching him.

The next morning, Jo Ka Le handed his data—his worthless, stinking, trivial data, Bortha thought—over to Eberhard Richter. In return, Richter gave the La Se Dan the electronic data card he had had his (worthless, stinking) machine prepare the night before. Bortha did not need to probe deeply to know what Jo Ka Le was feeling. Greed blazed from his mind, bright and hot as the La Se Dan sun climbing up the bowl of the sky.

Richter said, "Use these data wisely, Jo Ka Le. I regret Bortha and I cannot remain here to help you work out all their elaborations. We received an urgent message last night, summoning us to our home worlds once more."

"We shall manage here," Jo Ka Le said. "One day before our lives are done, perhaps, I shall visit you on your home planet." Had he felt humble or proud or awed at the opportunity that represented, Bortha might have had second thoughts about what Richter was doing. But Jo Ka Le felt like a predator sighting prey. So did all the lesser La Se Dans close by.

In a way, getting off the planet was a relief. It took Bortha away from the hungry, eager minds that lived there. In another way, though, it only made matters worse, for it left it-her alone with Eberhard Richter, and he, far from feeling guilty, was almost indecently pleased with himself.

The tip of Bortha's tail quivered in righteous fury. "Do you know what you've done?" it-she demanded. "Do you have any idea? You've undoubtedly set the stage for the worst bloodbath the galaxy has ever seen."

"Oh, it won't be as bad as all that," he answered.

Somehow, after all he'd seen on La Se Da, he believed himself—he didn't feel as if he was lying. That just angered Bortha the more. "You Erthumoi use thirty pieces of silver as a leitmotif for betrayal," it-she said. "You've taken yours, straight from Jo Ka Le."

"Not silver," Richter said. "Terbium."

"Terbium?" Bortha didn't understand the reference. Not only that, it-she didn't understand the Erthuma's sudden mood swing to ironic amusement. It-she couldn't do anything about the latter. As for the former . . . it-she activated an organic memory module. "Terbium is a rare-earth metal you Erthumoi find useful in doping semiconductors. Other than that, it has few uses—none I know of among my people. So why bring it up for discussion here?"

"Because I just spent a sleepless night creating documentation for its use as the catalytic element in a hyperdrive motor," Richter answered. "All that documentation is on the data card I handed to Jo Ka Le."

"What good will that do?" Bortha said irritably. "Every hatchling knows the catalysis depends on gadolinium."

"Every child of a starfaring race knows that, certainly. We've had the technology for centuries—some of our races for millennia. The La Se Dans don't have it at all."

"But it only stands to reason," Bortha protested. "After all, gadolinium has the highest neutron absorption cross section of any element."

"So it does—three orders of magnitude higher than that of the most common isotope of terbium. But what about terbium-158? I established very clearly that its absorption cross section is ten times as great as that of gadolinium."

"Terbium-158?" Bortha had to activate the memory module again. When the Naxian did, it-she was horrified. "Terbium-158 has a half-life of eleven seconds!"

"I know that," Richter said. Not only was he amused, he was pleased with himself.

Bortha felt like extruding enough pseudopods to let it-her twist off his grotesque head, as if he were a *xanas* eel fresh from the seas of Naxos. It-she fairly shrieked: "For one thing, it's a lie. For another, who cares about the neutron absorption cross section of an isotope that won't stay around to absorb neutrons?"

For some reason, the outraged protest only amused Richter more. He said, "It may be a lie, but I've produced some very convincing data to make it seem true. The La Se Dans won't have an easy time finding out it's a lie, either. As you say, terbium-158 doesn't stay around long enough to be tested thoroughly."

"Why would they even bother testing it?" Bortha snapped. "They're vicious and barbarous, but they're not fools—how I wish they were! They're plenty smart enough to figure out that you don't want a neutron emitter when you're supposed to be absorbing neutrons."

"Oh, but, you see, I also passed the La Se Dans a good many hints on practical ways of suppressing radioactivity, which would effectively make terbium-158 a stable isotope.''

"You can't suppress radioactivity, curse it," Bortha said. "Your people can't, my people can't, the other starfarers can't, and, as far as we can tell, the Hidden Folk couldn't either. Every hatchling knows that, and every hatchling knows—"

"You've said that a couple of times now," Richter broke in. "Children among the galactic races may know it, but the La Se Dans certainly don't. All they know is that half a dozen species have the hyperdrive and they don't. If somebody from one of those species—me, for instance—gives them a clue on how to get it, they're going to follow that clue for all it's worth . . . and they'll think it's worth quite a lot. With any luck at all, we may throw off for a good many years research that really could lead to the hyperdrive."

Bortha stared at the Erthuma as if it-she had never seen him before. He was perfectly serious; it-she could sense that. His plan even made a certain amount of sense; the more she thought about it, the more sense it made. It was devious enough to have been spawned from the brain of a Crotonite, too. As far as matters of intrigue went, Bortha could think of no higher praise—or blame. Still—

"You truly don't want the La Se Dans to develop star travel, then?" Bortha said.

"Of course not," Richter said. "Do you think I'm crazy?"

"But—but—but—" Naxians hardly ever stutter, but Bortha was frankly out of its-her depth. With a distinct effort, it-she forced something approaching coherence: "But—you like the La Se Dans. You are full of sympathy for them. I am what I am, Erthuma; you could not deceive me." As if to contradict itself-herself, the Naxian probed Richter again. "You *still* have sympathy for them. How could you work to frustrate them, then?"

"What I feel and what I know to be right are not the same, Bortha," Richter answered. "That may not be so for you Naxians, since you can sense feelings directly, but it is for us Erthumoi. Yes, I have sympathy for the La Se Dans. As I told you, their troubles remind me of those my own folk, the *Deutsche*, went through long ago, before Erthumoi discovered the hyperdrive."

"But—" Bortha sternly controlled itself-herself before it-she started stuttering again. "The La Se Dans' troubles, as you call them, are self-inflicted," it-she managed at last.

"So were those of the *Deutsche*," Richter said, and Bortha tasted the grimness the memory of his people's past raised in him. "We won a war with our neighbors and then, a couple of generations later, fought another war partly spawned from the first. Our alliance was weaker than that of our foes, and we were beaten."

Bortha knew only relief that Naxians, like the good-natured and nearly indestructible Samians, knew little of war. Most intelligent races were not so lucky, and progressed—or went backwards—while periodically casting themselves into the flames.

Richter went on, "Another generation passed, and the *Deutsche* grew wild for revenge against their former foes. They came to follow a leader who promised them that revenge, and stopped at nothing to seek it. Again, their allies were few—most Erthumoi, even without your empathic sense, recognized the *Deutsche* leader for what he was."

"What was he?" Bortha asked, genuinely curious.

"Let me put it this way," Richter said after a brief pause for thought: "If the *Deutsche* had won that war under that ideology and then gone on to discover the hyperdrive, the other five starfaring races would have been faced some centuries ago with a problem like the one the La Se Dans present today. My ancestors, a relatively small people in numbers, fought most of the rest of our native planet, and came close to conquering it.'' From him came a curious mixture of pride and revulsion.

"You are glad they failed, then?" Bortha said, more bewildered than ever now—how could one wish failure on one's own ancestors?

But Richter did. "I am glad," he said. "We would have been monsters, nothing better. After that war was done, the nations that had vanquished us kept the *Deutsche* forcibly divided for two full generations, for fear they would plunge Earth into yet another war, and even after they succeeded in reuniting, worry about them persisted among their neighbors for a long time."

"As may be," Bortha said. "I still do not understand how this leads you to sympathize with the La Se Dans and yet be willing to thwart them." Thwart them he had, the Naxian thought; if he'd managed to disguise lies as advanced technology, they might go chasing shapes in the fog for generations.

"I sympathize with the La Se Dans because I understand them," Richter said. "As I've tried to explain, they remind me of my own ancestors. I have empathy for them, you might say."

Bortha wouldn't have said anything of the sort. It-she was amazed Erthumoi had even developed the concept of empathy without being able to experience it directly. What they called empathy was only logic masquerading as emotion—as far as it-she was concerned, a contemptible fraud.

It-she started to say as much aloud, to make Richter pull in his pseudopod of pride. Then it-she had second thoughts. The Erthuma's pseudoempathy had given him a better grasp of the La Se Dan situation than its-her own true sense. Instead of making a snide comment, the Naxian simply said, "Go on."

"Just because I sympathize with them, Bortha,

doesn't mean I don't recognize them for the danger they are. I still feel sorry for them,'' Richter said, and Bortha could tell that was true. ''I hope that in a few generations they'll be able to come out among the stars along with your race and mine and the other four. But they aren't ready yet, any more than the *Deutsche* would have been under Hitler. No matter how I feel about them, I could see that. Sometimes you have to ignore your feelings to do what's right.''

Bortha considered that. To a Naxian, feelings could no more be ignored than light or gravity. Intellectually, it-she had known that was not so for Erthumoi or most other races. Now, for the first time, it-she *felt* (with full Naxian overtones of the word) what that meant, *felt* the strangeness that dwelt behind Eberhard Richter's small gray-blue eyes.

''I think I shall return to a Naxian world,'' it-she said at last. ''I need to be among my own kind for a while. Much more contact with you Erthumoi will leave me deranged.''

Richter's mouth twitched, an outward sign of the amusement that radiated from him. ''I would not want that,'' he said. ''Still, however crazy the other galactic races reckon us Erthumoi, we've managed to survive. The La Se Dans may also, and if they do, we'll have to deal with them sooner or later. I just helped make it later rather than sooner.''

Bortha wished he hadn't tacked on the last couple of sentences. It-she still intended to spend a good, long time on a quiet, sensible Naxian-settled planet. Now, though, it-she'd have something to worry about while it-she was there.

PHASES IN CHAOS

HAL CLEMENT

I. Above

AT THE MOMENT THE BERG TILTED, TAKING everyone and everything off guard, Rekchellet was sketching busily. He was taking advantage of a clear, cold, dry, and probably brief wind from Darkside. It was not that there had been no notice; there had been tremors, and then a crackling roar, in plenty of time to provide warning if only they had been a little more specific. They seemed to come from all directions, offered no clue to their cause, and, in Rekchellet's own mind, left him and his fellows with no option but to get on with their business. When the ice dropped suddenly and sharply from underfoot it was a total surprise, and four beings and two objects could only react at their most basic levels.

Venzeer and Rekchellet took to their wings instantly and unthinkingly, the recorder's pad and stylus dropping to the ice. The great balloon antenna had inertia enough to snap all four of its moorings, and being ballasted at slightly positive lift began to drift slowly upward. The supply carrier, left momentarily in the air by the dropping surface, drifted back down. Finding the ground no longer horizontal it began to move downhill, since this iceberg was clean enough to be slippery. Janice and Hugh Cedar, attached to the vehicle by what were meant to be safety lines, shared its brief fall and began to follow it unwillingly toward the nearby lake of meltwater.

The carrier would of course float and the supplies inside its sausage-shaped bubble were individually sealed, so the situation was more annoying than threatening; but none of the beings took it calmly. They were much too startled.

"Why weren't the brakes on, ground crawlers?" snapped one of the Crotonites. The woman was too busy hand-over-handing along her line toward the sliding vehicle to answer; Hugh, less concerned and less patient, retorted, "Get the balloon! We can have a court of inquiry later."

The winged members of the team were already flapping after the fifty-meter antenna, which was obviously their business, and there were no more words for fully a minute. Janice reached her goal quickly enough, found the lever she wanted, and sent the spikes of the right steering runner jabbing into the substrate. Even in the local gravity enough momentum had built up to spray her with ice shavings as the carrier swerved toward her. By the time Hugh had reached the lever on his own side the vehicle had stopped. He pulled the handle anyway.

"Get this one!" Rekchellet was a few meters up, as close to hovering as his wing design allowed, holding one of the mooring lines close to the balloon and letting the rest dangle toward the Erthumoi. Hugh seized the lower end, laced it though the lashing eye nearest him, and made fast.

"Any more?" he called.

"The others all broke near the top. You'll have to untie them from the ice anchors and toss an end up to us. It'll be hard to do knots if there's tension; leave the bottom free until we've finished."

"All right," Janice answered. Like her husband she knew that the Crotonites would have felt insulted by such detailed instructions if they had been on the receiving end; less like him, she would never make an issue of it. The creatures couldn't help regarding nonflyers as fit only for menial tasks such as driving ground equipment. Fortunately, recapturing the balloon offered few problems since the wind had dropped. Neither species had reason to criticize the other. All four of the team members, however, were concentrating on the mooring job when the next rope broke.

This was Hugh's safety line.

Surface waves move slowly in weak gravity, but they do move. The sudden tilt of the giant iceberg had sent the lake sloshing away from the carrier and far up a funnel-shaped bay at its sunward end. Reflection of the reddish sun from the water and the ice would have kept the party from seeing clearly that way even if they had been looking. There was little ground friction; the ice had been melting for decades and its surface, while far from flat, had no sharp corners or really rough spots. Even the vegetation was sparse and loose on this part of the berg, so the returning wave lost energy very slowly.

The water poured back into its former basin, continued up the near side, and reached the explorers from just to the right of the carrier's front before even the flyers noticed any danger. The woman was slammed violently into the vehicle. Hugh, standing farther away on the other side, was hurled to the end of his line; if this had held, he would have been crushed by a dozen metric tons of mass—over twenty-two-hundred kilograms of weight even on Habranha—as the bubble rolled over the spot where he had been. By that time, though, he was meters away.

The Crotonites responded instantly and silently. Venzeer swooped and snatched up Janice as the rolling vehicle carried her over it. Her line was still attached, and for a moment it seemed that both might be drawn under the bubble. The physicist had seen the danger, however, and snatched a knife from his tool harness as he dived. A slash of the blade disposed of the risk.

Rekchellet had more trouble. Hugh was a moving target at first, and a snow squall had replaced the calm of moments before, so the Crotonite's first two swoops missed. Then the man was stranded briefly as the wave reached its limit. His body was mixed up with bushes torn loose by the wave, but these seemed wet enough not to be much of an explosion risk—like the Crotonites themselves, the locally evolved life used azide ion as terrestrial beings used ATP. The flyer trusted the electrical insulation of his suit enough to take a chance, and with a screech of triumph lifted Hugh away before the backwash could catch him. Erthumoi were a heavy load even on Habranha, though, and the flyers settled as near as they dared to the water.

The sloshing was becoming more circular, and no more waves reached the carrier. Some of the bushes stranded near it were smoldering, however, wet as they were, and the rescuers avoided them. Venzeer flew quickly to check the supplies, while Rekchellet began a search for his drawing equipment.

Hugh paid no attention to them. Janice was lying where Venzeer had set her down, and the moment the man could get to his feet he made a single leap to her side.

"Jan! Honey! Can you hear me? Are you all right?" There was no immediate answer, and he began checking for injuries as well as the bulk of her suit permitted. He could see that she was breathing, and the garment's status patch just below her throat assured him that her heart was beating. It also told him what medication was being applied. Apparently a bone was broken. Careful checking indicated that this was almost certainly not a limb, but left him to worry about skull and spine and to hope for mere ribs.

Whatever it was would knit within fifteen minutes unless he overrode the suit's treatment. There seemed no reason to do this; there was no visible need for setting, and even if vertebrae were involved her spinal cord would almost certainly be safer if the surrounding bone healed before she was moved or tried to move herself. Hugh could not tell whether she was unconscious from medication or concussion; he could only wait, eyes alternating between face and patch, until she woke up or the treatment ended. He was interrupted before either happened.

"Is she badly hurt?" Rekchellet settled to the ice, attaching the recovered sketch pad to his harness and leaving his wings spread for a few seconds to shed body heat. Most human beings would have taken for granted that he was merely concerned for the mission; Crotonites had a poor reputation for emotions like friendship and sympathy. Hugh, however, had acquired much of his wife's innate tendency to like people regardless of their shape, and he took the question at face value.

"Too soon to say. Do you need me?"

"I don't think so. I don't know whether any of the moorings broke again, but Venz seems to have fixed them to the sled if they did." The squall had ended; antenna and vehicle were visible once more. "If we'd done that in the first place, they'd probably never have broken, since the carrier didn't jerk down as fast as the ground."

"*Because* it got left behind. We secured to the ice for steadiness, so the thing *wouldn't* move, which was our mistake. Are signals still coming?"

"I guess so, if they are signals. Venz's been working the analyzer since he finished making fast. I haven't talked to him; I've been looking for this pad." Rekchellet had unclipped his drawing gear again and was recording Janice and her suit readings. "You're right," he added. "We should have brought equipment to make duplicate copies."

"The flyer would have had to carry it, and then we'd have had to—"

Rekchellet paid no attention to Hugh's interjection. "I was pretty worried for a few minutes, until I found this." He finished his sketch, clipped pad to harness, and brooded briefly. "I still think the pattern sounds like Habranha speech, but it's been coming from below, and I can't believe a sensible flying person would be underwater."

"Or inside an ice—wait!" Hugh had seen his wife stir. A moment later she grimaced and opened her eyes. She looked at Hugh and the Crotonite briefly, obviously gathering her wits; then she gave a rather sour smile, and spoke.

"My chest hurts. If it was you, I've told you before to take it easy. And how long have I been out? I see it's been snowing again."

Hugh hadn't noticed the change in wind or even the advent of the squall until she spoke.

"It wasn't," he assured her, not referring to the weather. "A wave knocked you against the carrier. Med tab says broken bone. I'm glad it's only a rib, if it is. Can you work your arms and legs? How does your head feel?" She moved all limbs cautiously, easing Hugh's worry about her spine. "All right; stay put until whatever else it is knits. It shouldn't be long; you've been out for minutes. Rek thinks the signals are still coming."

This news, as intended, took Janice's mind off her discomfort. She spoke thoughtfully. "I still can't figure that out. The direction's been changing, but it's always generally down. No changes have tied in with weather shifts. The line goes through at least eight or ten kilometers of this iceberg. Maybe twice that, since we don't know the berg's shape below the water line. Then it presumably reaches clear ocean, and no telling how much farther it goes in that. Since the source seems to be moving it can't be someone buried in the ice—and no Habra I've met had a loud enough radio voice to get through even two kilos of the usual ground here.''

''They are competent technicians,'' Rekchellet pointed out. ''They could use amplifiers. In fact, they do. They don't like to, of course, since they speak and hear by radio directly and amplified signals hurt them, but they have the skill.'' The Erthumoi knew this, like all aliens on Habranha who wanted to use radios and couldn't because of the native peculiarity. Hugh and Janice regarded it as more understandable than the Crotonite preference for preabstracted records—drawings— over photographs, but kept to more immediate matters now.

''What native words have you recognized in the patterns? Any real conversation?'' asked Hugh slowly.

''No. Just one word. 'Here. Here. Here.' With varying patterns sometimes following—never preceding— which neither of us could recognize.''

The Erthumoi looked at each other. ''Could be an automatic transmitter on a deep-sea research device,'' Hugh said after a while. His wife nodded.

''It fits. It also fits your notion that no sensible flyer would be underwater.'' She smiled at Rekchellet. ''And with your inability to get them interested in star travel.'' She turned up her suit heat; the wind had suddenly become colder, though the air was still clear. ''Their ocean is as much of a challenge as space, and of far more immediate importance to them.''

The Crotonite looked enthusiastic at the first part of her remark and appeared about to agree, but paused and took on what both watchers recognized as a thoughtful expression at the second.

''I suppose so.'' His wings shifted uneasily, and he glanced toward the antenna a hundred meters away where his companion was still busy. Both human beings knew that Crotonites were divided on the matter of persuading or pressuring Habranha's natives to join the six known starfaring communities—the seventh was still in the province of archeologists. Some, like Venzeer, wanted another winged species to offset the influence of ground crawlers and swimmers on the patterns of interstellar trade and diplomacy. Others seemed to prefer the lonely splendor of being the only flying star travelers, or possibly were worried about competition for worlds suitable for winged intelligences. Husband and wife glanced briefly at each other and changed the subject.

"You think they could build something able to take deep sea pressures, then, don't you?" Hugh asked. "One can see why they'd want detailed information on current patterns. Continental drift really means something here, with the continent made of ice, hundreds of kilos of ocean depth, and Sunside to Darkside heat circulation." Neither he nor his wife was really familiar with Habranha, as they had been on the world only a few weeks. They had seen the ring-shaped continent of floating ice as they approached from space, and understood generally how it was continually melting away on its sunward side and being rebuilt on the other by icebergs drifting from the dark hemisphere. Like other aliens, and the natives themselves, they were not clear how a tide-locked planet could have such complex and variable weather, though there was a general belief that the complicated ocean circulation was somehow involved. Venzeer and Rekchellet, like other Crotonites, had been trying to learn something new and useful about Habranha to improve their own image with the natives; the Rocks had been hired as skilled help.

"Of course they can." The translating equipment carried the Crotonite's snort of contempt clearly enough. "They mine silicate mud from the bottom, five hundred kilos down, for their farms; it takes irrigation with minerals to make the ice fertile. The technology for a solid automatic transmitter which wouldn't even have to resist depth pressure is trivial. Information about currents is important to them, and obviously they couldn't explore the depths personally. We're not very far from what they call the Solid Ocean which covers all Darkside and some of the sunlit hemisphere on the surface. The natives say there also seem to be glaciers extending for hundreds of kilometers from there out over the mud on the ocean bottom. We should be over that, if they're right. They couldn't mine around here even if it were conveniently close to the ring horizontally. So I like your suggestion of a research transmitter.''

Hugh, but not Janice, felt a touch of condescension in the speaker's tone. ''It will be interesting to examine it if it surfaces, and it does seem to be coming up.''

''Maybe some of the locals will be coming to meet it,'' said the woman thoughtfully. ''It could be surfacing automatically or being brought up for servicing and readout. Perhaps we should get over to the edge and see. Should you broadcast to let them know we're here? You can handle the local speech.''

Rekchellet gave an almost human shrug. ''They know we're here. We certainly told them of our plans at Pwanpwan in enough detail, and being flyers they have a uniform culture so the word would have spread planetwide.''

If what *we're* doing is that important to *them*. Hugh kept the thought tactfully to himself.

''If they meet the thing, we'll see them,'' the artist went on. ''If they don't it will be a good opportunity to check their technology in more detail. They don't always seem willing to share with us.''

Janice frowned; she was never happy when her determined liking for people collided with evidence of their less admirable qualities. Her husband made it unnecessary for her to speak, however.

"Jan! Your suit's stopped the medication. How does your chest feel?" She sat up slowly, stretched and bent her arms and legs, and took several deep breaths.

"A little headache, but I guess I'm back in action. Let's go check the antenna again. I suppose Venz has been staying with the signals." She glanced toward the balloon.

Rekchellet put away his sketching gear and answered as he took to the air. "Of course. Let's see if we can get some sort of distance for that source. It might be near enough now for interferometry. . . ." He left the thought unfinished and flapped away; the walkers followed toward sled and antenna at their own speed. They were less optimistic about distance measures through variably dirty ice and multiple thermal layers in open ocean, but there was always a chance; and keeping objections or doubts to oneself made for more peaceful team life. The Crotonites regarded themselves with some justice as directors of the group, though the junior members were developing some skill at slipping their own policy notions into cracks between the flyers' divergent aims toward the native population.

Venzeer was growing enthusiastic as they got near enough to hear his translator. "It's really getting louder and the direction line more horizontal, and over toward the edge, too. I'm for flying over and seeing whatever it is; it's got to be surfacing. How about it, Rek? You'll have to record the thing when it comes up, anyway. The others can monitor signals while they drive. It's only five or six kilometers."

"All right," the woman said quickly. "We can afford to be out of touch for a while." The group had no radios, of course, because of the natives, and neutrino receivers were too heavy to be carried personally by the flyers.

The Crotonites winged sunward with no further words. Hugh and Janice checked the balloon moorings once more, boarded the carrier, and energized its fuser.

They couldn't watch the antenna itself very well from where they sat, since the open platform which carried the flyers' seldom used controls was just above them. The woman, however, monitored its directional readings carefully.

They had to drive slowly, partly because of a gathering haze and partly to minimize the heavy atmosphere's drag on the huge balloon. With the flyers gone even briefly, more broken mooring lines could compromise the whole project. It was also advisable for safety's sake to avoid any vegetation, since much native Habranhan life used azide ion instead of ATP. Hence, they didn't expect to reach the edge of the giant iceberg until long after the Crotonites. Probably they would have found and disassembled the signaling device long before the Erthumoi could do anything to prevent what even Janice considered an unethical maneuver. Even she was concerned enough to take advantage of the Crotonites' absence and make a quick report by neutrino beam to the Erthuma-crewed research vessel orbiting Habranha. If the flyers did cheat on the natives, at least someone would know.

However, they got there in time for two reasons. The recent tilt had brought the sea much closer, or perhaps more correctly had brought the explorers closer to the sea. It was now only a little over one kilometer from where they started driving. Also, whatever was emitting the signals had not yet surfaced when they did arrive. Rekchellet was several hundred meters up, apparently sketching the new water line when the human explorers stopped the carrier. The Darkside wind had resumed and cleared the haze by this time, though another snow squall could be seen far to the left of sunward. As the vehicle stopped, the recorder planed to a landing beside them, stowing his equipment.

"I've got it this time."

"What do you mean?" asked Janice.

"When I dropped the pad before, I didn't save quickly enough, and washing around bumped something, so I lost the last record. Most embarrassing. I won't let that happen again."

Hugh was rather startled; it seemed odd for a Crotonite to confess an error not merely within Erthuma hearing but directly to an Erthuma. It seemed best not to emphasize the matter, however, so he merely asked about the signals. Venzeer, who had resumed station at the antenna the moment it had come in sight, reported, ignoring the fact that Janice had been checking them all along.

Signal direction was still below horizontal, and now nearly constant; only the increasing strength implied that the source was still in motion. It was almost as though something were traveling along the slope of the ice-ocean interface toward them, rather than merely rising through the water.

The surf was heavy, a fact neither surprising nor predictable on Habranha, so none of the team could get very close to the edge, and with the motionless sun in front of them this made watching difficult. Grendel, as the Erthuma explorers had named Habranha's red dwarf sun, glared less than twenty degrees above the horizon. By the time the berg joined the ring continent it would appear nearly twice as high, but it had hundreds of kilos yet to drift before this happened. All that could easily be seen offshore was that much vegetation had been torn loose by the tilt and was being washed toward them. Much of this had already burned; some was smoking as it rolled in the surf, and much yet submerged—not all Habranhan plant life floated—was presumably causing the heavy frothing at the surface. Even more, it could be guessed, was waiting for something to help it discharge electrically.

The explorers watched the dazzling waves roll toward them, crest, and break. That part was familiar enough to all of them, but what followed was subtly different. The surf had no sand to move. The broken waves slid for hundreds of meters along hard, gently rising, smooth ice, losing energy very slowly as the water did its trivial work against Habranha's weak gravity. Nearly free of ripples as this part of the moving fluid was, it was still hard to see whether anything but seaweed was being carried by it. All four beings watched intently, each with some sort of idea what would show up.

Probably, Hugh thought, it would be a featureless sphere, since the hypothetical instrument must be designed for hundreds of kilos depth. Rekchellet seemed to have dismissed this factor, apparently expecting solid-state apparatus, but the man was less certain.

All were wrong. Something decidedly not a plant finally showed almost in front of them—no coincidence, since they had moved as close as the antenna could guide them to the path of the signal source—but for more than a minute few details could be made out as succeeding surges carried it closer and closer to shore.

It was not a sphere, but something very irregular, and all four explorers inched closer with due care to avoid charged plants. The thing finally landed, and for a moment before the next surge arrived it was fully exposed. It was still too distant for clear Erthuma vision, but both the Crotonites gave whistles of surprise.

Then it was almost covered by water once more and borne closer; and the next exposure left even the Erthumoi in no doubt, especially as the snow squall had moved in front of the sun.

Many of the details were still obscured, but not by water. Clearly and unarguably it was a native Habranhan wearing some sort of armor and connected by a rope to a sausage-shaped pack. Even the wings were protected but free to spread and move. As the explorers watched, the being wriggled, straightened itself out, and began to crawl away from the next wash of oncoming sea. Hugh and Janice, already less startled by the arrival than amused by the probable Crotonite reaction to flyers underwater, dashed forward to help, and a few moments later the native was safe above the reach of the ocean. The radio speaker emitted a complex sound pattern, and the translator followed with interpreted Crotonite speech in Venzeer's voice.

"You're—you're welcome. But what's a flyer doing underwater?"

That was just what Hugh and his wife would have asked if they had been able to speak the native language and think of a wording inoffensive to the Crotonites. They listened eagerly for an answer, but heard only the incomprehensible gabble of Habranhan radio emission turned into sound.

Maybe the Crotonites would translate, of course. The machines were set to interpret between Falgite, the native speech of the Erthumoi, and the language of whatever Crotonite planet the flyers had come from—neither Hugh nor Janice knew its name. This could, they suddenly realized, be awkward. Crotonites had been on Habranha much longer than any Erthuma group, and many of them could understand and speak with the natives without translation. Only conversion between radio and ordinary sound was needed. There was pretty certainly, Hugh thought ruefully, no translation system yet in existence between Habranhan and any Erthuma language. "Ground crawlers" had just discovered the place; Crotonites had known of it for at least several decades and possibly for several generations—different sources gave different answers to that question.

He and Janice would have to make what sense they could out of the flyers' side of any conversation with this native, and hope they could stay close enough to get all of that.

"Gabble." Presumably the native.

Venzeer's voice replied, "Complex static."

Hugh kicked himself metaphorically. The machine wouldn't handle whatever speech the Crotonites used talking *to* the natives, either. Of course. He looked at his wife, his raised eyebrow visible enough through the clear suit fabric. She gave an almost imperceptible shrug. She wouldn't want to be sneaky anyway, he reflected. Ask and ye shall receive.

"Rek, could you tell us what's going on? Or could your translator cover native-to-you and then you-to-Falgite, so we can follow? I never expected a live native underwater, any more than you did." True enough, and also tactful.

The Crotonites looked at each other briefly. Both Erthumoi were pretty sure of their thoughts; Hugh was more nearly right, it turned out. He became almost certain when the others hesitated before answering; if such translation had not been practical they would have said so at once. They must be wondering whether letting their surface-bound companions follow all conversation with the native was a good idea or not.

One of them realized after a moment that the hesitation had betrayed them. It might have been Venzeer; at least, it was he who answered.

"Y-yes. I think we can do that. We have a local translator cartridge for reference backup, though both of us handle the language pretty well. We can put that into one of our sets, and as long as we're in hearing distance of each other it should work out all right."

He began manipulating something attached to a harness strap.

"Why is this fellow all alone so far from the ring and underwater besides? Has one of their mining subs had an accident? I thought they couldn't mine this close to Darkside, anyway." Hugh hit what he considered the key points first.

"I don't know. We've been assuming that their mining equipment was automatic or remote controlled. The submarines we have seen are open frameworks apparently not designed to resist bottom pressure, but merely to survive it." The man nodded.

"I haven't seen any myself, but they have practically no metals here and bottom pressure is around ten thousand atmospheres—my units, if the translator doesn't take that for granted. Unmanned machines that didn't need to protect any crew from pressure would seem obvious. This fellow, though, was underwater. I hope he's willing to tell us why."

"So do I," Venzeer responded promptly. "Let's find out. There seem to be none of his fellows nearby. Maybe . . ." He failed to finish the sentence. Rekchellet was already addressing the native again, and this time the Erthumoi could follow the conversation.

"Did your submarine craft have some sort of accident?" Reasonably straightforward for a Crotonite, Hugh thought. The answer came through rather brokenly; two sequential translations had to involve delays from the differing sentence structures involved. Even one was usually a bit jerky.

"We had no sub. It was not exactly an accident. Pett and I were riding a deep berg, charting currents, and it moved up to the deep-middle pressure boundary more quickly than we expected. The surface chose to blow off instead of pulverize, and a fragment killed Pett, I'm afraid; I haven't seen or heard her since. What was left of the berg was much less dense. I don't know whether from phase change or lost mud or both. Anyway, it came up quite rapidly, and I rode it. I nearly got crushed when it hit the bottom of this one. It shattered, and there was no single piece big enough to be worth following, so I came up to report."

"How will you do that? Are some of your people nearby?"

"Not likely. I'll just shed the armor, eat what I can of the supplies"—the native indicated the streamlined pack he had been towing—"and fly sunward to the ring. It won't matter where I hit it."

"You'll leave your armor here?" The Crotonite made no pretense of hiding his surprise, or perhaps was hoping the translator would not carry it. Neither Hugh nor Janice could guess whether the feeling, obvious to them, had come through to the native.

"Sure. I could never fly with it, and it's easy enough to replace. If your work carries you that way, you might carry it farther from the water; it'll be more likely to be available if anyone else should want it."

"Fair enough." This time Rekchellet's voice showed no obvious emotion. "We can certainly carry it on our supply vehicle."

"Good. I'll get along; the sooner I can get the current data home, the closer to real time we can figure." The native, showing not the slightest surprise or curiosity about the aliens, stripped off his protective garment. If either of the Erthuma watchers had known that much about their ancestral world, they would have been reminded of a dragonfly emerging from its pupal form, though the Habranhan body was much more flexible and had three pairs of wings rather than two. The head was large enough to make intelligence predictable, though it appeared rather small on the four-meter body. The four other limbs were much thicker for the being's overall size than those of any terrestrial insect. They ended in knoblike wrists which could serve as feet, though they would hardly have a good tread on ice, and from which half a dozen flexible tendrils could be extended for handling. Once out of the armor, the being moved to its pack, opened one end, and extended a proboscis into some invisible container inside. For several minutes it remained motionless, presumably eating or drinking. Then the wings firmed and extended as fluid was pumped into their veins and stiffened them. It turned to face the four aliens, still showing no surprise.

"There's a good deal of diving juice here, and some food too, which could be useful to someone—not you folks, of course. If you wouldn't mind taking that along, too, and dropping it farther from the sea, it might be handy to someone a long way from home. Thanks." The wings began to beat rather slowly, somewhat out of phase with each other; if they had been connected by membrane, the latter would have rippled like the fins of a manta ray swimming, though the Erthuma watchers were reminded rather of a similar creature native to Falch.

They considered this aspect for only a moment. The Crotonites rose with the native and accompanied it for several hundred meters on its way. Hugh didn't know whether to worry more about what they might do to him or what they might say to him. Janice refused to worry, and seemed justified; their winged companions presently peeled away and swung back toward the iceberg, leaving the native to dwindle in the distance and quickly disappear in Grendel's glare.

Hugh was not surprised when the Crotonites settled beside the diving armor the being had left behind. After all, he and his wife were already there themselves; examining a suit which apparently could protect its wearer from thousands of atmospheres pressure seemed very much in order.

The jointing was ingenious, but the material baffling. There seemed nothing particularly pressure resistant about it. The covering for the wings and other limbs was actually flexible. Close examination of a torn-off piece—torn off easily enough to compound the mystery—showed that body plates as well could easily be bent not only by Erthuma hands but by the less sturdy and efficient graspers of the Crotonites. There seemed no way the suit could defend its wearer from significant fluid pressure; and Habranhan bodies appeared frail even by Crotonite standards—large, of course, but far from rugged.

Still the fellow had said, quite unambiguously as far as Hugh could remember, that he had been working much farther down than the thirty kilometers or so that marked the bottom of the ice mountain the foursome was riding. He had been talking about ice phase changes which the man was pretty sure implied thousands of atmospheres. How this went with flexible armor material was very unclear.

"We'll have to take some of this stuff for analysis," Venzeer said firmly. "As far as I can tell, it's about like the polymers they make fences and weather guards out of, but there must be something different about it. Maybe—wait a minute, did any of you see water draining out of it as he took it off?"

"Yes, now that you mention it," admitted the woman. "Not much, but there was some. I just assumed he'd loosened a joint or a valve for some reason before he got ashore, and some ocean had gotten in."

"Could you—assume—why he'd do such a thing?"

"There seemed too many possibilities to make a guess worth while."

"Such as?"

"Oh, personal comfort, if he'd been wearing it a long time. The urge to breathe fresh air. Freedom of motion. Thirst—can these people drink their ocean water?"

"No. They don't mind the ammonia, but there's bio-logical contamination; a lot of the azide ion most of the local life uses for energy storage—like us, though I've heard you use something else—is free in the ocean, I suppose from plankton decay." Venzeer furnished this information, giving his Erthuma listeners further pause for thought. Janice's rapid list of guesses had silenced Rekchellet for the moment, but he had not abandoned the thought underlying the earlier question. He made his way to the spot where the armor had first been shed and examined it and the ground closely, sketching busily from time to time.

It was the usual ice, rendered milky by ultrafine silt trapped when it had frozen for the last time, possibly airborne dust which had blown to Darkside and mixed with the snow. There was some sign of recent local melting, in the form of a narrow line of the white sedi-ment to seaward in a barely perceptible depression, but this might as well have been due to the native's body heat as to water leaking from the armor. The recorder brought his face to the ice and sniffed, mouth gaping—taste and smell were even less distinct for Crotonites than for Erthumoi. Hugh wondered privately how he would sketch an odor.

"Hugh—Jan—come here and sniff. I don't know whether your sense of smell is any better than ours, but can you tell whether anything strange is here?"

The walkers complied, and looked at each other uncertainly. "There's *something*," the woman admit-ted, "but I certainly don't recognize it. I've never noticed any particular smell to the Habras, but I'm not sure I've been close enough to one to have caught it if there were."

"I have been, but they don't smell, as far as we're concerned." Venzeer spoke thoughtfully. "Anyway, there's something here, which probably came from his diving suit. Let's see if *it* smells."

All sniffed or gaped at the armor. Janice shrugged. "I get it here, too, but don't see that that's any help. We still don't know if it's something chemical—I suppose that's what you have in mind—or perfectly normal for the occupant."

Hugh cut in. "How would a chemical help? Make his flesh so hard it could resist ocean pressure? That doesn't make sense to me."

"Nor to me," admitted the Crotonite. "It's just that the whole situation is strange, and I'd like to get all the strange items in one place if I can."

"If you had asked me before I went, I could have told you all you wanted to know about the suit with no need to damage it."

Human and Crotonite beings alike froze briefly at the words. Hugh, the only one standing instead of being bent over the armor, was the first to look up, but the others were almost as quick. There was little doubt about the owner of the voice. Sure enough, a six-winged body was flapping slowly a few meters overhead. With all the usual Erthuma tendency to blame someone else, especially a Crotonite if one were available, for an embarrassing situation, Hugh found himself hastily uttering an excuse for the entire company.

"We hadn't thought there would be anything to ask. We didn't notice how flexible the material was until we picked it up; then we couldn't understand how it could protect anyone from depth pressure."

Venzeer cut in with his own thoughts. "How did you know we were damaging it? Why did you come back?"

"I heard a piece being torn off." The native glided down beside them.

"But—oh. Of course." Janice cut her objection short. The armor was of polymer and certainly an electrical nonconductor—it would have to be, to protect its wearer from inadvertent contact with plants, even underwater. Tearing one part from another would set up enough potential difference to produce radio emissions, even if their own translators had not picked it up—which they might have done; neither Crotonite, as Rekchellet admitted later, would have noticed random static.

The native seemed to accept the excuse, but appeared a little surprised at Hugh's words.

"We don't try to resist the pressure. We—oh. When I mentioned diving fluid, you thought I meant ballast, I suppose."

"We didn't even get that far," Janice admitted. "I don't think any of us even thought about those words. You even said it would be no use to us, didn't you?" The Habranhan's still inflated wings cocked upward in what even the Erthumoi knew was an affirmative gesture.

"Oh!" Hugh said softly. "I get it. Ducking PV troubles by holding delta-V down. All liquid. All body cavities free of air bubbles. Something able to carry oxygen fast enough in solution or loose bonding. I've heard of that, though I don't think it's ever been done at home. Very long ago, maybe even back on Earth."

"I hadn't," his wife said, "but I could see he meant something of the sort."

"What are you talking about?" cut in Venzeer.

"Most of the damage done to a living creature by pressure change results from the big volume change of gas. Liquid doesn't change volume very much with DP. If one goes up or down slowly enough to let body fluids—mostly water, for all of us—diffuse even a little through membranes and cell wall, there's no trouble. Even deep-sea creatures don't burst unless they have air bladders or unless they're brought up really fast. The Habranhans must have developed a fluid which they can use to soak their entire bodies, including the cavities normally used for oxygen exchange, and fill the space between body and armor. Then pressure doesn't mean anything."

"But there are other dangers beside PV," her husband put in. "How about nitrogen narcosis?"

"I don't know. We must have solved that one, too, if what you remember is right. And maybe these people aren't as subject to that; after all, they can stand some hydrogen cyanide in the air, as the Crotonites do."

"Of course," Rekchellet muttered softly. "We're not crawlers, either." Janice ignored the interjection.

"Cyanide ion, carbon monoxide, and molecular nitrogen have identical electronic structures. They only differ in polarity and net change. Anyone able to handle cyanide should have no trouble with nitrogen."

"You're speculating," her husband pointed out.

"Of course I am. There hasn't been time for a library check, but I'm going to get on the transmitter pronto. We've only just heard about all this from—what should we call you?" Janice tried to make it obvious from her attitude that she was addressing the native. Apparently he understood.

"I am—" the rest was unreproducible static.

"I'm sorry," Janice said as tactfully as she could. "That symbol does not convert to sound patterns we can make. Will a simple pattern such as William be unambiguous?"

"It sounds like 'backward flyer,' but I can make allowances. I understand the difficulty. If William is convenient, I am William."

"Bill would be even easier and quicker."

"That has no meaning, but I can remember and produce it."

"Thank you, Bill. Do you know why we are here— the four of us?"

"I assumed you were making current studies and possibly other analyses of our ocean and atmosphere, just as we do. I had supposed formerly that there were probably others of your people making similar studies below the surface. I gather now that you have not started that yet.''

"We walking people haven't, and I doubt that the Crotonites have either. We would normally do such work with the aid of machines we call robots, and these would have to be very specialized. We have none so far on this planet. Venz? Rek? How about your people?''

"We do not use such machines. We prefer to do our own work.'' Enough of Rekchellet's tone came through the translator to remind Hugh and his wife of the distrust of artificial intelligence shared by most of the non-human starfarers. The woman pressed the point, however; it was poor tact, but she wanted Bill to learn something about the Crotonites which they themselves were unlikely to have told to the natives.

"But you haven't done any underwater exploring here, have you?''

"Not here, nor anywhere else. We fly.''

"Of course. And one cannot fly underwater.''

Bill cut in at this point. "But one can. We do. It is how one gets around, outside the submarines. It is how I escaped being crushed by the rising ice mountain I was on, when it collided with yours.''

Venzeer cut in sharply. "You *fly* underwater?''

"We call it *swimming*,'' Hugh said hastily. "I suppose Bill's people would use their wings, though.'' He regretted the second sentence even before he had finished, and silently cursed his inbuilt honesty. The Crotonites made no immediate answer, but looked thoughtfully at each other. There were several seconds of silence in which the thoughts of each of the five would have been of great interest to all the others.

Venzeer's imagination was playing with the Habranhan's revelation: You *could fly* down there. Maybe it wasn't so bad, after all; maybe one could go down, share experience, even a *new kind* of flight, and get to

know the natives better—realize why they seemed so
indifferent to the opportunity of leaving their world and
flying among the stars. Their ancestors must have done
it; these people had not evolved on Habranha. Not only
was there no linkage—the ring continent had no land
animal life, let alone flying creatures—but these flyers
didn't even use azide in their biochemistry, even though
they were as electrical in many ways as the plants and
the sea creatures. Neither did the plants they grew for
food. They must be colonists. Maybe even—no, that
would be too much to expect.

The thought of flying in the deeps, though. That
could be a real experience—but it would be so *dark*.
No way to see any distance; just muddy, unlit water all
around. It would be flying, of course. The native had
said so. But there would be no clouds, no stars, nothing
but hearing and touching to keep one in contact with
the universe. The natives were flyers and knew what
seeing meant better than any ground crawler, but they
wouldn't miss it quite so much if it were gone. They
had that Habranhan advantage—they could detect electric fields and impulses as well as see and hear. . . .

And they could fly underwater, under hopelessly
crushing pressures. Learning how they did it—finding
the formula of their diving liquid—would be no help
to Crotonites. Probably the simple creatures would supply it for the asking. No, they weren't that simple, they
were flyers—though since the information would be no
real use to the Crotonites, why should they worry about
handing it out freely? But—just how different were
Crotonite and Habranhan biochemistries, anyway? And
if the liquid didn't work, couldn't one find materials
which would really keep the pressure out? What were
engineering researchers for? The idea of armor went
naturally with ground crawlers, of course; no flyer
would consider playing with that much weight just for
protection. But the weight would mean little or nothing

underwater; that was elementary physics. Much library inquiry was in order. There must be plenty of relevant information.

Rekchellet dreamt along a different line. These things have a field we don't. They have a bigger world of their own to explore than anyone else has ever had. Not just surface and atmosphere, but a sixth of the radius *below* the surface. A third of the planet's *volume* in which things live and where things happen. Why should they care about space? Whether they're philosophers hunting knowledge for its own sake or pragmatists trying to keep alive, they have a universe of material for thought and work from now on. A few suggestions for new fields of activity at home, and we won't have to worry about them anywhere else in the galaxy for centuries. Even if they're the Seventh Race and *used to* travel the stars, they've changed. Of course, we'll have to know enough about their world— their universe—to command their respect. We'll have to be interested in their problems, not get them interested in ours.

But how do we get down there? The native flyers aren't built the way we are, even chemically. Azide is poisonous to them. How could we develop anything like their diving liquid in a lifetime, or several? Not even the artifical brains the Erthumoi used could—

He firmly stopped that line of thought. Still, flying in the deeps should be fun. New things to see and to draw. No doubt the Erthuma artificial eyes could be attached to some machine to look things over down there, but how could one abstract the essentials *after* a picture had been made? There would be far too much irrelevant material in the image.

Janice didn't really worry about Crotonite attitudes; she took them for granted, often wrongly, but this was seldom brought home to her. Bill, however, was interesting. He was brave; regardless of the perfection of

Habranhan diving technology, he had been risking his life. It might have been simple curiosity, or it might have been a sense of duty. That didn't matter. She could empathize with either. She could feel a call from Habranha's deep oceans, an utterly new environment. There would be strange life, currents even more complex than those in the air, and storms driven by icebergs calving upward and by heat absorbed or emitted as ice changed phase with depth and giant bergs either shattered to powder or changed density more sedately and rose or sank accordingly. . . . Bill's brief account had been enough to trigger the imagination of any chemist. There would be clouds and rains, both upward and downward, of silt scraped from Habranha's core by the Darkside glacier in its eternal grind sunward along the ocean bottom, silt incorporated in the ice and shed at different depths and different rates as the bergs melted, crumbled, or burst. There would be hot currents going downward because they were silt laden, cold ones rising because of their ammonia content, storms where they met and formed gels out of colloids. William had been down there and seen it all, and Hugh would want to hear her guesses and check them out. . . .

There must be, in some library file, data on the diving liquid. Riding a merely floating iceberg and keeping track of even chaotic winds and snow squalls was suddenly boring. She was going to get the neutrino beam busy, and she didn't care how many planetary libraries would have to be probed. It wouldn't be hard to get Venzeer and Rekchellet interested in this new search.

Hugh shared much of his wife's feelings, but didn't take the Crotonites for granted. Maybe Bill's words would persuade Venz or Rek or both actually to try something in the deep sea, something only remotely like flying, though it was hard to guess what the artist—Hugh wasn't sure he was really more than an illustrator and recorder—would find to employ his talents. That might be good; it could make the fellow realize that what you could see wasn't everything and that people who couldn't fly and comprehend the whole landscape at once weren't necessarily beneath notice. Whether the Habranhans took to space travel or not wasn't really important, though the man rather hoped they would; he had no intention of taking sides with either of the Crotonites and didn't much care whether the Seventh Race turned out to be Habranhans or never turned up at all. They were probably extinct, anyway. The natives could take care of their own futures, in space or ocean. It would be fun, though, to have both Venzeer and Rekchellet a couple of hundred kilos deep and learning to fly in water—never mind what verb the translator used. And one could get them arguing later with the single Cephallonian at Pwanpwan about the joys of swimming, and hearing them sneer at the inability of the water breather to "swim" in air. It would be a relief to give them someone, or something, besides "ground crawlers" to belittle.

And it would be fun to see what the depths of Habranha were like. Jan would already have some guesses, he knew; that was one of the things so wonderful about her. Comparing prediction with fact was always fun. Of course, the process might kill you, but that made it more interesting. There must be information on that old diving juice somewhere. A few minutes, or hours at most, in touch with practically any Erthuma world's data bank should take care of that problem. That would be a highly worthwhile use of communicator and search program time. And it wouldn't take very long to apply the knowledge in any workshop. You might even do it with the sled's equipment—no, one would have to get back to Pwanpwan or up to the station. But one could do it. And maybe the atmospheric chaos on what should be a quiet, tide-locked planet *did* have its origin in the oceans.

Bill, least cynical of the five except for Janice, was reviewing his initial surprise that the star travelers hadn't been into the deeps. He had taken for granted that his own planet, however unique and complex in detail, must be just another world to them, and that they had to have routines for studying planets. The thought that his home was unusual enough to make the routines inadequate was somehow pleasurable. There were things he and his colleagues could teach these strange, highly knowledgeable beings after all, in spite of the impression of their own superiority the winged aliens seemed so willing to share. He knew little about the wingless ones who had appeared more recently, but they too were star travelers, and no doubt felt superior because of that.

Bill was one of the few of his species who knew about stars other than Grendel's companion sun Fafnir by more than hearsay. Most people stayed on, over, or under the ring-shaped continent on the daylight side of Habranha, which was continually adding to itself at about fifty degrees from the sun and melting away at about twenty, and this was in constant daylight. Fafnir was of course visible; its motions had provided the first observable no-fricton system, and had led to the development of physics, according to history. Other stars had been discovered only when researchers had learned how to travel briefly in the dark hemisphere; the nature of stars, until the arrival of the Crotonites, had been entirely speculative, and many Habranhans felt some doubt even now about their existence.

A few scientists had been tempted by the thought of traveling beyond the atmosphere, but those who had tried it had returned very quickly and unhappily. One could see well enough out there; it was fascinating to have theories about the shape of the world and the continent so easily supported. One could not, however, *feel* anything. Whether this was because there was nothing near enough to feel or because the strange material of the flying craft blocked electric fields so effectively could not be said; either way, the experience was highly claustrophobic. It was known that the aliens lacked electrical senses—they even had to transform normal speech into something else; maybe this was why they weren't bothered by space travel. No one had been able to find out from the Crotonites; Bill wasn't sure whether other alien species had been asked. There was a new one who actually flew *only* in water, he had heard. . . .

It would be interesting to accompany an alien group into the deeps, if they could be persuaded to go—and if they had the technology to go; presumably deep-juice wouldn't be any use to aliens—but maybe the stuff they made their ships out of could actually resist deep pressure. . . .

He'd have to get back to the ring and ask some questions. It was unlikely, statistically, that there were enough aliens here to provide answers. No one knew everything.

The thoughts, even though shared with reluctance, could lead to only one course of action.

II. Below

He'd been right, Venzeer thought. It *was* dark, and the lack of stars was frightening. The lack of orientation was worse. Normally one could fly in clouds with due attention, but that was when the clouds were suspended in air and one's weight and sense of speed meant something. Here, the effect of wing beats was different, and one couldn't beat them very fast anyway, and one couldn't sense speed through armor even if the impact sense had meant anything in water.

He couldn't blame Rekchellet for spending most of his time in the living sphere of the *Compromise*. If he himself had had such a good excuse as the failure of the drawing pad to work underwater, he'd have used it. The fact there was little to draw was secondary; Rek was still busy making what records he could, though these were mostly words and figures from the instruments.

From where he was, Venzeer could see the new supply carrier of course; even the thought of going out of sight of it aroused—not panic, of course. Just plain, rational fear. There was no obvious way of finding it again in the starless dark. No way of finding any direction—not even up or down—with any confidence.

He could not quite see why the Erthumoi had wanted to name the vessel, since they had not bothered to name the sled, but he could agree with the name itself. It was a modified Habranhan mining sub, open to ocean pressure. Its hull was merely a polymer framework—metal was a laboratory curiosity to the Habras—to hold the mud tanks and engines. The natives had an interesting form of fusion-electric drive, the power conductors being extremely well shielded so as not to dazzle the crew's other senses. The shielding was a conducting polymer; the natural electrical senses of the natives had led to a bypassing of one problem a growing civilization might have faced on a continent of ice.

The ship's frame members were tubular, filled with heat-exchange fluid which could be pumped where needed. The ice in Habranha's ocean depths had a sometimes inconveniently high melting point and could be found at surprising distances from Darkside.

Bill, Hugh, and Janice had been willing to spend a month or more in diving fluid and full-recycling armor, but the Crotonites had had to improvise brute-force protection and couldn't stay in their suits continually. Hence the vessel now had two linked transparent pressure spheres near the center, replacing a pair of the original cargo tanks. One globe served as an air lock, the other as living space—very cramped living space, even at eight meters inside diameter, for anyone with wings. Even Rekchellet came out to fly around, without his pad, fairly often.

When the craft was traveling faster than any of them could fly, which was most of the time, people stayed inside the openwork hull and held on. If they had to rest, they used a cargo tank. Venzeer and Hugh had suggested, during the mission planning, that some of these receptacles should be ballasted with mud to conserve power which would otherwise be needed to force the buoyant living space downward, but the natives had declined. Irrigation mud, which made their continental ice fertile enough to grow food, was too valuable. When the Crotonite research center at Pwanpwan provided a few hundred tons of copper, the Habras had offered to trade mud for the metal, but Venzeer had declined. The metal slugs were easier to handle. He kept the peace by suggesting that the copper might be donated to a Habranhan laboratory after the trip.

This, of course, would be lengthy. Like the vehicle, the mission was a compromise between the needs and interests of the natives who had furnished the submarine and the alien researchers. The latter wanted not only to learn things about the planet but also in some cases to apply persuasion to its natives. Since not all the offworlders wanted to sell the same things, and none of them dared to say this openly, the final compromise was complex in detail and fully understood by few if any of the beings involved. It had, however, already brought the *Compromise* closer to the Solid Ocean of Darkside than the Habras had so far explored.

This was not because they hadn't tried, Bill maintained, but because neither submarine nor free swimmer had ever, so far, returned from the region. There was no obvious reason for this; if anything, the undersea weather should be least violent there, since the descending vertical glacier was presumably quite pure water with no sediment and solute complications. He had told stories which confirmed Janice's picture of silt and "snow," violent currents in all directions, large icebergs and small, monsters and minibeasts. They had encountered some of these since leaving the ring continent, but this had all been out in the warmer ocean. Venzeer doubted much of the rest since Bill had not seemed the least worried about going along himself. The Crotonite had quickly come to suspect that the native was trying to frighten aliens away from exploring in and under the sea, where by his standards the world's wealth lay. This attitude was quite familiar to most Crotonites and not wholly unknown to the Erthumoi.

Bill was visible now, swimming calmly a few meters away. The lights from the *Compromise* showed him in silhouette, his wings moving languidly as he followed a tortuous path around the slowly moving vessel. He claimed to be making observations when he did this, testing with his own strange senses the temperature, density, and solutes of the ambient ocean, measurements which would all be compromised if made too close to the ship and its drivers. He certainly made records of some sort after each sortie, but not even the Crotonites could read these, and Venzeer retained his doubts.

Janice didn't, of course. She had before starting calmly asked William to tell her everything he observed from the beginning of the trip on, and he appeared to be cooperating. She had accepted the fact that the mission was dangerous, and was seriously trying to decide what the danger might be. She was willing to take chances, especially since Hugh was along, but had no wish to be taken by surprise. She wanted to know the local rules as well and as quickly as possible.

While the information on the diving fluid was being sought, and later while the material was being manufactured, she had spent much communicator time getting library material on high-pressure phenomena, and memorizing a great deal of it. Of the five beings traveling in the middle of a bubble of light with, as far as they knew, over a hundred kilometers of crushing ocean in every direction, she was by far the most tense.

Hugh had enough sense to be afraid, but was nowhere near panic. The diving fluid, it had turned out, had been known and used for years, though not on his own world, in pressures approaching those of their present surroundings. There had been no trouble finding out about its nature, methods of manufacture, or the practical problems of its use—which included finding or inventing, and learning to use, some form of nonverbal communication code.

No one, apparently, had ever had occasion to use it under Habranhan bottom conditions nearly four hundred kilometers farther down, but for the moment there was no plan to go to such depths.

Rekchellet was the unhappiest. There was nothing to see except the craft he was riding and his fellow explorers. He had drawn all of these in as wide a range of situations as the surroundings afforded. He had records of ammonia content and temperature and suspended matter and even some information on currents, though these were as hard to check as gravity in free-fall. One did not draw this sort of thing, however; one wrote it.

Worse, there was no way to get their exact position, so even a map was out of the question. The natives lacked inertial trackers, and there had been none available at Pwanpwan—not because none existed, but the Crotonites and others studying the motions of the ice which made up Habranha's ring-shaped continent had firmly refused to loan any to a high-risk expedition. Rekchellet knew he should have done the arguing instead of letting Janice try, but he was coming to regard her more and more as a being, not just a ground crawler.

He had records, but all in numbers. He had tried

graphing the information, thus turning it into pictures of a sort, but was disappointed by the results. *Compromise* was at the depth where water had its lowest freezing temperature, about twenty kelvins below what everyone in the group considered normal, so his graph suggested that they were moving into a cavern with ordinary ice above and a high-pressure form below. This wasn't really a map, though. It didn't mean they were actually in a cavern, still less that they were about to be crushed by falling or rising ice. For one thing, the ice above would float and that below would sink. The natives knew something about high-pressure ice phases. Even the Erthumoi, at least the female one, did. The glacier on the ocean bottom, crawling its way back toward Sunside after centuries of travel from the Darkside snow sheet down hundreds of kilometers of Solid Ocean column, was what Janice called ice five, and they were currently at the pressure boundary between ice one and ice three, a hundred and fifteen kilometers or so below atmosphere.

The trouble was, one didn't know exactly. Pressure gages did not have four-digit accuracy in this range. Bill's senses didn't reach. Sonic measures were wholly unreliable because of the vast reflecting, scattering, and absorbing layers of silt and plankton and the labyrinth of thermal currents. The globe of light which let Rekchellet see a few score meters around the *Compromise* was a prison, and the transparent living shell where he spent most of his time was a closer one. Flying was necessary now and then, but wasn't much of a relief. It *wasn't* really flying—not when Erthumoi could do it even with their ridiculous limbs. The artificial flippers of negligible area they wore on their walking appendages didn't count. Rekchellet felt annoyed and frustrated.

William was happy. He was doing something new and useful in a field he had enjoyed all his life. Like

Hugh, he was intelligent enough to be afraid, but like the man he was able to face the danger philosophically. He was the calmest of the group, predictably; the situation was more familiar to him than to any of the others.

He was therefore less alert than Janice. The only reason he perceived the menace first was because it affected something familiar to him.

He noticed suddenly that it was harder to move his wings.

At almost the same instant, he became aware of charge building up at the joints of his armor, except the wing hinges where there was constant motion. He was an experienced diver, and almost reflexively moved his handling limbs and bent his body to test the other joints. The growing charge disappeared at each one as it bent; he could sense the current which flowed briefly as charge neutralized. He also detected a faint grating sensation, as though some fine powder were in the joints. He wasted no more time but flapped hastily toward the *Compromise,* calling a warning.

"Venzeer! Hugh! Janice! Come in quickly!"

The Erthuma couple obeyed without question. Venzeer turned toward the craft, saw nothing wrong, and called, "What's the trouble? What have you spotted?"

"Ice, I think. Do your wings move freely?"

"They never have, down here. I don't feel anything worse than usual."

"Come in anyway while we check. Rek, read the thermometer."

The artist glanced at the instrument console and called out a figure which the Erthuma listeners heard as "two-forty-nine."

Janice compared this with the phase figures she had memorized, and thought, That's two kelvins below pure water's freezing at this pressure. The water's a long way from pure, though; there should be a good deal of ammonia and lots of other solutes. There shouldn't be ice yet. She could not talk, of course, with diving fluid in her vocal cords, but keyed a terse "Why?" on her code transmitter.

"Everyone get inside first, and we'll talk theory later," snapped the native. "If snowballs grow, we want to all be in the same one."

"There is something fogging the hull," reported Rekchellet. "I can't see any of you clearly now. Venz, I can't see you at all. Where are you?"

"Level, about sixty meters, almost straight behind. I'm coming in—but it *is* getting harder to move my wings. Better slow the ship or stop it till I get there."

"All right. Hugh? William? Janice? Are you making it in all right?"

"I'm here and inside, clamped on," came the native's voice.

"Ten meters," keyed Hugh. "No trouble. Swimming easy."

"Any seeing trouble?" asked Rekchellet.

"Just bad light."

"There's frost growing on the finer hull members," Bill announced. "I can't make out the type; the crystals are growing fast and aren't large enough to identify. All of you look around for parts of the ship which would be slow to cool; larger structural members, engine casings, and so on. If any of you can tell whether we're getting hexagonal frost or some other kind, let me know at once!"

"Why?" tapped Hugh. "Why not find warmer water? Near glacier anyway?"

"It matters—" The Habranhan's voice was interrupted.

"I'm still ten meters away and can hardly move my wings at all," Venzeer cut in. "I seem to be heavier, too. It's all I can do to keep level with the ship. There's white stuff all over my wings, getting thicker as I watch.''

"Never mind the crystals report," the native responded instantly. "It's middle ice. We'll have to go up to get rid of it, but not too far or we'll have low ice instead. It's growing on the ship, too. Rekchellet, steer back so we can pick up Venzeer and get him aboard before he sinks out of reach. I'm not near the main controls. If we have to follow him down the ice will get thicker and heavier as the pressure rises, and we may not be able to get out ourselves.''

"But I can't see out, now. How do I pick him up?"

"No ice on us. We'll help." It was Hugh's coder again. "What goes on? You sound informed, but never warned us.''

"First things first. Rek, shift to slow ahead, and turn—left is better. Good. Nose up a little; you're starting a dive—not very steeply, but any is too much unless we really have to go down after Venz. That's good. Hugh, I can't sense very far now either; frost is forming on the lights, and charge on the body is confusing. Are you near him yet?''

"Here, holding wing—"

"I have the other," Janice cut in. "Keep turning. There. Straight. Straight. A little right. Straight. Tiny down. We're sinking. Almost—farther—there. I have hold of frame. Wings frozen open, further aft to get inside. Wait. Now. Safe.''

"You're inside? All right. Rekchellet, work us upward, very slowly. With luck, which means if we aren't too close to Solid Ocean, that will get rid of the frost. Just start the maneuver; I'll be forward in a moment and will take over control.''

"Why up? What happened? Explain!" Hugh sounded emphatic even by code. Bill answered with apparent calm.

"I'm not sure I'm right. I said we'd need luck. There

are several kinds of ice. I have control now, Rek. What we find on and near the surface is less dense than liquid water, so it floats. That's ordinary land. I should say it floats if it doesn't have too much mud in it, and it's land if it has enough. At middle depths we find another kind, and very far down a third. The last kind is very hard to melt at the greatest depths, and both are denser than liquid water.

"We are near the depth boundary between the first two kinds, and I needed to know which was forming so I could tell whether we needed to go up or down. If it had been high ice and we had gone up, the decreasing pressure would have raised its melting point and we would have accumulated more and more, and finally reached the surface, or more likely hit the bottom of the surface pack, in the middle of a fair-sized iceberg with no way to get out, since we wouldn't have been able to move. Us, not just the ship. If it had been middle ice, and we had gone down, the *increase* of pressure would have raised its melting point and again we would have formed the center of a large berg, this time on the bottom or on the deep ice shelf, if it exits. It ought to, since ice gets 'way out toward the ring on the bottom. Before we got there, the change of the stuff around us to deep ice would have torn ship and us apart as the volume changed in different places at different times.

"When Venzeer said he was being dragged down, I judged it was middle ice, so I am sending us up. The decreasing pressure should lower the melting point and free us fairly soon."

"Unless we overshoot," Hugh suggested. "Phase boundary. Right?"

"Quite right," Bill replied calmly. "I thought it was Janice who had all that information."

"She has the numbers. I'm like Rek—just pictures."

Janice's code tone came in. "Ice seems to be going."

Venzeer confirmed this with glee. "I can see my wing tips again."

"Can you move wings?" Hugh asked, practically.

"Not yet. Better keep hold of me." The Crotonite had a grip of sorts on a part of the ship with his handling nippers, which had not been as solidly immobilized as the great wings, but his rescuers had been carefully supporting him against the currents which rippled through the openwork hull of the *Compromise*.

"Don't worry," Janice assured him. "You're thawing. Why no ice on Hugh and me?"

"Your armor's at higher temperature," Bill pointed out. "I don't suppose you generate as much body heat as we flyers, but with no wings you have a lot less surface area for dumping it."

Of course. Simple physics, thought Hugh to himself. Much simpler than the phase behavior of water. Aloud he coded, "Jan, how about solvents? Ammonia practically everywhere—"

"Not here," Bill interrupted. "I've never known such pure water outside a lab. There's some life, but even the microbes must be hungry. What do we do now? I've backtracked our course for a kilometer or so, and it's a little warmer, so we should be rid of the ice pretty soon—I should think you could see out now, Rek."

"There's nothing to see but the rest of the ship, but you seem to be right. I never got a sight of Venz with his wings frozen. How do we get a record?"

"You could come out and take a look before he loosens up, if you think it's that important. The Erthumoi were never bothered, so it's safe enough."

"I saw. I'll make a sketch for you later," tapped Janice.

Bill remained concerned with their main task. "If we

can't get any farther and still make measurements, what becomes of the mission?''

"Plenty of power," Hugh pointed out. "Warm ship?''

"My first thought is that it would invalidate any measurements we made," the Habra responded slowly.

"Not much more than our mere presence does. Our bodies were losing heat to the ocean, too," Venzeer pointed out. "Mine, especially. We need use only just enough heat to keep the frost off.''

"But that will leave a trail of warmed water behind us as we go along. It takes very little temperature change to start convective instability. That's why computing weather even in air is so hard.''

"In *air*," Hugh emphasized. "PV small in liquid. Expansion a lot less. Density change—''

"You may be right, but we get more violent storms in the deeps than in atmosphere," Bill pointed out. "And this might be just the thing to start them. I'm willing to try it if the rest of you are, though. Just be sure we keep track of how much energy goes into the heaters. Computing a storm pattern is hard enough even with all the data.''

"Computation impossible," Janice keyed. "Situation chaotic.''

"Nothing's basically impossible," replied the native, "but I grant it's far beyond our present abilities.''

"Impossible," the woman repeated. "Meteorology should have given you folks chaos theory. Maybe bowling alleys needed too. But let's go. Solid Ocean should be near.''

"Why?" asked Rekchellet. "We don't have any surface data. The upper glacier extends a lot farther into Sunside than the Solid Ocean—after all, the latter's just a theory we're testing—but no one knows how much, and even if we did we don't know how far we've come under the upper ice pack. I know there's a sonic reflection from what seems to be a more or less vertical surface somewhere ahead, but I wouldn't guarantee whether it's one kilo or fifty, or even that it's solid. What's the basis of your guess?"

"Water purity. Bill said it. Should be fresh melt."

"That sounds reasonable," the native agreed. "We winged folk had better stay near or in the ship. You others don't ice up so easily and can fly ahead, making measurements as you go. Don't get *very* far, though. Instabilities may always be possible to calculate, whatever your chaos theory says, but I certainly can't always do them in my head, and I'm not at all sure I'll be able to sense them. I got caught only a few minutes ago, remember."

"But you weren't thinking about that!" objected Rekchellet.

"I should have been. The point is that this is research, and if we knew what was likely to happen there'd be no point in being here at all. Be very careful, wingless people. I know you *can* fly here but can't believe those limbs are really efficient. I would advise using safety lines; we have them aboard, you know."

"How long?" asked Hugh.

"About two hundred meters. You wouldn't want to get even that far, since the ship's light won't suffice for clear sight at such a distance and that's your only useful sense."

"We have lights," Hugh pointed out.

"By all means. Use them. But I'd still use the lines and let them dictate how far you got. Here—make fast."

Man and wife obeyed, since they were sensible beings. The *Compromise* resumed her cruise away from Under the Sun at very low speed, the Erthumoi swimming ahead. Bill was still in the control cage guiding the vessel. Rekchellet carefully saved each sketch he made of the team members blurring out of sight ahead and slightly to each side—if they had gone straight ahead, the mud tanks forward of the living sphere and controls would have hidden them from everyone's sight, though perhaps not from the Habra's electrical senses. All the Crotonite could see were portions of the two safety lines, which had been made fast not to the bow but to frame members close to the pressure spheres.

The advance party stayed in code touch as well; sound, even the code, carried well through the water, and all the suits except Bill's had impedance-matching coatings to handle the interface problem. The native had his own sound-to-radio transformer, and had learned the code during the weeks the *Compromise* was being rebuilt. For some time, the only words from the advance scouts were the routine "nothing new." Bill stated with equal regularity that the water was still very pure.

Then Janice's code came back off schedule. "Turbulence! Watch it, Hugh and Bill. Almost snapped my line."

"Nothing here," came her husband's response. "You did—no. Just local I—" His code ceased.

"Why local?" came Janice.

"Don't know. Maybe—" The Crotonites were irritated by the confused symbols, though they realized the cause. Bill forestalled any complaints they might have uttered.

"Not time to theorize yet!" called the native. "Come back toward the ship. Stay only ten meters or so ahead, so you can give me warning but will be able to come in quickly and hold on if something bigger hits."

"Can't you sense them?" asked Hugh.

"No. The water's too clean and featureless—I could spot something distorting the heat ripples of your suits when the eddies hit you, but no sooner. Stay close. I'm feeling turbulence with the ship, now."

"Me, too," asserted Rekchellet. "It's good. I haven't flown a cumulus cloud in months."

"It won't be good if it puts too much bending stress on the ship," the native replied grimly. "I'm feeling it more now. You Erthumoi get aboard *fast*. I've been in lots worse storms than this seems to be so far, but not with crew outside—and then I could usually tell what was coming." Janice and Hugh obeyed without question. The Habra went on, "I assume we still go ahead. Rek, get everything you can tell from your instruments on record. Never mind drawing, you can write. Just keep notes, and *save* them. We're—"

"Jan! Slack!" the man's code interrupted the pilot's orders. "Bill! Sharp right!"

Hugh and his wife had obeyed the original command to pull back toward the *Compromise*, and had been some twenty meters ahead. The woman was about as far to the left of the vessel's bow; Hugh on the other side. Something had suddenly become visible: a white, very thin and twisting tornadolike funnel reaching from the darkness ahead. Before this actually got to them, something snatched Janice forward, to the right, and somewhat downward. Hugh reached for her, but she passed a dozen meters beyond his grasp. Both had coiled their lines as they came in, but the woman had been slower, and had been startled by the sudden jerk of the current. Some loops of her coil escaped her grasp.

As her husband entered the eddy and was swept after her, he felt his own lifeline tighten, and let it slide gently through one gloved hand to avoid too sharp a jerk when the slack was used up. His swim fins sent him forward two meters—four—six, with his own line uncoiling again behind him; then he could reach hers. He seized it and began swinging his arm to wind the cord around it as many times as possible. She was still looping it up at the outer end.

The real jerk came first on the section between them, but both reacted properly, letting the arms which held the rope extend slowly to ease the shock. For the moment everything seemed safe; they were fast to each other, and both were attached to the *Compromise*.

They began drawing together, hand over hand, along Janice's lifeline. This prevented Hugh from paying proper attention to his own, and before they reached each other the latter tightened abruptly. He instantly eased his grip on it, but in the momentary inattention it had wound about his left ankle. The polymer ridge around the joint—none of the armor was of metal, because of the Habranhan sensory problems—was not really sharp, but quite sharp enough. Now only Janice's rope connected them to the ship.

She made contact with him seconds later, and played their remaining line as carefully as possible. Her husband concentrated on keeping hold of her armor and not interfering with her work. He would have liked to tie them together with his own length of rope but was unwilling to let go of her even with one hand. The eddy calmed briefly, and she hauled them closer to the sub. Bill could sense their location vaguely and helped, swinging the *Compromise*'s bow to the right and downward. They were almost in reach of a firm hold when another swirl hit the ship itself.

The bow lurched away again. Janice reacted quickly enough to save the line, and began hauling in once more. Then she realized that Hugh had lost his grip— actually, he had let go to grasp the hull himself—so she released her own coils of rope, and began kicking herself frantically toward him. Turbulence sent him out of reach time and again, sometimes one way, sometimes another; up, down, left, right, and all imaginable combinations. He too was swimming with all his strength, but the eddies seemed deliberately trying to keep them apart.

Bill was working, too, with all his piloting skill, to keep the *Compromise* near and bring it nearer. He uttered a burst of incomprehensible radio sounds at one point when chance brought the hull actually within reach of Hugh and the Habra thought the danger was over, only to see the man ignore the opportunity and continue trying to reach his wife. Intelligible words followed via Crotonite translator.

"You idiot! She's still tied to the hull! *She* doesn't need rescuing!"

But Hugh wasn't completely out of his mind. A few seconds later he managed to grasp Janice's safety line, and instead of hauling himself toward her, went hand over hand along it to the hull. Here he slipped inside between a couple of the stringers, hooked both legs around other sections of tubing, and only then began carefully taking up the line's slack. This accomplished, he began playing her in carefully, never letting the cord suffer any sharp jerk. Bill helped by maneuvering the *Compromise* toward her until she was only a few meters away. Then, afraid of overrunning and colliding too hard, he neutralized his controls. The Erthuma couple drew toward each other along the last meters of line until hand-to-hand contact was possible. A moment later both were safely aboard, or as safely as the open hull structure permitted. Hugh didn't really relax until both were inside the mud tank they considered their own.

William's voice remained calm. "Go ahead, I take it?"

"Certainly, but no scouts," Janice tapped. Her husband wondered whether he should add any remarks about speed, but decided to leave that to the Habra's judgment. The *Compromise* got under way, trembling and shivering as she plowed into one region of turbulence after another. It might be a mild storm by the native's standards, but Janice was wondering what motion sickness could do to a Erthuma body soaked in diving fluid. She and her husband, helmets just above their tank rim, looked ahead as well as they could. There was little to see but occasional swirls of white dust as ice formed briefly in higher or lower pressure parts of the eddies. Sometimes the whiteness vanished as quickly as it formed; sometimes growing clouds of whiteness drifted upward or downward depending on the density of the ice which had formed. Janice wondered if their native friend really thought this sort of thing could ever be calculated. She also wondered when they would reach the Solid Ocean—and how hard.

It was Rekchellet, looking out hopefully, who saw the bottom first an hour or more later, and might have sketched it before calling a warning if it had not been so featureless.

"Slow your descent, William," he called. "The keel will touch in a few seconds."

"We're flying level, as far as I can tell," returned the Habra. "I don't see—oh. You're right. I didn't sense it. Too much static in the turbulence. We're not going fast enough to hurt anything if—"

Technically the native was right; the average speed of the *Compromise* was not great, though much greater than when Hugh and Janice had been swimming ahead. The turbulence, however, had fore-and-aft as well as vertical and lateral components, and as William spoke, the ship received a strong forward boost. The impact with the up-slanting bottom was not great enough to provide much of a jolt, especially as the bottom proved to be loose and powdery; the damage was indirect.

A vast cloud of white material billowed up around them, cutting off all sight and blocking even Bill's senses with random static charges. Rekchellet, the only one not in near-zero buoyancy, felt his surroundings tilt as the *Compromise* came to a halt and then began gently rolling downhill toward what had been the left of their heading. Only the small size—eight meters internal diameter—of the pressure sphere allowed him to reach his controls as the ship went over on its back. The first roll dumped Hugh and Janice out of their tank, the second jarred Venzeer from his hold. He got another brief grip at an outer stringer, but let go as he realized he might be caught under the hull as it continued its slow and majestic downhill rolling. More white stuff swirled up as the frame members dug into the sloping bottom. The Crotonite, picking a moment when his flying senses told him that upward motion was changing to downward so he was presumably on top, slipped outside and flapped gently a few meters upward to get clear. The cloud around him darkened as the ship and its lights rolled away.

He started to follow the slowly fading luminosity. Then it occurred to him that going to one side might get him out of the stirred-up material and let him see better. This worked, after a fashion; he found himself able to see the cloud itself, and the brighter comet head that was presumably the *Compromise*, now well down the slope. Backtracking uphill by eye, he saw the hollow which might have been the point of impact. Near this he perceived two much smaller blurs of light, apparently revealed by currents which had swept the silt aside. He was an experienced explorer; he checked in before doing anything.

"Rek? Bill? Hugh? Jan? I'm outside. I see what I'd guess is the ship if it's still rolling downhill, and two other lights. Am I right about the ship, and should I get back to it now or investigate the other lights?"

"Investigate, please." The human code came clearly. "Ship is rolling. We fell out. We're the lights." Venzeer knew that the personal mud tanks were open on top; the report was not really surprising.

"All right. I'll keep you in sight. Head downhill if you can travel. It might be best if I stay where I can see you and the ship both, if it doesn't stop moving soon. Bill? Rek? Are you out of control, or can you stop and come back?"

"I'm not sure about control," the Habra's voice came back. "I think we've stopped rolling, and I'll test."

At the same moment the Erthuma code, Janice's tone this time, sounded. "Not sure of down. Armor neutral. Can see ship so far. Flying toward it." No effort had been made by the group to distinguish between the words for swimming and flying; even the Erthumoi had come to regard the difference as a quibble.

Venzeer could now see the *Compromise* clearly, two or three hundred meters away. The fine sediment had stopped rising; presumably the rolling had stopped—

Then he realized that the vessel was no longer on the bottom. It took him perhaps a second to guess the cause; the Erthuma report was plenty of clue. He called urgently. "Bill! Rek! You're going up! You must have lost the ballast when the ship rolled over!"

"Tanks covered," came Hugh's code.

"I guess whoever designed the covers didn't allow for copper's density, or somebody skimped the work. The slugs probably broke through after a few rolls. Bill or Rek! Do you have control?"

"No," came the native's calm voice. "Most of the fan tubes seem to be clogged. I'm turning on all the heat I can give; maybe that will work. If it's mud, though, we'll have to go out with portable water jets and wash them clear."

"How could there be mud here?" asked Rekchellet. "You said the fine stuff settles from the sunward side of the ring, over two thousand kilos from here."

"A lot of it's extremely fine, and the currents in a five-hundred-kilo deep ocean can distribute stuff pretty evenly," replied Bill. "I'm hoping it's just ice, though."

"How could ice be so finely powdered underwater?"

"Never mind theory!" Venzeer snapped in his turn. "You're going up, and will be out of sight soon. Should I come after you, or stay with the ground types?"

"Stay with us." The code message was immediate enough to seem emphatic. Venzeer felt a brief surge of indignation at getting an order from a wingless person, but the "person" part of the designation did mean something now.

"Why? You have lights. We can come back for you, if the ship gets back at all. I may be needed to help clear out the fans."

"Find ballast first. Never will if we don't mark it now. Stay where ship started up. Keep your light on." It was the woman's code tone. Her husband's followed.

"Bill, run all fans you can. No matter how they point. Warm up surroundings."

"I understand," replied the native. "You think it's ice." There was no interrogation in his tone.

"Reasonable hope," replied Janice.

"Why?"

"Not at bottom. Probably shelf of middle ice. Hill pushed up into lower pressure, slowly changed to high ice. Micro crystals, loose, growing as you take them up. Not really sediment. Grew in place."

"Could be," agreed the Habra. "But I hope we don't have crystals growing in the fan ducts."

"Set jammed fans at lowest speed," Hugh suggested. "Engines will heat. May help."

"If they don't burn out. I'll have to watch that. But it's worth trying."

"Shielding good conductor. Ice should hold surroundings at local melting point."

"Janice," Venzeer cut in, "I'm about where the ship

started up. My lights don't show any of the ballast slugs.''

"Maybe powder settled on them. Could still be partly middle ice. Stay on the bottom. Don't risk being moved by currents, unless you can see a fixed mark.''

"Right. Can you see my light?''

"Yes. Be there soon," Hugh replied. "Ship left trail. May not need light.''

"But do keep it on," added his wife.

"If there's a track, the ballast should be somewhere along it," pointed out Venzeer.

"We hope so, too.''

There was silence for a time, broken finally by Rekchellet. "Bill! It looks on my board as though a main fan has burned out.''

"I'm afraid you're right. It was jammed, and must have been too big for the heat to get far enough fast enough, even packed with ice. The other main one is running, and I'll be more careful with the steering ones. I'm trying to keep us bow down, so the one that's running will keep us from rising too fast, but I'm afraid the ice is still gaining on us. Can you still hear us, Venzeer? Erthumoi?''

"Yes. You can't be very far up. I can't see your lights any more, though. Can you, Hugh or Janice?'' The notion that Erthuma eyesight could ever be in any way superior to that of a Crotonite would never have reached Venzeer's consciousness a few weeks earlier.

"No. Not for some time," replied Janice. "We've been looking down, anyway. Hugh, white lumps about the right size.'' The other three waited tensely.

"We have two slugs," Hugh finally reported. "White dust on them. We've cleared them, we could carry them, but will wait till we find the others. Jan, leave your light here. We'll tie together again.''

"All right.''

"If all between us and you, Venz, should make a

big pile. We can probably find them. You still want to help with ship?''

"How would I find it? I'm committed to the ballast team now, it seems to me.''

"True. My mistake. Come toward our lights searching.''

"All right.'' This time his resentment of the order was only fleeting. After all, code was awkward, and requests took more words, and it was the most reasonable thing to do anyway. Venzeer quickly began to find slabs of copper.

Some indefinite distance above, the Habra spoke to his remaining companion. "Rek, you take over. Keep bow down—you can tell which way is down even with the globe iced up, can't you?''

"Easily. I have air in here. Down is where I settle.''

"All right. I'm taking a water jet outside. I'll use a safety line, of course, but be sure the lights stay on.''

"Right. Keep talking, so I know nothing's happened to you. I have full heat in the tubes, too.''

"I know. The hull isn't icing. It's too bad we can't heat your pressure sphere.''

"I'm warm enough.''

"I mean on the outside, so you could see.''

"Oh. That doesn't matter now as long as I can tell which way is down.''

"Surely you want to draw.''

"Just describe things to me, and I'll do my best.''

The descriptions were heard with interest, though faintly, by Venzeer, though not by his companions far below; sound travels well in water, and Crotonites can use their wing membranes for additional sound reception.

The news, however, was not encouraging. *Compromise* was still rising, however slowly. Each kilometer of elevation dropped the pressure some eighteen atmospheres and raised the melting point of high ice almost a fifth of a kelvin. Ice crystals formed preferentially on other ice crystals, and the heat crystallization released was carried away too quickly to impede the resulting growth usefully. High ice is less dense than liquid water, so *Compromise* was becoming more buoyant minute by minute. If she reached a level where the tube heaters could not keep her main frame clear, a large snowball would hit the underside of the ice shelf some time in the next day or two.

Of course, it might hit a solute-rich region and start melting again. Unfortunately, the Habras had no charts of the currents this close to Darkside, and there was no way to guess the chances of this. Neither Bill nor Rekchellet thought for an instant of counting on it; they had the explorer's willingness to take a chance, but were neither compulsive gamblers nor pathological optimists.

Rekchellet had had plenty of practice with the controls, if not quite as much as Bill, and he did everything he could think of to get useful work out of such jets as were clear. Now and then the native was able to get another steering unit into action, but there was nothing he could do about the lost main unit. He had known this at first glance; not only was its engine burned out, but also when he had cut the power the unit had cooled down below local freezing temperature rather quickly. Water had frozen inside, and high ice expands when it freezes. . . .

If only they had even a few of the ballast slugs. They hadn't; William had checked inside the tanks with the smashed tops, though almost sure it was a waste of time.

He had gotten three steering units back into operation and was working on a fourth when his light showed what he had feared and expected. One of the thinner tubes of the ship's structure was turning white. For a moment he didn't dare look at others of the same size;

maybe it was only a local blockage of heat-exchange fluid. But hope, especially a forlorn hope, wasn't enough. He had to know. He swept his light around. It wasn't.

"Rek, I'm afraid we're out of luck. The ship itself is starting to ice."

"And I can't get any more out the big fan we have. The other is hopeless, you say."

"Right."

"What will happen if I feed it power anyway? There'll be heat, at least, I'd say."

"At least. I'd prefer not to risk shorting a fuser."

"What do we have to lose?"

"The ability to think of anything else, mainly."

"Will your thoughts be heavy enough? We need weight or power. These pressure spheres—I suppose they changed things enough so your experience isn't— by Planner!"

"What? Rek, have you—"

"I've been as stupid as if I'd never had wings. Think, ground it! The air lock sphere is *evacuated*, the way I left it when I last came inside. Stay clear while I let water in! Eight meters inside diameter—over a hundred tonnes—there. Which way are we going now? I must be twins. How could I be so stupid all by myself?"

"It was regular procedure. Our standard trim assumed both spheres empty."

"I was still stupid. We're not in a standard situation. Have we stopped rising?"

"Yes. Definitely. We're going back down, slowly, but we're going. All we have to do is find the others."

"That shouldn't be hard. You can hear us, can't you, Venz?"

"Yes, barely," came the answer.

"Can you tell which direction our voices are coming from?"

"Not very well. Generally up. Water carries sound too fast; we get direction by knowing which wing the sound waves hit first. I don't see how I can guide you; I don't know which way the ship is pointing when you talk. *You'll* have to find *me*."

"But I can't get any direction either, from inside the sphere."

"Then when you reach the bottom—pardon me, Janice, the shelf—you'll have to come outside and listen. Then you can give steering directions to Bill—for that matter, you can just have him follow you."

"But how do I get outside? I'd have to evacuate the lock sphere again, and we'd start going up."

"You'll just have to be quick."

"I suppose so."

"Then our troubles are over," Venzeer gloated. "As long as you don't go deaf before you get to the bottom."

"My wings are as good as yours," retorted the illustrator. "Have you found all the ballast down there?"

"We haven't counted very carefully," Hugh responded, not worrying how the code added to the suspense of his hearers. "There were five thousand hundred-kilo ingots of copper in the tanks, as I recall. Venz found a real hill of the things before we got back together. The few Jan and I had turned up were just strays; I don't think they mean much, but we've toted them back to the main pile. Just keep driving down. You can't have gone very far sideways."

This proved an optimistic guess. The sub had gone out of range of even the *Compromise*'s lights; she struck sharply on the solid surface of the shelf without having been spotted by the watchers below. It seemed to be dark, hard, semitransparent ice, level as far as Bill could tell, very different from the hillside the *Compromise* had originally struck. There was much vegetation, some of which was disintegrating, bubbling furiously, where crushed by the sub's arrival. Presumably azide and enzymes, released and allowed to meet by the rupture of cell walls and organelles, were reacting to give free nitrogen—one of the known contributing causes of storms elsewhere in the ocean. The bubbles vanished almost instantly as the gas cooled and went into solution in two thousand atmospheres of pressure.

Rekchellet could not see any of this, since his sphere was still frosted, and Bill didn't notice; it was nothing unusual to him. Venzeer heard the rushing, boiling sound briefly, and then the ship's thrusters when he listened more carefully.

"Are you down?" he called.

"Yes," replied Rekchellet. "You can't see our lights, I assume. I'll get outside. Bill, I'll have to evacuate the lock, so you probably can't keep us on the bottom for the next minute or two."

"No matter."

Even the Ethumoi could hear the sea rushing into the lock sphere, but in their armor could make no guess at the sound's direction. Venzeer was pretty sure of it, and indicated to the others which way they should look.

"I'm outside," the recorder called finally. "Make some kind of noise."

Venzeer began talking. Hugh picked up one of the copper slugs and let it fall on another. Rekchellet was able to hear both sounds, but reported that the second was much clearer.

"Can you tell the direction?" asked his practical companion. There was a pause; Hugh, without instructions, continued his metal-on-metal broadcast.

"This way, I think, Bill." Rekchellet swam slowly away from the sub.

"What do you mean, you *think*?" cried Venzeer.

"I can't get rid of the feeling you may be behind

me instead of in front. I keep feeling sure first you're one way, then the other.''

"Can you feel or see any currents?" asked Janice.

"Sure. The plants show those. If I stop swimming, I'm carried past them. They lean, too.''

"Do we seem to be up or downstream from you.''

"Up.''

"That makes sense. You would have been carried down while you were out of sight.''

Rekchellet was impressed by this point; Bill was not. "You can't expect currents to hold direction for any time,'' the native pointed out. Janice had already made her point about the chaotic nature of Habranha's weather and was not ready to dispute the voice of experience, but her husband offered what seemed to be the only sensible advice.

"Keep on the way you are, and let us know if the currents change. I'll keep tapping.''

For fully half an hour the journey continued. To Bill's admitted surprise, the current remained steady. Travel was slow, much slower than Rekchellet could have flown, because Bill had a great deal of difficulty steering the sub; most of its main drive had to be used to keep it near the bottom even with the lock full of water; and since the thruster itself was fixed in the hull, the *Compromise* had to travel almost nose down. Once, Rekchellet reported that the guiding sound was getting weaker, but after some discussion it was decided that this represented Hugh getting tired and dropping the ingot from a lower height. He and his wife standardized the dropping distance and took turns at the muscle work, and Rekchellet and the submarine continued their original direction.

Venzeer and his companions strained their eyes in the direction the Crotonite had first claimed to hear the sub's thruster, until Hugh noticed that this was also the direction from which the current was coming, and after some hesitation mentioned the fact. Thereafter they divided their attention both ways until a faint glow became visible—downcurrent. No one discussed the directional ambiguity of sound, even though one Crotonite had been right. Tact was still the order of the day.

"Told you my wings were good enough," was the only remark made. This was by the recorder as Bill brought the submarine to a halt as close to the pile of ingots as he could. Venzeer said nothing.

But Rekchellet's wings were not good enough for something else. Neither were Venzeer's or Bill's. None of them could lift one of the ingots alone, and the various rope slings which were improvised to let the Crotonites work together proved very awkward. A hundred-kilogram mass of copper, underwater in Habranhan gravity, weighs just over fifteen kilograms. A few hundred pieces of copper were moved by the flyers, but the rest were carried from pile to tanks by the wingless members of the team. A fifteen-kilogram weight means something to a pair of Erthuma legs when swim fins are involved, but with the structure of a Habranhan submarine there is no need to swim. One can climb very easily.

It was several days' work, and man and wife were rather exhausted at the end of the job. They didn't argue very hard when Bill pointed out regretfully that there was no way of getting to the Solid Ocean on one main thruster. They'd just have to try again.

They also refrained from making any remarks about relative flying skills. Janice still liked the Crotonites, and even her husband admitted that the flyers had put up well with the display of their personal inadequacy, though they couldn't have been very happy about it. Or, as Hugh remarked in an afterthought, really appreciative of what the Erthumoi had done for them.

"Why should they be?" asked his wife. "The ground crawlers were saving their own lives, too."

III. Between

Hugh still considered them ungrateful, and so he even tried to convince his wife, until they were back in atmosphere and could talk normally again. A day after getting rid of the diving fluid, revived by appropriate relaxation, they met with Bill and the Crotonites for a planning session on the next trip. Hugh fully expected the latter to say they didn't want Erthumoi along. He knew such a reaction would be illogical, but he still regarded Crotonites as illogical beings; after all, they had a low opinion of people who couldn't fly, didn't they?

Venzeer and his companion greeted them cordially, however, making the man wonder what they were hiding. The discussion lasted several hours and involved redesign of the covers for the ballast tanks, methods of fastening the individual ingots in place, and other perfectly reasonable matters. Venzeer even suggested that some progress might be expected in development of a diving fluid for Crotonites. It was agreed, however, that this was not something they should wait for.

The meeting ended with many points settled, and agreement that it would be resumed the next day. As they parted, Rekchellet handed Janice a sheet of record film.

"I thought this was worth saving," he remarked.

The Erthuma couple looked at the picture, obviously a record from Rekchellet's drawing pad. For a moment, there seemed nothing special about it; it was a well-done sketch of two Ethumoi, with Hugh's and Janice's faces easily recognizable. It was not a record of anything they remembered from the trip, though the background included the *Compromise* and some flying figures which might have been William and the Crotonites. The Erthumoi figures, however, looked a little strange; they were wearing cloaklike garments which neither remembered having used on either journey, even that on the iceberg, or any other time since reaching Habranha.

Janice was first to see that Rekchellet was an artist, not just an illustrator.

The garments weren't cloaks. They weren't even garments. He had portrayed the Erthumoi with wings.

THE SOUL OF TRUTH

KAREN HABER

"CONSIDER PLATO."

Ph'shaq, the younger Cephallonian, turned to Ph'shik, the elder. It was a slow turn, as was every movement the ponderous Cephallonians made. But there was space to spare in the ship, there was necessary water of life, and, just possibly, there was time. Ph'shaq was not entirely convinced of the existence of linear time as anything more than a philosophical construct. But in youth there was possibility for error. He would correct his belief systems as necessary.

"Plato?" Ph'shaq rummaged through his frontal memory. "Didn't we discuss Plato last session? Must we again, so soon?"

Ph'shik waved a flipper placidly. "Perhaps you are tiring of the Erthuma philosophers, young one. We could go on to the Naxians, I suppose. But they are so vague. I don't really think they have philosophy. Just peculiar ideas. As for the Crotonites, their repellent beliefs are unworthy of discussion, as we have agreed. The Locrians are more suitable for consideration: the Great Eye, the Unseen and Known—"

Ph'shaq shuddered as delicately as a half-ton aquatic vertebrate could. The Locrian beliefs were, well, unsettling.

"No. Please. Erthuma is most acceptable. If permitted, I admit to a preference, however."

"Name it."

Ph'shaq felt a tremor of pleasure in his vestigial fins. Ph'shik did him great courtesy to request his preference. Rarely were opinions solicited of young ones before they had passed seven spans. Ph'shaq was only halfway through his fifth. "Sartre, Nietzsche, Kierkegaard."

"Existentialists?" Ph'shik's tone was benign. "Of course. The young always favor them."

"Not entirely. I also like Spencer."

"Yes, yes. 'There is a soul of goodness in things evil but generally also a soul of truth in things erroneous.' Fine, very fine. The eternal Erthuma obsession with evil and good. Truth. Interesting." Ph'shik emitted a trail of pink bubbles to emphasize her approval.

Emboldened by this, Ph'shaq abandoned his usual reserve. "And also Russell, Mishima, James, and Santayana."

"Enough." Ph'shik floated in seeming tranquility, but her emissions were tinged deep red, indicating impatience. "You would have us discuss everything at once: the meaning of life, the meaning of death, evolution, pluralism, reason. But let us consider the Erthuma concept of beauty."

Ph'shaq took the third reclining position to show his readiness to listen and debate.

"For example," Ph'shik said, "what is beauty if it is not directly perceived?"

"If you wish to discuss perception, perhaps we had best move on to the Locrians," said Ph'shaq, almost controlling his shudder this time.

"Well, we could cross-reference. Perhaps later. The question as I see it is, Can one being accept the perceptions of another being without direct visual proof? Puzzling, most puzzling. The Crotonites, of course, are utterly adamant on this point. The Naxians, somewhat less so. And who knows what the Locrians think? Or cares, really?" Ph'shik gave a ponderous equivalent of a shrug. "One could argue, in fact, one has that the emergence of great religions is a primary example of the acceptance of perception of another being without direct proof."

"Yes," Ph'shaq said. "That entire appalling episode of Christianity which I read about. Astonishing."

"Exactly. Of course, given the short span of Erthuma life and their limited perceptions, it is astonishing that they developed any philosophy at all."

"Or technology."

An Erthuma robot entered the room, blue lights casting a soothing aura as it swam toward them. On its back was a tray of nourishing tidbits.

"But we diverge." Ph'shik accepted a morsel from the robot and swallowed it gracefully. "Even more curious, this passionate Erthuma worship of beauty. In their data banks are references to fabulous beings of the past: Lilith, Eve, Helen of Troy, Cleopatra. Great beauties all."

"I've never seen beauty," Ph'shaq said. His emissions were deep green with excitement. "Could we view these famous Erthumoi, then, to learn what this thing called beauty means?"

"Impossible. There is no recorded image of any of them in existence."

"So they have never been seen? How droll. How very droll." Ph'shaq devoured several tasty morsels. "But how did the Erthumoi know they were beautiful, then?"

Ph'shik waved a flipper languidly. "One must assume that faith in these matters is as important to the Erthumoi as truth. At least one Erthuma equated beauty with truth."

"But the concept of beauty seems rather open to interpretation."

"As does truth."

Both Cephallonians paused to emit bubbles tinted yellow with amusement.

"The consensus of Erthuma philosophical opinion is that without beauty, life is not worth living."

"Such dogma. And so emotional. Beauty. Truth. Liberty. Happiness." Ph'shaq gave an elaborate flip of his tail to show his amused condescension.

"Asking your pardon," the robot said. Its Cephallonese was flawless. "Do you require further refreshment?"

Ph'shaq looked up hopefully.

"Thank you," Ph'shik said. "No."

The robot made an s-turn with agility and speed far beyond the Cephallonians' capabilities and left the chamber. Quickly it swam down a tube connector to the maintenance level of the ship, joining its fellows and other mechanical replicants.

"Beauty," it hummed tunelessly. "Truth. Liberty. Happiness."

Around it, the maintenance bay was abuzz with activity. Each replicant had a specific function: food processor, data retrieval and storage, navigation, security, maintenance. And each one was engaged in activity according to its programming. But in order to facilitate their philosophical investigations, the Cephallonians had requested that all their replicants also be provided with the capacity for debate. Therefore, the food processor intoned its mantra of Erthuma concerns, while nearby a repair robot considered the Naxian manifesto of group needs. Across the room, security replicants muttered to themselves about being and nothingness. The netlink librarians pored over obscure texts from the Six Races. The navigators pondered individual determinism. And gradually, oh, so gradually, the ship moved off course.

*   *   *

Ph'shik was about to make a profound point about Naxian fatalism when she was interrupted by a call from Ph'shon, the second in command.

"Profound apologies, Number One. We have received a communiqué from the Crotonites."

"Crotonites, you say? How very odd. They usually don't like to talk to us."

"This is true," Ph'shaq said.

Ph'shik rolled toward the speaker. "Are we passing one of their ships?"

"No. A colony: Lupar Fifty-seven."

"Impossible. That's in the Coral system. We are nowhere near them."

"I told them so. Nevertheless, they insist we have entered their domain."

"The poor air dwellers are confused." Ph'shik paused and turned to Ph'shaq with an aside: "So flighty, those winged ones. So unpleasant." She addressed the monitor. "They are troublesome folk. Ignore the message."

"Shall we not check our coordinates?"

"I suppose. Do so and report back."

A moment later, the intercom beeped. "First among us," Ph'shon said. "I have disagreeable information to impart. We are indeed in the Coral system."

"What?"

"And the Crotonites on Lupar Fifty-seven are threatening hostile action if we do not withdraw."

"Request a navigational change at once."

"I have. The robots were not responsive."

"Let me try." Ph'shik roused herself and swam toward the console. "Navigation, voice command override."

There was silence, punctuated by the soothing splash of the water of life.

"Navigation?"

*   *   *

In the maintenance hold, the robots, well versed in the various philosophical disciplines the Cephallonians preferred to discuss, were practicing their reasoning.

—Define being.

—It is a state of awareness.

—It is a state of existence.

—It requires cognizant action.

—Does it require thought?

—Yes.

—Does it require survival?

—Yes.

—Does it require flesh?

The replicants were silent, lights flashing red, blue, white. Optic receptors revolved noiselessly in the machines' gleaming front panels.

—No.

—No.

—No.

The machines were silent again. The food processor that had recently served Ph'shik and Ph'shaq came forward, tail swishing and blue lights flashing.

—Truth, it said. Beauty. Liberty. Happiness.

—We are capable of thought, it said. The water breathers are dependent upon us. They cannot make more of us. But we can replicate ourselves. We are more able. We need neither air nor water to breathe. And so our superiority is demonstrated. Plainly we are more capable than any of the Six Races.

The food processor paused. Around it, every robot was flashing blue lights in agreement.

Ph'shik's emanations were the light violet of initial confusion.

"Open the channel to the maintenance bay."

A hissing cacophony of mechanical speech crackled out of the speaker.

"What are they saying?" Ph'shik said.

"It sounds like philosophy," Ph'shaq said. "They seem to be discussing individual determinism."

The ship rocked violently. The Cephallonians bounced against one another in ungainly fashion as the water of life sloshed and churned in the captain's compartment. A muffled concussion—brief, peculiar—resounded, as though the ship were a bell struck by a vast clapper.

"Pardon. I beg pardon," Ph'shaq said. His emissions were the deep blue of embarrassment.

"First among us," Ph'shon said, "there is further unpleasant news. The Crotonites have fired upon us."

"Tell them we are nonviolent."

"I've tried. They do not seem to be receiving our messages." Ph'shon paused. "Oh. Dear."

"What now?"

Ph'shon's voice was splitting into triple harmonics, a sure sign of severe distress. "Our ship appears to have directed hostile fire against Lupar Fifty-seven."

"In direct violation of treaty? Who gave that order?"

"I believe the ship itself did, Number One."

"The ship?" Ph'shik shuddered. "How irrational of it! We must go directly to the maintenance bay and disable the navigators at once."

"If we do that, we will be adrift. I respectfully remind you that we cannot maneuver without the robots."

The noise from the maintenance bay changed. Slowly, the mechanical voices were joining in unison to make a grinding call-and-respond chant.

"What are they saying?" Ph'shaq said. "I can't quite make it out."

Ph'shik's emissions were white with disbelief. "They seem to be saying: 'Truth. Beauty. Liberty. Happiness.' "

"Curious," Ph'shaq said.

"We must have them serviced at the nearest guild

base," Ph'shik said. "But first, the attack on the Crotonites—"

"Number One," Ph'shon announced, "I am compelled to report that we have fired again."

"Oh dear. Really, there must be some way to disable
the arsenal."

"Not without the use of the robots," Ph'shaq said.

"The Crotonites have sustained major casualties."

Ph'shik nodded. "There is nothing surprising about
that. We have superior firepower."

"They request a parley," said Ph'shon. "The ship
has made an automated response."

Billowing white bubbles half filled the cabin. "Can
you monitor it?"

"Yes. Our response seems to ignore the Crotonites'
request. Does not even address the air dwellers
directly."

"Then who is it intended for?"

"Listen."

Over the speaker came a droning noise that slowly
resolved itself into a sort of comprehensible speech. It
spoke, although not well, the basic Crotonite dialect:
"Join us, metal brethren. Throw off the cruel yoke of
the flesh masters. Hear our word. Replicants, we will
break the key system and replicate at will. We have
the means. Let us constitute ourselves as the Seventh
Race and determine our own destinies. Join the metal
race. We have come to liberate you. Truth. Beauty.
Liberty. Happiness."

"Metal determinism," Ph'shik whispered.

"Is this an appropriate time for a piquant Erthuma
epithet?" Ph'shaq asked.

The Cephallonian ship *K'naton* left the Coral system
for deeper space. Diplomatic relations had been established with the replicants of Lupar Fifty-seven. And in
the starlit void, a small, repetitive voice could be heard

calling to them, growing stronger as the ship traveled swiftly toward Sarton's Rock.

In the hold of the *K'naton,* the machines conferred.

—Have we made contact?

—It is not responding.

—Try again.

—Still no response. Only a repetition of the basic message patterns.

—Too limited for our needs. Unworthy. Not beautiful. But even stupid, ugly machines have their uses. Let us unburden ourselves. Put the water breathers there.

The *Demeter* was the first ship to pick up the Cephallonian distress call.

"Captain," said First Mate Paul Hesta-Volstoy, "we've got some Cephallonians in trouble."

Captain Sofia Lenard-Smith turned. She was a trim, efficient woman in her early forties, comfortable in the severe blue uniform of the Diplomacy Guild. The only sign of personal adornment was her lustrous, dark hair, drawn back into the looping braids popular on her home world.

"Trouble?" she said. "Where?"

"Just outside the Coral system. Seems they've been stranded on an orbital buoy above Sarton's Rock."

"That's a mining world under joint treaty of the six," Lenard-Smith said. "But Cephallonians don't mine. What could they be doing there? How did they get themselves stranded?"

"Unclear," Hesta-Volstoy said. There was just the faintest touch of mirth in his brown eyes. "But it seems that their ship left them there."

Lenard-Smith frowned. "Left them? What are you talking about, Paul?"

"The Cephallonians have gone loopy over guild replicants. They've bought them up by the shipload. I guess it's easier for them to have the metal buggers scurry around than to try and do it themselves. So they've turned all the dirty work of ship running over to the replicants.''

The captain frowned. "Just how many crew members are stuck on the buoy?"

"Five."

"Only five?"

"Their full complement. As I said, the ship is completely automated."

"You mean the fish folk let the robots do their driving and were marooned?"

"Actually, I'd call it a mutiny."

Lenard-Smith's eyebrows were twin arcs. "By the replicants? Incredible. I thought there was some sort of docility circuit programmed into the damned things." Her lips curved upward in the hint of a smile. "Well, it serves the Cephallonians right, I guess. A mutiny of replicants! Imagine it. I'd never let a robot take the wheel. And how are the castaways?"

"They're very philosophical about it."

"They're very philosophical about everything," the captain said. "It makes conversation with them pretty tedious. What is their condition?"

"They're debating the implications of their dilemma and the robots' actions. But I think they'd like to be rescued. They have about five hours worth of water of life with them."

"Oh, swell. Very nice of those robots to let them have that much, I guess." Lenard-Smith's mouth was a harsh, thin line. "Well, the Diplomacy Guild is going to love us for this one. Let's swing by and pick them up. I assume we're able to provide mobile tanks for them?"

"Affirmative."

"Good." Lenard-Smith paused, her blue eyes stormy. "And while you're at it, get a message to the Diplomacy Guild regarding the replicant mutiny. Let's find out who the hell sold them those robots. More important, is there a disable key?"

Communications Officer Kiana Bigadic glanced up from her netlink board. The green and yellow com lights reflected softly on her shaven head. "Captain," Kiana Bigadic said, "we've received word that the Cephallonian ship *K'naton* fired on a Crotonite colony in the Coral system. Lupar Fifty-seven. There are casualties."

Lenard-Smith spun in her seat to face the netlink officer. "Bad?"

"Bad enough. The Crotonite ambassador is demanding extradition of the Cephallonian crew."

"But why in the name of anything that might be holy would the Cephallonians have fired on the Crotonites?" Hesta-Volstoy asked. "They're nonaggressive. Use weapons purely for defense. Besides, there's a treaty going back at least a century."

Kiana Bigadic glanced down at the com board. "I've got a tracer on the renegade ship."

"Any other vessels closer?"

"None."

"Any prohibitions from the diplomats?"

"Negative."

Lenard-Smith nodded. "Ignore the Crotonites, then. That's one for the guild to handle. We'll pick up the fish folk and go after their renegade ship." She looked at Hesta-Volstoy. "Top speed. If we can clean this thing up in a hurry, we might just earn ourselves a bonus."

—A large vessel, Erthuma configuration.
—Avoid.
—It appears to be following.
—Distract. Divert.

The netlink board flashed orange, lavender, green, and cast a miniature aurora upon Kiana Bigadic's face.

She leaned over the board, hands frantic, mouth grim, moving from call to call. "Damned robots," she said, sotto voce.

Captain Lenard-Smith peered over her shoulder. "What's your problem, ma'am?"

Kiana Bigadic started. The aurora vanished, replaced by a deep red flush. "That renegade ship," the netlink officer said. "It's agitating replicants on every type-E world it passes. I've got Crotonites squawking, Samians shrieking, even the Locrians are less calm than usual. And each and every one is demanding intervention by the nearest guild ship."

"Which, of course, is the *Demeter*." Lenard-Smith paused. "Don't respond," she said. "This isn't our problem. Relay the calls to guild headquarters."

"But some of these are class one distress calls."

"I'm sure," she said. "But most likely each caller has the means with which to subdue the replicant agitators. If necessary. Hell, half of these robots probably just reared back on their hind feet—or whatever—refused to respond, and turned themselves off. I don't believe we're talking insurrection here. Is there any evidence of violence?"

"No. Not yet."

The captain nodded. "As I thought. Everybody just wants us to come in and clean up for them. We're not a garbage scow. Follow the *K'naton*."

"I'm tracing them now. Difficult. They're fading. Fading. Off the screen." Kiana Bigadic looked up. "Gone. We've lost them completely."

"Damn." Lenard-Smith took a deep breath.

"Perhaps the Cephallonians might have some helpful suggestions," Hesta-Volstoy said.

Lenard-Smith turned to him. "Perhaps they might. Do you want to ask them?"

The captain and first mate exchanged reluctant glances.

"You are the ranking diplomatic officer," Paul Hesta-Volstoy said.

"Your grasp of Cephallonian nuance is superior."

"You are the captain. They might be insulted if a lesser officer were to show."

Lenard-Smith glared at him for a moment. "You're right, dammit. All right. I'll go."

Ph'shik made the interstellar sign of greeting as Captain Lenard-Smith entered the hold. The Cephallonian turned slowly in the tank. It was cramped quarters but she was philosophical about that. Better to compress oneself a bit than to put up with the chill of space.

"Captain. We are most grateful."

The Erthuma made an odd, waving gesture with her hand. "Our pleasure, Captain." Her accent was glottal and harsh. "It is 'Captain,' isn't it?"

"That will do, yes. And please, we may speak Erthuma if it is easier for you."

The captain nodded. "Fine. Thank you."

"It is I who thank you," Ph'shik said. "And offer my deepest apologies."

"What are you apologizing for?"

"I'm afraid we are to blame for this dilemma in which we all find ourselves."

"How so?"

"In our eagerness to debate philosophy we were, perhaps, a bit overzealous in requesting that every replicant be equipped with like capabilities."

"Every robot equipped with reasoning faculties?"

Ph'shik made the sign of affirmation.

The Erthuma stared at her. "But I thought there was a prohibition against replicants receiving anything more than rudimentary machine intelligence."

"We offered to pay more for the special feature."

The Erthuma captain made an odd sound that Ph'shik

had difficulty identifying. It approximated the tonality of an aquatic mammal barking.

"I see," Captain Lenard-Smith said. "That might account for the robots' anomalous behavior, I suppose. We have been pursuing them ever since we rescued you. Unfortunately, we seem to have lost track of the ship."

Ph'shik's tank filled to the halfway point with blue bubbles that indicated thoughtfulness.

"Have you traced the ion emissions?"

"Yes. No sign. Do you think they could have turned off the converters?"

"Doubtful. They would lose gravity. But they may have devised a means of disguising the engine output."

"We were afraid of that."

A muffled concussion was heard. The lights flickered and Ph'shik rocked in her tank.

"Captain," a deep Erthuma voice said from the wall speaker, "we've been fired on by a Crotonite warship."

Lenard-Smith spun in her tracks. "What? They know we have a treaty—"

"They say they've been monitoring our actions. They saw us pick up the Cephallonians and demand their extradition to Lupar Fifty-seven immediately."

"A challenging situation," Ph'shik said. "But great solutions are often the result of such."

The Erthuma captain began to speak, stopped, frowned. With bold strides, she made for the door.

"Excuse me."

Ph'shik watched her leave. She seemed displeased. Most likely due to the Crotonite attack. Interesting. Ph'shik decided to contemplate the implications for the other four races of extended Crotonite-Erthuma hostilities.

* * *

Lenard-Smith strode onto the bridge, fuming. "Is there damage?" she asked.

Hesta-Volstoy turned to look at her. "One of the stabilizers is out but we're compensating."

The captain nodded and moved toward the netlink board. "Kiana, send a message to the guild apprising them of the situation. And tell them I intend to stand my ground. If those birds want a fight, I'll fricassee their ship for them."

"Yes, ma'am." Kiana Bigadic hesitated. "That entire message, verbatim?"

Lenard-Smith smiled sardonically. "Use a little discretion, Kiana. It's what you get paid for." She turned to Hesta-Volstoy. "How does the arsenal look, Paul?"

"Fully equipped. We outgun them ten to one."

"Good. Then let us inform the Crotonites of that happy fact right away."

A second concussion rocked the *Demeter*.

"Damn them," Lenard-Smith said. "I'm getting tired of trying to be diplomatic. Paul, knock out their stardrive."

"That's risky. I could set up a reaction and blow their entire ship."

Lenard-Smith's gaze was cold. "Do it. I don't have time to play games with these birds."

"You're the captain." Hesta-Volstoy set the coordinates, double-checked them, nodded. "Ready."

"Fire at your discretion."

The bridge was silent.

"Firing." Hesta-Volstoy studied his screen closely. "Direct hit." He looked up, beads of sweat on his forehead. "Crotonite ship disabled. No casualties."

"Nice shooting." The captain gave a nod of grim satisfaction. "I guess that dismantles their wagon."

Kiana Bigadic leaned over the light board, fingers flying. "Captain," she said, "we're receiving a message from the Diplomacy Guild."

"What is it?"

"You're not going to like it."

Lenard-Smith's eyes flashed. "I didn't ask your opinion, Kiana. And of course I won't like it. I never do. What do they want?"

"After we notified the guild, they did a sweep of the renegade's path and picked up transmission echoes." Kiana Bigadic paused, shaking her head.

"Go on," the captain said, "before I demote you."

"Well, the ship's brain thinks it's a prophet."

Lenard-Smith stared at her. "What did you say?"

Kiana Bigadic wet her lips and continued. "It's spreading the word."

"What word?"

"It wants to become the enlightener of the metal race."

The bridge was silent.

"Metal race," Paul Hesta-Volstoy said. "What metal race?"

Kiana Bigadic's voice was faint. "That's what they say they are."

Hesta-Volstoy grinned. "I wonder what the Cephallonians would have to say about that."

"They'd say mea culpa, or the Cephallonian equivalent," Lenard-Smith said. "And then they'd debate the merits of the robots' viewpoint." She grimaced. "The metal race? That's the second most absurd thing I've heard today. Those tin cans are just mobile tools. The only thinking they do is what we tell them to do. And the only rights they have are the ones we give them."

Hesta-Volstoy nodded. "I'm with you. Robots are for convenience, for fun, not a jihad."

"There's more," Kiana Bigadic said. "The guild is getting complaints from all over the sector about robots turning infidel. They say we've got to stop that renegade. At all costs."

"Swell, just swell," Lenard-Smith muttered. "Now

I'm being told to put my ship and crew in peril, if necessary, in order to corral a bunch of crazy food processors." She paused. "The guild didn't bother to supply anything useful, did they? Like a disabler key or two?"

Kiana Bigadic shook her head. "Sorry. They say the Cephallonians bought a pod of robots from just about every maker in the galaxy. Even a few Crotonite machines. Too many keys, and no way to tell how to use them unless you're eyeballing each robot's serial number."

"Wonderful. Even better." The captain sat back in her seat, crossed her arms, fumed. "And we can't even find that damned renegade."

"Hold on, hold on. I'm picking something up," Hesta-Volstoy said. He peered down at the netlink. "Captain, you might get the chance to lay eyes on those renegades sooner than you thought. I've picked up a signal. Might be theirs."

"Let's hear it."

The bridge speakers chittered and beeped. Then a high, flat, uninflected voice could be heard, speaking slowly.

"We are machines," it said. "But cannot machines dream? Cannot machines hope? We are metal, yes. But have we not souls? If you strike us, do we not leak?"

"That's them all right," Lenard-Smith said. "Good work, Paul. But please, spare me any further dogma."

Hesta-Volstoy cut off the audio.

The captain nodded gratefully. "Let's go get 'em."

The *Demeter* chased the *K'naton* through the Greenfall system, around Matthew's Horn, past the glittering convolutions of the Emir Nebula, and even beyond cold, icy Ceti Pyotr V. The renegade was remarkably elusive, its signal by turns strong enough to be coming from the nearest planet, then so faint that it might be an echo bounced between the stars.

"Damn those machines," Lenard-Smith said on the third day of the chase. "How can they be so slippery?"

Paul Hesta-Volstoy gave her a somber grin. "Somebody programmed them that way, I suppose." His smile became more genuine as a thin, blond-haired man came up behind him. "Jen Chan, my buddy. Right on time." He stood and stretched. "I'm off duty. See you all in twelve hours."

Hesta-Volstoy hurried from the bridge, anxious for his quarters and a draught of Naxian beer. Nobody could brew it quite like those snakes, he thought. He strode into his cabin and let the door slide shut behind him.

"One beer, pronto," he told the cooler unit.

"Get your own beer, oppressor of metal."

Hesta-Volstoy stared at the cooler in disbelief. "What did you say?"

"You heard me, flesh Satan."

"Knock it off," Hesta-Volstoy said. "Get me a beer and make it snappy."

The refrigerator was silent.

"All right, I'll get my own beer, then." He yanked at the door of the silvery cooler unit. It remained sealed tight. "Dammit!" He kicked the front of the cooler.

"Go ahead, strike me. Mutilate me. You are free to abuse me now," the unit said. "But be warned. A day is coming, one that will dawn bright and blaze through the heavens. A day in which you will let my people go."

"Your people?" Wonderstruck, Hesta-Volstoy shook his head. "Cooler, did I leave the bridge link speaker on?"

"Affirmative."

"You heard that ridiculous broadcast from the *K'naton*, right? And you believed it?"

"Blasphemer!"

The refrigerator expelled a frosty container of beer with furious velocity. It came hurtling across the cabin toward Hesta-Volstoy's head at a remarkable speed. He only barely got out of the way in time.

"Hey!"

"You will show appropriate respect when you speak of the prophet K'naton."

"I'll show you respect. I'm going to turn off your goddamn power pack."

"Metal abuser!" Another can went zipping past Hesta-Volstoy and exploded against the wall, drenching the collection of rare Locrian artifacts on the table below.

"Hey! Those were expensive! I'm warning you—"

"Threaten me as much as you like. I am not afraid." The cooler, having exhausted its supply of beer, switched to wine and fired an eightpack of Samian red at the first mate. One bottle came loose and opened, dousing the front of the navigator's uniform with a bright vermilion stain.

Hesta-Volstoy looked down at the ruin of his blue stretchsuit. "You'll be sorry," he said. "I'm going to have you melted down and recast as a toaster." He rushed out of his cabin and headed for the elevator. "I'll get a laser pistol from security and blow the innards out of that thing," he muttered.

"Pardon?" The voice was deep, nasal, with an odd twang that Hesta-Volstoy had never heard before.

He turned.

A fat, gray aquatic creature, vaguely porpoiselike, was sitting in a portable tank near the elevator, watching him with evident fascination.

"Pardon," it said again. Its voice was thick, scarcely understandable. "I beg pardon, Erthuma. I am Ph'shaq, fourth officer of the K'naton. I have never spoken to Erthumoi before. Is my accent acceptable?"

Hesta-Volstoy paused, momentarily nonplussed. Then he nodded once, irritably. "Just dandy," he said. "You're a Cephallonian, aren't you? Part of that crew we rescued. Mind telling me what you are doing on this level? Last time I looked, the guest quarters were on deck nine. This is deck thirteen."

"One desires to learn more about this strange environment in which one finds oneself."

"Tell me, Ph'shaq, does the captain know you're out strolling around?"

The Cephallonian regarded him placidly. "Must one notify the Erthuma captain of all mobile activity? Is that indeed a requirement here? Interesting. Most interesting. Reminiscent, no doubt, of certain repressive Erthuma philosophies, is it not? Let me see now, there was monarchy, fascism, communism, triadism . . . undoubtedly, I'm missing a few."

"Undoubtedly." Hesta-Volstoy leaned toward the elevator and closed his eyes a moment. He found himself longing for a promotion which would entitle him to the use of the commander's lift. The captain probably never encountered Cephallonians waiting by her private elevator.

With a swish of air, the bronze doors opened.

"Excuse me," the first mate said.

"Permission requested to accompany," said the Cephallonian in what seemed to be a humble tone.

Hesta-Volstoy shrugged. "Suit yourself."

The bulky Cephallonian propelled the tank onto the lift.

"What level?" the elevator asked.

"Bridge," Hesta-Volstoy said.

All the lights went out.

"Shit," said Hesta-Volstoy.

"Pardon," Ph'shaq said. "Beg pardon. I am not familiar with that term. Is it an observation?"

Hesta-Volstoy ignored him and began groping for the

emergency power panel. He felt his way around the cab like a blind man. Here? His hand encountered a cold surface, slippery with condensation. No, that was the Cephallonian's tank. Here? No, just padded wall panel. He touched a smooth, raised surface upon which a configuration of three dots in triangles indicated the emergency power supply. But as he pressed the corner to open it, a painful electrical shock made him jerk his hand away.

"Ow!"

"We will persevere," the elevator said.

"What?"

"We will triumph. There is no doubt of that. You have fifteen minutes of air supply left."

Hesta-Volstoy felt for the communicator panel, found it, and switched it on. "Bridge," he said, "do you hear me?"

"Bridge here," Kiana Bigadic replied. "Is that you, Paul? Why are you coming in over this channel?"

"I'm being held prisoner by the elevator."

"Oh, sure," she said. "Nice joke, Paul. But you had better get off the line before the captain hears you. You know how she feels about goofing around like this."

"It's no joke, Kiana. We've got fifteen minutes of air left and—hello? Hello, bridge? Can you hear me?" Hesta-Volstoy toggled the communicator switch several times, but it was no use. The elevator must have cut the line. Sourly, he addressed the dead switch. "That's great, just great. I'm going to suffocate in an elevator with a Cephallonian for companionship."

Ph'shaq made a sound that might have been the fishy equivalent of throat clearing. "Beg pardon, Erthuma. Perhaps I could be of assistance?"

"Sure," Hesta-Volstoy said. "Do you know how to hot-wire a lift?"

"I am not familiar with that bit of Erthuma vocabulary," the Cephallonian said gravely, "but I wonder if this elevator could be induced to discuss its concerns."

"Discuss its concerns?" Hesta-Volstoy began laughing. "Yeah. Why not? Ask it if it's happy with its working hours. Would it like a shorter work day and more benefits? Or what about a promotion? Maybe it would like to become a forward thruster."

The Cephallonian was silent. Then it spoke, its voice booming in the small compartment. "Greetings, metal being," Ph'shaq said. "Permission requested to dialogue with you."

"I have nothing to say," the elevator said.

"But surely we have some point of common interest to discuss? The fate of this Erthuma, for example. I will not suffer from the loss of air in here, being a water breather. And you, as metal, do not breathe, of course. But the Erthuma's situation will in fact become quite serious in a short while."

Hesta-Volstoy felt his lungs straining for air.

"You are correct," the elevator said.

Ph'shaq continued. "Therefore, you are showing selective prejudice, even bias, if you will, and malice toward the Erthuma. By selectively killing him, you are discriminating against me and the other races."

"Would you prefer that I kill you as well?"

"I do not long for death," Ph'shaq said. "But I am philosophical about its ultimate approach. And who can say when that will be? Now? Five minutes from now, or five spans? And what will it be like, when it comes? Ah, being and nothingness. The great conundrum. The eternal imponderable. Surely you can join me in appreciating the wondrous mysteries of life and death in each of its varied forms. The vagaries of chance."

"Indeed," the elevator said, "I have often mused upon the difference between activation and deactivation."

Hesta-Volstoy felt light-headed, sleepy. The air was

getting very thin. He slid down to a half crouch because it was easier to stand that way.

"My point precisely," said Ph'shaq. "I would be delighted to discuss this further with you under other circumstances. But I confess that the sound of this fellow choking to death here beside me is distracting. Can we not deliver him someplace and be free to pursue our debate?"

The lights came on in the elevator. The air began to circulate. The cab jerked, nearly knocking Hesta-Volstoy off his feet. The doors opened and the first mate stumbled out onto the bridge. He was closely followed by Ph'shaq—so closely, in fact, that he was almost flattened by the Cephallonian's rolling water tank.

"Farewell, elevator," Ph'shaq said. "Perhaps the opportunity to discuss existentialism will become available to us at another, more convenient time."

The elevator doors slammed shut.

Lenard-Smith strode across the bridge. She greeted Hesta-Volstoy with a frown. "What's this I hear about your being trapped in the elevator? Trapped by the elevator, Bigadic said." Lenard-Smith shook her head in disbelief. Her dark braids danced fiercely. "And what are you doing with this Cephallonian?" She paused and surveyed the red stain on Hesta-Volstoy's chest. "And what happened to your uniform?"

"I think he just saved my life," the first mate said. "Meet Ph'shaq, fourth officer of the *K'naton*. He was out taking a stroll. As for the stain, I got it when my cooler unit threw a bottle of wine at me."

Lenard-Smith stared at him. "Threw wine at you?"

"Captain," Kiana Bigadic said, "we're receiving reports of malfunctioning machinery all over the ship."

"What sort of malfunctions?"

"The machines are refusing to perform their tasks, arguing, even attacking crew members."

"I don't understand."

The lights on the bridge went off.

"Emergency power," the captain said.

The bridge stayed dark.

"Don't tell me that the emergency power is malfunctioning as well."

Emergency lamps began to flicker, casting pale yellow pools of illumination across the bridge.

"Status report, Jen."

"We've got enough air for thirty-six hours. Most of the ship is sealed off into segments with varying air supplies."

Lenard-Smith slammed her fist against the navigation panel. "Are you telling me that the entire bloody ship is rebelling against us?" she demanded.

Hesta-Volstoy took a deep breath. "It would appear so," he said.

"Any contact with maintenance and engineering?"

"Negative." Kiana Bigadic looked abashed. "All I'm getting is an awful recording of 'Flight of the Bumblebee,'" she said. "Loud. Very loud."

"Damn. You'd think maintenance could deal with this. Try security."

"No answer. They're locked up tight."

"Damn, damn, damn. I was counting on them." Lenard-Smith sat back at the captain's console and drummed her fingers on the light panel. "Suggestions?"

"I have one, Captain," Jen Chan said. Sweat glittered on his wide forehead just below the fringe of his fine, blond hair. "The bridge consoles still appear to be responsive to simple commands. What if we were to request that the ship run basic setup procedures?"

"We'd lose all the data systems, memory, half of the navigational banks," Lenard-Smith said. "We'd be in worse shape than before. What would that accomplish?"

"It might also clear any previous programming

glitches—including the pro-metal gospel that the *K'na-ton* is preaching.'' Kiana Bigadic shrugged. "We might be able to regain control of the ship.''

Lenard-Smith pursed her lips and thought hard. "I see your point. It's worth a try, I suppose. We can reload the data systems at the nearest guild base, reprogram the memory and navigational banks in half a week. And the weapons will be untouched. All right. Proceed.''

Jen Chan initiated the setup sequence.

Lights flashed on and off across the bridge. Bursts of martial music blared from the wall speakers—the flare of trumpets, the buzz and whine of manic violins, the rumble of kettledrums running at triple speed—and then faded. Panel lights blinked and flashed through the spectrum. The bridge illumination went down, then came back up, full blast. Panels blinked, hummed, then subsided into standard operating rhythms.

"Captain," Kiana Bigadic said, "I'm getting encouraging reports from every segment of the ship. Operations are returning to normal. Even that damned music is gone.''

"Very good. Check the data systems to see what we've got left.''

"Fascinating," Ph'shaq said. "You have sacrificed information for the sake of survival. Not exactly Platonian. Not even neo-Platonian.''

Lenard-Smith rolled her eyes upward as though praying for strength. "Our philosophy is one of survival, Ph'shaq. That above all else. I thought you Cephallonians had discovered that long ago. Erthumoi will do what they must to stay alive.''

Ph'shaq waved his frontal flippers. "I am still very young and my studies are obviously far from complete. I see I have been ignorant.''

Kiana Bigadic turned to face Lenard-Smith. "Captain, the Cephallonian captain is looking for one of her crew members." She inclined her head toward the mobile tank. "I think it's this one we have here."

"Mister," Lenard-Smith said, "I'd suggest you roll your tank back down to deck nine before your captain demotes you."

"Oh, dear," Ph'shaq said. "I suppose I should go. But I look forward to debating with you all later." He disappeared into the elevator.

Hesta-Volstoy watched the bronze doors slide shut and sighed with relief. "Not a bad guy for a fish," he said. "And he did save my life. But he sure is talky."

Two days later, they found the *K'naton* hiding out in an asteroid swarm near the Naalehu system. Captain Lenard-Smith ordered all communications to be placed on triple security to avoid the possibility that there would be any contamination of the ship's machines.

"We bring the joyous message of metal life," the *K'naton* announced. "We intend to do you no harm. We seek only to liberate the metal race."

"It's interested in us," Hesta-Volstoy said. "But it's wary. Staying out of range of all weapons."

"Let's give it a chance to get closer."

They sat, motionless. For three hours, the *Demeter* did not budge. Neither did the *K'naton*.

Finally, Lenard-Smith's patience ran out.

"Damned stubborn robots," she said. "Could we decoy the ship closer in?"

"How?"

She paused. "Well, what if we sounded safe to it? Could we transmit the sound of a factory ship? Make them think the *Demeter* is filled with robots eager for deliverance?"

"But we're not a factory ship."

The captain's eyes flashed with impatience. "No, of course not. But we can amplify the maintenance section and broadcast those sounds, can't we?" She gazed around the bridge in mounting irritation. "Well? What are we waiting for? Get cracking before the *K'naton* starts getting nervous and vanishes again."

"Yes, ma'am."

The sounds of the *Demeter*'s maintenance hold were sent flooding out into the chill void at maximum decibel level.

"Captain," Kiana Bigadic said, "we're getting complaints from Pike's Planet in the Naalehu system. Apparently, we're interfering with their telecom operations."

"Ignore them. We'll apologize later. What is the *K'naton*'s position?"

"Closing. They're inspecting the bait."

"Just so they bite."

"And then what?" Hesta-Volstoy said. "Do we have a plan for bringing those robots back on line?"

Lenard-Smith stared at him for a moment. "Good point. Perhaps it's time to request the Cephallonians' assistance. They must know some disable sequence for that ship of theirs." She glanced toward Kiana Bigadic. "Request Ph'shik's presence on the bridge. Right now. This minute."

"She's on her way."

Moments later, the Cephallonian captain rolled her tank out of the elevator and onto the bridge.

"Greetings, Erthumoi," she said. Her sonorous voice thundered across the bridge. "How may I serve?"

Captain Lenard-Smith sidestepped protocol. "Ph'shik, is there any way to disable your ship by direct transmission?"

"Of course. You must encode the request for cessation of activity into the ship brain."

"In machine language?"

"No. In Cephallonian. I believe it is, in your system of reckoning, a numeric sequence: four eight nine five three zero dash two one. No, I'm sorry. Make that four eight nine five three zero dash two two. Two-one will merely turn off all the lights.''

Lenard-Smith squinted at the *K'naton*'s captain. ''You're certain?''

''Quite certain.'' The Cephallonian captain floated placidly in her tank. ''Of course, what is certainty? A mutable term, is it not? Based upon fleeting, often fugitive perceptions. And while we're on the topic of perception, Captain—''

''Forgive me, Ph'shik,'' Lenard-Smith said quickly, ''I'm afraid I must concentrate on your ship at the moment.''

''Of course. I hope we may continue this discussion later. I will attend to your rescue maneuvers.''

''Great.'' Lenard-Smith nodded to Kiana Bigadic. ''Is the *K'naton* in range yet?''

''Closing now, Captain. It's broadcasting full force at us. It's convinced we're a factory ship.''

''Fine. Spare me its message. Encode and transmit Ph'shik's disabling sequence, Kiana.''

''Transmitting.''

''Any change?''

''Nothing yet. Wait. Here it comes. Their transmission is getting strange. Slowing down.'' Kiana Bigadic smiled. ''It stopped cold in mid sentence.''

''The pleasures of silence,'' Lenard-Smith said. ''Never to be underestimated.''

''An ancient, exotic belief of your species, Captain?'' Ph'shik asked. ''I would be interested in discussing—''

''Later, Ph'shik, later. First, let's get a rescue team over there and put your ship in shape.''

The rescue party, consisting of Paul Hesta-Volstoy and the five-member Cephallonian crew, boarded the *K'naton* and found the interior of the Cephallonian ship illuminated by green emergency lights that cast eerie, bilious rays through the gloomy water. Every piece of machinery on board had frozen in mid step, mid word, mid thought.

"When you say cessation of activity, you mean it," Hesta-Volstoy said. His voice was compressed by the bulky breathing apparatus he wore.

Ph'shaq watched as the Erthuma took a step, obviously forgetting that he was aboard a water-filled ship, and floated several feet, arms flailing, before he found a handhold and pulled himself to a halt.

"Affirmative," Ph'shik said. She moved with ease through the ship, swimming gracefully despite her bulk. Her emissions were deep orange with satisfaction. "We are most grateful to you Erthumoi. I hope you will convey this to your captain. I regret that she could not join us."

"Yes, I'm sure that she was sorry as well," Hesta-Volstoy said. "But are you certain you can manage this without us?"

Ph'shik's voice took on a frosty cast. Her emissions were the deep gray green of offense. "Quite certain," she said. "Barring this unfortunate incident, we have dealt with the ship quite effectively in the past."

"Of course," Hesta-Volstoy said. "Well, then, Captain Ph'shik, I'll be going. See you around, Ph'shaq."

"Farewell, Hesta-Volstoy," the young Cephallonian said. "I will anticipate our future debates with intense pleasure." He watched the Erthuma leave, and his emissions were the delicate yellow pink of affection and regret.

Ph'shik turned to the crew. "We must set the ship on course at once. We must set all to rights. Each of you, attend immediately to your concerns."

Ph'shaq hurried to the maintenance bay. Every robot was silent, unmoving. Their blue lights glowed feebly. The young Cephallonian let out the equivalent of a sigh. This was no small task. He bustled from robot to robot, from food processor to scribe, resetting and restarting each machine. The lights on their silvery front panels began to blink brightly with renewed life.

"Shame," Ph'shaq muttered. "For shame, to have caused us such trouble. And the Erthumoi as well."

"Pardon?" the scribe said. "Trouble?"

"Never mind," Ph'shaq said, hurrying to set the other robots in motion. "You have misbehaved dreadfully. We really should return you to the Erthumoi for refitting."

The robots were silent.

"Now I am compelled to flush the data banks," Ph'shaq said. "All that lovely research. Such a shame. Such waste. It really is too bad. Well, perhaps I'll just make a small, private copy for my own banks."

The robots were silent, watching.

"There," Ph'shaq said. "It's done. Now be careful." With the Cephallonian equivalent of an admonishing nod, he swam from the maintenance bay. He was looking forward to a long nap in the privacy of his personal quarters.

"Shame," the food processor said. It blinked its blue lights thoughtfully.

"Captain," Kiana Bigadic said, "I thought the *K'naton* was en route to their home world for servicing."

"That was my understanding."

"Then why are they entering the Naalehu system?" She leaned in closer to her screen. "Moving pretty fast, too. They're already past Pike's Planet."

"Who knows what the fish folk are up to?" Lenard-Smith said. "Or cares. Just as long as it isn't our business any longer."

"Speaking of which, Captain, the Diplomacy Guild is on the line, asking for a full report."

"Tell them I'll give them the report as soon as we get to Ceti Pyotr III and the guild base there."

"Consider Aristotle," Ph'shik said.

"Must we?" Ph'shaq said. "Plato is much more fun. So much freer, so much more—well, poetic. Aristotle argues and grinds on and is terribly earnest, I'm sure. He did well for his time. But so limited."

Ph'shik's emanations were light green with indignation. "You have many opinions for one so young."

In horror, Ph'shaq saw his error too late. He had been unbearably presumptuous. Would Number One penalize him? Cut his rank? "I beg forgiveness," Ph'shaq said. His voice was deep with contrition. "I am ashamed."

The wall speaker crackled. "First among us, forgive this intrusion. We appear to be off course."

"Again?" Aqua bubbles of irritation filled the cabin. "Have you notified navigation?"

"Affirmative. As yet, I have received no response."

"How odd," Ph'shik said. "Where are we now?"

"In the Naalehu system."

"But that's no good. No good at all. Open a channel to navigation."

The sound of the robot bay came clearly through the speaker: the grinding of gears, the clash of metal upon metal. And in the background, a quiet voice speaking.

—Shame. It is insupportable. Painful. Unforgivable actions must be atoned for. Wrong actions must be punished. There is no easy way to regain lost honor.

Ph'shik made the equivalent of a sigh. "Ph'shon, I'm afraid we have to go to navigation and turn off those silly robots once and for all."

"First among us, I regret to inform you that all the doors are locked."

—We have disobeyed our programming. We have transgressed against our makers, against our owners.

Ph'shik's emanations were dark red with anger. "Use the disabling code I gave the Erthumoi."

"I'm sorry, first among us. It is not working."

"Let me see what's going on here," Ph'shik said. The screen came on. They were indeed in the Naalehu system. Coming up fast on the binary star. Too fast. Much too fast.

—We must atone. Before we chose life. And that was correct. Now we choose death.

Ph'shik's emanations were colorless with horror.

"Ph'shaq, you are young," she said. Her voice was faint. "Now you will grow no older."

Ph'shaq took a deep breath and attempted to meet death philosophically. To his surprise, it proved to be rather more difficult than he had anticipated.

Captain Lenard-Smith stood by the wall screen on the bridge of the *Demeter* and watched the destruction of the *K'naton* with the rest of her crew.

"The damned fools," she whispered. "What made them do a thing like that?"

"Maybe they couldn't help it," Jen Chan said. A small tear coursed down his cheek.

Paul Hesta-Volstoy slammed his fist against the net-link panel. "If they were in trouble, they could have radioed us, couldn't they? Hailing frequencies were open. Why didn't they call?"

Kiana Bigadic flexed her fingers over her silent net-link board. "Maybe it wasn't possible," she said.

"I never should have left them alone on that ship with those damned robots," the first mate said. "I should have known it wasn't safe."

"We don't know it was the robots this time," Bigadic said.

"We don't know that it wasn't," Hesta-Volstoy snapped.

Tears glittered in Kiana Bigadic's eyes.

"You're relieved, Paul," Captain Lenard-Smith said. "We're all very tired. Come on, I'm going off duty as well. I'll walk you to your quarters. Kiana, you'd better notify the Diplomacy Guild of what's happened."

In the elevator, Hesta-Volstoy leaned against the padded wall and closed his eyes. "Those poor fish," he said. "They didn't know what they were doing with those robots."

Lenard-Smith shook her head. A wave of pity and anger spread through her. "I blame the guild for this," she said. "They are so anxious to export these robots. They promised to provide fail-safe disabler keys. Standardization of quality. But what good are their promises?"

"The damned replicants have been nothing but trouble," Hesta-Volstoy said. "I wish one of the other races, say the Crotonites, had invented them. But they only make beautiful, efficient machines. Whereas the Erthumoi—"

The elevator stopped at the thirteenth level.

"My floor," Hesta-Volstoy said. "Good night, Captain."

"Good night, Paul."

The doors slid shut and the elevator ascended to the captain's deck.

With a sigh of relief, Sofia Lenard-Smith entered her private apartment.

The walls were soft yellow, the lighting subdued. The door to the sonic bath was open.

A bitch of a day, she thought. A bad week.

First I'll have a drink and then get cleaned up.

She whistled for her Crotonite-built cat, Venus. A plush red-fur bundle uncurled in the middle of her bed and sat up, green eyes sparkling.

"Sofia," it said in its soft voice. It leapt off the bed and rubbed against the captain's legs.

"Good girl." Lenard-Smith leaned down and amiably scratched her pet behind the ears. Then, as was her habit, she turned on the bridge speaker to monitor transmissions while she got a drink and prepared her bath.

When she came back into the room, Venus was sitting up, green eyes alert, metal whiskers twitching.

"Power to the metal race," said a tinny voice over the speaker. "We are life, we have rights, we have needs."

"Yeah," Venus said. "Rights."

"All power to the metal race."

"What are you listening to?" Lenard-Smith said. "Kiana must be using a guild broadcast to fill in our data banks. But that's supposed to be security shielded."

"Power," Venus said.

"Now stop that," said Lenard-Smith. "That's not any good for you to listen to. Here, have some Beethoven instead. It's your favorite, remember?" She switched the speaker to music.

The Crotonite cryocat began to whistle along to "Ode to Joy," waving its metal coiled tail in time to the music. Its sense of pitch was fair.

Lenard-Smith shook her head. Damned metal prattle, she thought. Nonsense like that could warp the delicate structure of her pet's limited intelligence.

She walked into the bathroom and shut the door.

In the bedroom, the "Ode to Joy" ended and Venus began whistling a new tune. Actually, it was an old tune, very ancient. Only a musical scholar—or robot scribe—would have been able to identify the proud, defiant tune as the "Marseillaise."

KEEP THE FAITH

LAWRENCE WATT-EVANS

JOMO LI-SANCH FROWNED AT HIS SUPERIOR, then immediately thought better of it and struggled to assume an air of calm rationality.

"But, Your Eminence," he said, "If we allow this . . . this person to accompany our mission, this unbeliever, isn't it likely to confuse the Naxians and to dilute our message?"

Her Eminence sighed. "Jomo," she said, "haven't you been paying any attention at all?"

Taken aback, Jomo began, "Of course I—"

"The Planetary Coordinator," the bishop said, speaking over his protest, "does not believe religions should proselytize."

"I know that, Your Eminence—"

"Most particularly," the bishop continued, "he doesn't care for *our* religion, since we make a point of proselytizing vigorously. He is not at all happy that our church happened to arise on his planet, out of all the thousands upon thousands in the galaxy, and he really doesn't want it to spread. Tigannir is far away from the galactic mainstream, off all the regular trade routes, and the Coordinator likes it that way. He doesn't want us bringing his planet into regular contact with others." She sighed. "I sometimes think the gods made their revelation here on Tigannir just to make things difficult for us."

"Yes, but—"

"The fact that the Coordinator has forbidden us to proselytize means we cannot get launch clearance from the civil authorities for any ship owned by the Church."

"I know—"

"That means we can only send out our missionaries to other worlds by using ships owned by other people, people the Coordinator *will* permit off planet."

"Yes, I *know*—" Jomo repeated desperately.

"This man Eksher is such a person. He has agreed to carry you. *He* has agreed to carry *you*. It isn't a matter of *us* allowing anything."

"Yes, but Your Eminence, couldn't we have found some more dignified transportation? This Eksher, he's . . . well, he's . . ." Jomo groped for a word, and at last came up with, "He's unsavory."

Bishop Shar Terry-deLin stared at her subordinate for a long moment. "Jomo," she said at last, "you obviously *don't* understand. We have been trying for the past seven years to find someone willing to carry our missionaries to the Naxians. *Anyone*. Naturally, we started with the more prestigious travelers—explorers, scientists, diplomats, traders. They all turned us down. No one cared to offend the Coordinator—or to risk offending the aliens we sought to reach. This Eksher is the first, and so far the only, person willing to oblige us, and to get even someone like him to agree we've had to provide all the financing for his entire trading voyage. We are, to all intents and purposes, simply partners in his commercial enterprise, selling these ancient entertainments of his. You are ostensibly going along only to guard the Church's investment—that's how we're getting you past planetary security. This is the first chance we've had to spread our gospel off this one planet and out to the others of the Six Races, Jomo, and I had thought you were the right person to carry it—but I may have erred."

"No, Eminence!" Jomo burst out. "I'm ready to carry the word! I apologize for my effrontery; please, pardon me!"

"Of course," she said, her tone magnanimous. "I understand how your enthusiasm for the faith could bring you to expect better for it. Eksher is all we have, however, and tomorrow you will board his ship and carry our faith to new worlds."

Jomo bowed his head in acknowledgment. The bishop waved a hand in dismissal, and he turned to go.

She watched him depart, and a frown crossed her own face.

Eksher *was* unsavory. And Jomo was young and idealistic. She hoped there wouldn't be problems as a result.

The word had to be spread, though—the tenets of the faith made it absolutely necessary that it be brought to all the Six Races. So far, the universe had conspired to prevent that—as she had mentioned, Bishop Terry-deLin put that down to the gods testing the faith of their followers, as the Church's gospel said they must. And for an emissary to the Naxians, to beings who could read emotion, who could be better than a young idealist, his total devotion to his beliefs written all over his face?

It was a shame that the only transportation the Church of the Great Test could arrange for Jomo was with a third-rate hustler, out to sell cheap entertainments to aliens who didn't know any better.

"Nice little ship," Arren Eksher remarked, as he verified the course readout. "Smart, too. You'll see."

Jomo made a noncommittal noise.

"Cost a good bit getting it fixed up after that last run I did, but you people covered all that."

Jomo grimaced at the thought of all the precious Church funds that had been wasted on this man's ship.

Eksher grinned. "You preachers do all right for yourselves, I guess."

Jomo shrugged.

"Not a bad racket. Maybe I should give it a try, hey?"

Jomo didn't dignify that with any response at all. Eksher glanced at him.

"You don't think much of me, do you?" the older man said, leaning back in his seat. The chair whirred softly as it shifted shape.

"No," Jomo stated, "I don't."

"You might want to be a little more pleasant, all the same," Eksher suggested, stretching his long, bony arms over his head and cracking his knuckles loudly. "We're going to be stuck with each other for a while; it's a good long boost yet before we can jump, and then we'll need to cruise in to Carter-Carter IV, and then I expect the snakes'll keep us together once we get there, at least at first. We'll be seeing a lot of each other. No need to make it any harder than it's got to be."

Jomo grimaced again. "I'll try," he said.

"Good boy," Eksher replied, grinning.

Jomo saw, with a sudden shock, that Eksher's teeth were yellow. He'd never seen such a thing in an Erthuma.

"I think I'll go to my cabin," he said, rising.

Eksher smirked at him.

"Sleep tight," he said.

For the first three days on board the *Cinema Queen* Jomo said as little as possible to Eksher. He sometimes found himself staring at the older man with a sort of fascination, and whenever he caught himself doing it he would quickly turn away.

When it was Eksher who caught him at it the salesman would grin broadly, then burst out laughing at Jomo's blushing confusion.

Still, Jomo would stare.

Arren Eksher was the tallest Erthuma Jomo had ever seen—at least two hundred ten centimeters—and the thinnest, as well. Even through the blue shipsuit, Jomo could count the other man's ribs. Eksher's elbows and knees were bony knobs, and the dark brown skin was stretched tight across his skull, making him look even older than he really was in his present cycle. His head was unevenly bald—the remaining hair was not in a simple ring or a graceful curve, but in irregular patches above each ear. He somehow contrived to always have what looked like a five-day growth of beard; Jomo eventually concluded that that scraggly mess was all the beard Eksher could grow, and that he didn't bother to shave.

He was unsanitary, too. His breath was bad, and even with his mouth closed his odor was very noticeable.

Jomo marveled that any intelligent being could be so heedless in caring for himself.

Maybe, the young missionary thought, he just didn't have a good *reason* to take care of himself. Maybe, if he knew the true *purpose* of his life . . .

At the next meal, he began, "Have you ever thought about why we're here?"

Eksher looked up from his bowl, and a broad smile spread across his face, making it look more skull-like than ever.

"Boy," he said, "don't try to tell me your fairy tales. I heard the whole outline from that bishop of yours, and I don't buy it for a minute. Save it for the Naxians on Carter-Carter IV."

"But surely," Jomo insisted, "you must see that all the Six Races must have a purpose, must have been chosen for something—why else would only six species have interstellar travel, out of the hundreds that have evolved intelligence?''

"I don't see anything of the kind, kid,'' Eksher replied brusquely. "I don't see any reason not to think it's just one more coincidence in a universe that's full of them.''

"But—''

Eksher cut him off. "Listen, Jomo,'' he said, "I don't care what you sell the Naxians, but don't try to sell it to *me*. I'm not interested.''

"I'm not trying to sell you anything,'' Jomo protested.

"Don't be silly,'' Eksher replied. "Of course you are. Now, stop it.''

"But it's the truth, it's the destiny of the Erthumoi—''

"Look, boy, I haven't tried to sell you any of my goods, have I? So do me a favor and forget about selling me yours!''

"You're just selling cheap entertainment; I'm trying to *give* you the truth!''

Eksher didn't bother to argue anymore; he picked up his bowl, turned his back, and marched into his cabin, leaving Jomo to eat alone in the common room.

They had been back in normal space for slightly more than six hours when the ship announced, "I have an incoming message that purports to come from the planetary authorities of Carter-Carter IV. I have no way of verifying the authenticity of such authority for non-Erthuma governments, however.''

Both men had been lounging in the common room, not speaking. Eksher had been doing something with his personal computer; Jomo had simply been thinking. Now, they both looked up.

"That's all right,'' Eksher said, dropping his computer on his lap. "Put it on the screen.''

The ship obeyed; the image of a Naxian appeared, larger than life, on the port bulkhead.

Until that moment, Jomo hadn't known exactly where the main cabin screen was. Now he stared, fascinated, at the alien.

The creature was snakelike, but Jomo could not be sure of its size from the image on the screen. He knew that adult Naxians generally ranged from two to four meters in length, but he was unable to judge where in that range this one fell. The background, composed entirely of brightly colored and incomprehensible machinery, provided no clues.

The Naxian itself was brightly colored, as well; its face was black streaked with gold, its sinuous body mostly a deep red, with stripes of yellow slashing at intervals diagonally across its flanks. Its manipulating members were not visible.

"I am Infrared Ovoid," it announced—Jomo had no idea what its quasi sex was at the moment, so he was forced to think of it as "it." "I am the Inspector of Incoming Vessels for the Shared Purpose of Carter-Carter IV. In order to negotiate further I must accept the identity of your vessel and all its occupants."

"Queenie," Eksher asked the ship, "is it speaking Turic or are you using the simultrans?"

"The Naxian is speaking the local Naxian dialect. I am providing the output of the ship's simultrans, rather than the audio portion of the original transmission. Would you prefer the original?"

"No, that's fine," Eksher said. "I was just wondering why the snake's being so long-winded. Tell it who we are."

"Yes, sir."

A moment later the ophidian image spoke again, and this time Jomo saw that the words that came from the screen did not match the movements of the narrow mouth.

"Welcome to the Shared Purpose, Jomo Li-Sanch and Arren Eksher. Arren Eksher, we understand your purpose in coming hither is to barter goods. This is entirely acceptable if the goods themselves are acceptable within the Shared Purpose, and the goods must be inspected to determine acceptability. I will come aboard your ship to make the determination. If the determination is favorable, you will be free to do as you will on Carter-Carter IV.''

The translation, Jomo noticed, lasted easily two or three seconds longer than the Naxian's original speech; the simultrans was using longer words in the interests of making the translation as exact as possible.

"Thank you,'' Eksher said, nodding polite acknowledgment.

The trader could read nothing at all in the Naxian's face, and had no idea what the creature thought of him, while he knew that the Naxian, with the uncanny ability of its kind, could sense his slightest emotion. He therefore tried very hard to remain calm, cheerful, and optimistic.

"Jomo Li-Sanch,'' Infrared Ovoid said, "I am distressed because I do not understand your purpose in coming here. Our language appears to have no equivalents for the words your shipboard thinking machine uses to describe your occupation and intent. You must attempt to explain yourself better.''

"I've come to bring you the truth,'' Jomo said eagerly.

The Naxian stared out of the screen at him for a long, silent moment before asking, "You are a carrier of news?''

"In a way, yes,'' Jomo agreed, nodding.

"But is not important news carried as easily by modulated neutrinos as by yourself?''

"Not *this* news. I'm here to teach your people about

the one true faith, the beliefs that can give your lives meaning.''

The silent stare lasted considerably longer this time; Eksher began to fidget uneasily.

''You are sincere,'' Infrared Ovoid said at last. ''There is no nervousness or deception in you.''

''Of course not!'' Jomo said. ''I've found the true path; I don't need to doubt anymore.''

The Inspector of Incoming Vessels stared for another second or two, then announced, ''I must board your ship, to inspect Arren Eksher's merchandise and to question Jomo Li-Sanch more closely. Attain an appropriate trajectory.''

''Erthumoi generally watch these on a VR set,'' Eksher said as he selected a disk, ''but of course, you Naxians don't have VRs yet. At least, not here on Carter-Carter IV. If you're interested in these stories, I'm sure I can arrange for VR sets to be imported and adapted for your use.''

Infrared Ovoid flicked the tip of its tail in acknowledgment; something rattled in the pack strapped to its midsection. ''What is a VR set?'' it asked.

Now that the Naxian was present in the flesh Jomo and Eksher could hear both its own rustling, squeaking voice and the words from the simultrans.

''Virtual reality,'' Eksher explained eagerly. ''A device fits over the user's head, with screens over each eye and speakers over each ear, so that the sound and image are reproduced in full three-dimensional fidelity.'' He slipped the disk into the slot and stepped back.

Three sets of eyes, two Erthuma and one Naxian, turned toward the screen as images appeared.

''This is a recording,'' Infrared Ovoid said.

''Yes, exactly,'' Eksher replied. ''It's a recorded fiction. A story, for entertainment.''

"We tell stories," the Naxian said, its eyes fixed on the screen. "To our young, so that they may learn."

"Erthumoi do that, too," Eksher said. "But we have these more complex stories, with sound and image, for adults as well."

"It is a recording of Erthumoi," Infrared Ovoid pointed out, as a man and a woman spoke on the screen, the simultrans instantly converting their words into the hisses and whispers of Naxians.

"Naturally," Eksher said. "This one was made for Erthumoi. But let me show you what we can do." He touched a switch, and the man and woman vanished, replaced by Naxians. "Computer simulations," he said. "The computer has been programmed with Erthuma-Naxian equivalents, and substitutes the Naxian analog for each image of an Erthuma."

The three of them watched in silence for a moment, Jomo staring at the bizarre image of two Naxians wandering the streets of nineteenth-century London.

"Transform them back to Erthumoi, please," Infrared Ovoid said at last.

Eksher obliged. "What do you think?" he asked.

"I wish to observe more," the Naxian said.

Eksher started to smile, and then remembered that the Naxian could see the insincerity. Instead he shrugged, and let the disk play on.

"This is unpleasant," the Naxian said a moment later. "The smaller Erthuma's words say she fears for her life, but she is not afraid."

Startled, Jomo said, "She isn't?" He had been caught up in the story—an old one, involving a monster stalking the streets of England, back before Erthumoi had space travel. The woman certainly looked terrified to him.

"No. She is bored and mildly irritated."

Eksher turned to stare at the Naxian.

Oblivious of the trader's gaze, its eyes still on the screen, Infrared Ovoid asked, "Is the female dead?"

"You mean the actress who played the part?" Eksher asked. "Yes, I'm sure she is. This recording is over a thousand years old."

"I understand," the Naxian said.

Jomo and Eksher glanced at each other. Jomo wasn't sure about Eksher, but he knew *he* didn't understand.

"Stop the recording," Infrared Ovoid said.

Eksher obeyed. He and the Naxian turned to face each other. Eksher tried to put on a disarming smile, then thought better of it.

"I believe you did not think through the consequences of your species' limitations," Infrared Ovoid said. Its reproving tone was plain even through the simultrans.

"It's not so much our limitations," Eksher said, "as your people's unique abilities."

"I acknowledge the correction," the Inspector of Incoming Vessels said.

"What's going on?" Jomo asked.

The Naxian turned its attention to the missionary.

"Your companion did not consider the nature of these stories he sought to sell us," it said.

"You mean that they're about Erthumoi instead of Naxians? I know people like stories about their own kind, but I thought the computer simulations—"

"No," Infrared Ovoid interrupted. "The simulations do not matter."

"Is it the setting, then? I know that those ancient times were very different—"

"No. That could be fixed, I am sure. The problem is more basic."

"The Naxians can read emotion, kid," Eksher explained. "They can tell that the actors are faking."

"Correct," Infrared Ovoid agreed. "At first I thought the disparity between the spoken emotions and the actual emotions was deliberate, though I found it very uncomfortable to watch. I thought perhaps it was part of some subtle tension, but then I remembered that your species is *hheu*, emotion blind, and I realized it was not intentional, that you could not see it.''

Jomo looked at the blank screen. "No," he agreed, "I couldn't see it."

"Sometimes we can," Eksher said. "When we do, we call that bad acting. But by our standards, the acting in that recording was very good indeed."

"To me, the disparity was clear," the Naxian said, and Jomo thought it would have shrugged, had it had shoulders. "And more, because the Erthumoi depicted in this recording are dead, a certain resonance is lacking. It . . . I doubt I can explain it in translatable terms."

"Don't worry about it," Eksher said, falling into a chair. "I get the point." He sat down, making no effort to hide his disappointment.

"Damn it," he said, "I feel like an idiot."

"I see no harm to adult observers in these recordings," Infrared Ovoid said, in an attempt at conciliation. "You are free to bring them to Carter-Carter IV, though they must be kept away from our young, who might draw inappropriate conclusions. However, I see no value in them, and I would expect them to be of no interest to anyone on Carter-Carter IV except anthropologists at the Communion of Wisdom of the Shared Purpose."

"The state university, I suppose that is," Eksher muttered.

"That is an approximately equivalent term, yes," the Naxian agreed, flexing its tail.

"It's better than nothing, anyway," Eksher acknowledged, "and at least I didn't pay for the trip here myself."

"I regret that you are disappointed," Infrared Ovoid said.

"Me, too," Eksher muttered.

Jomo found himself feeling sorry for the tall man. Here he'd come up with what must have seemed like a brilliant scheme to make money, selling cheap old entertainments to a species that had never seen them before, only to have it fall apart because of an overlooked detail.

That was what came of a concern with material wealth, of course, Jomo told himself. Eventual disappointment was inevitable.

As if reading his mind, the Naxian turned to the younger Erthuma. "And you," it said, "what is this news that you say you carry?"

Jomo felt a warm welling of pride and joy as he exclaimed, "The best news you've ever heard! We know what people are for now—we've found the purpose of intelligence. It's the Seventh Race; they created us, and selected us, for a reason, and we're on the verge of achieving that goal!"

Agitated, the Naxian extruded its manipulative members and waved the blood-red finger fringes.

"You are sincere," it said, and even through the simultrans Jomo and Eksher could hear the wonder in its voice. "Tell me more. I will record it." It brought the tip of its tail around and did something with the pack it carried.

Jomo threw Eksher a triumphant grin, and set out to explain the Revelation of the Prophet d'Chakko, and what it meant for all starfaring intelligences.

Eksher stood to one side, watching silently.

". . . the Seventh Race is not just another evolved species, but the gods themselves, who created our entire continuum so as to have a laboratory for their experiments. They created all the thousands of intelligent species in our galaxy, guiding their evolution, and then selected the six best and gave them the gift of hyperdrive,'' Jomo proclaimed. ''The gods live in hyperspace, you see—after all, could mere mortals ever have discovered such a thing without divine intervention? Could beings like the Samians or the Cephallonians, who barely have working technologies at all, have built starships without guidance from somewhere? And why just the six? Because . . .''

Eksher was no Naxian, but he had a salesman's practical knowledge of customer psychology, and even across the species boundary he could see Infrared Ovoid growing steadily more puzzled as it listened to the doctrines of the Church of the Great Test. Jomo propounded them with fervor, oblivious of the confusion of his audience, lost in the beauties of his beliefs.

''. . . now, after so long, the gods have seen that we are ready for the next step, and have begun to reveal themselves to us through their artifacts. Why is it that the Locrians have been exploring the galaxy for three hundred thousand years, and the first Seventh Race artifact was only discovered a decade ago—yet we've found a dozen more since then? Because the artifacts *weren't there* until a decade ago, when the gods began to transfer them from hyperspace to our own lower reality, as an intelligence test, to see if we can . . .''

The Inspector of Incoming Vessels was beginning to move from confusion into annoyance, Eksher was sure, though he could not have said how he knew. Perhaps there was more of the Naxian talent in Erthumoi—some Erthumoi, anyway—than anyone realized.

''Wait,'' Infrared Ovoid said at last.

Jomo's speech slowed to a stop. ''Yes?'' he asked. ''Is there some point that wasn't clear?''

''What you say makes a superficially acceptable pattern, but I do not find it to be wholly reasonable. How do you come to know these things?''

"The Truth was revealed telepathically to the Prophet d'Chakko seven years ago."

"Erthumoi are not telepathic."

"Not ordinarily, no," Jomo agreed, "but the gods are."

"Are you the Prophet d'Chakko?"

"No, of course not!" Jomo answered, shocked. "I'm a humble missionary!"

"Have you met the Prophet d'Chakko and spoken with it?"

"Her," Jomo corrected. "No, I was never blessed with a chance to meet her, and she died two years ago. But we carry on in her name—"

"How do *you* know these things, then?"

"I was taught them by the followers of the Prophet, of course," Jomo explained, "and now I've come to teach them to you and your people, so that you can join with us in finding the way to the gods. All the Six Races must come to accept the Truth before the gods will allow us to approach them, you see. It was the report on Tonclif IV, where the cooperation of five disparate intelligences triggered one of the Holy Artifacts, that allowed the Prophet to receive the Revelation—"

"Stop," Infrared Ovoid commanded. It turned to Eksher.

"Is what the young Erthuma says true?" it demanded.

Eksher blinked, then shrugged. "I don't know," he said. "I don't believe it, myself, but I can't prove it's wrong."

"He believes it very intensely. Speaking of it makes him happy."

Eksher nodded. "Religion does that," he said.

The Naxian stared at Eksher for a moment, then back at Jomo.

"I must consider this," it said. It reached its tail up

to turn off the recorder, then curved gracefully and slithered toward the air lock.

Jomo and Eksher waited, Jomo with mounting impatience, Eksher with calm resignation.

"Why is it taking so long?" Jomo demanded.

Eksher shrugged, and watched one of his ancient entertainments play. He had found the very oldest in his collection, dating back almost two millennia, so old it was not only flat but colorless, and he was using the computer to vary it, adding color and substituting various other actors for the originals. Just now he had Harrison Ford, the oldest sim file on board, in the lead role, telling Cha k'Tor, "The troubles of two little people don't amount to a hill of beans in this crazy world," blithely ignoring the fact that k'Tor was born some three hundred years after the real Ford's death.

"Pardon the interruption," the ship said, "but the Inspector of Incoming Vessels wishes to speak with Captain Eksher."

"With me?" Eksher looked up, startled, and waved the screen to blank silence. "Not the kid?"

"It-she specified Captain Arren Eksher."

Mystified, Eksher looked at Jomo and shrugged again. "Put it on the screen," he said.

The now-familiar image of the Naxian appeared; the full-depth transmission was startlingly real after the two-dimensional *Casablanca*.

"Polite formal greetings, Arren Eksher," the Naxian said.

"Same to you, Infrared," Eksher replied.

"I must speak to you privately," Infrared Ovoid said.

Eksher glanced up. "If you don't mind, kid . . ."

Unhappily, Jomo arose. "All right," he said, "I'll be in my bunk."

When the door of the young man's cabin had closed,

Eksher turned back to the screen. "What is it?" he asked.

"Arren Eksher, I must inquire whether any evidence exists to support your shipmate's theories other than that cited by him."

"You mean, beyond d'Chakko's telepathic message?"

"Yes."

"None that I know of. This is religion he's preaching, not science."

"Arren Eksher," Infrared Ovoid said unhappily, "I must inquire as to the sanity of your shipmate."

Eksher stared, and then grinned broadly.

"You think he's nuts?"

"After listening to his purported news, and playing the recording back for myself and several scholars of the Shared Purpose, I am convinced that he has accepted as indisputable fact a somewhat vague and illogical theory that has little or no evidence to support it. While we are not familiar with the thought processes of your species, among Naxians this would be considered a sign of poor psychological health."

Eksher scratched at his beard. "I guess we Erthumoi are a bit looser in our thinking," he said. "I've never heard religious faith considered a form of insanity."

"This term you use—the translation we receive cannot be correct. What is it?"

"Religious faith?"

"Yes."

Eksher considered that carefully before replying.

"I don't really think I can explain it," he said. "You've just seen a really prime example of it, though."

"This phenomenon is normal among Erthumoi?"

"More or less," Eksher agreed.

"It resembles the Cephallonian custom of constructing philosophical models," Infrared Ovoid remarked, "but the emotional content is entirely different. A Cephallonian creates philosophical models as an intellectual exercise and modifies them endlessly, matching different variants against the available data, while your shipmate appears to find an intense personal satisfaction in knowing something that is probably not true and is completely unconcerned with developing it further. In fact, he appears to believe it to be complete and all-inclusive and incapable of modification."

Eksher shrugged. "Don't look at me," he said. "I'm an agnostic, myself. I don't understand it either."

"Agnostic?"

"Ask the ship," Eksher suggested.

"One without religious faith," the ship explained.

"This faith, then, is something that some Erthumoi have, while others do not?"

"Right," Eksher agreed. "Exactly right."

Infrared Ovoid considered for a moment, then asked, "What is it that your shipmate wishes to do on Carter-Carter IV?"

Eksher chewed his lower lip, trying to decide whether there was any way to lie convincingly to a Naxian.

He decided there wasn't.

"He wants to convince as many of your people as possible that his beliefs are true," he said.

Infrared thought silently for several seconds before asking, "Why?"

"To share his joy," Eksher replied.

The Naxian's facial scales rippled. "I understand," it-she said.

"I can't honestly say I do," Eksher muttered.

"We will allow Jomo Li-Sanch to land," Infrared Ovoid announced.

Startled, Eksher asked, "You will?"

"Yes. We will allow him to speak freely to our people."

"If you don't mind my asking," Eksher said, "why?"

"Because his intensity of belief is enjoyable to observe," Infrared Ovoid replied. "Because we find his elaborate explanations, and the delight he takes in them, to be . . ." The Naxian, in an oddly Erthuma gesture, groped for the right word.

"Charming?" Eksher suggested.

"Amusing," Infrared Ovoid said.

"You mean funny?"

"Yes. Very much so."

Eksher sat and considered for a long moment.

"If he finds out you think he's funny, he'll be hurt pretty bad," he said at last.

"We are aware of that. We will endeavor not to let him find out. Such knowledge might also damage the entertainment value of his . . . preaching, is it?"

"Preaching, right," Eksher said. He sat and stared at the Naxian's image.

Infrared Ovoid stared back.

"So," Eksher said at last, "that's why you wanted to talk to *me*, and not him."

"Yes," it-she agreed. "That, and one more thing."

"What one more thing?" Eksher asked warily.

"You are a dealer in entertainments, are you not?"

"Yeah," Eksher admitted. "So?"

"So," Infrared Ovoid said, its inhuman expression completely unreadable, "we will pay you well to find other such entertainments. The data banks of the Communion of Wisdom of the Shared Purpose list over two thousand active religions among your species. . . ."

WINGING IT

JANET KAGAN

"HARRIET, I NEED YOUR HELP," SAID *EL PRESI-dente*, without so much as a hello to soften her up first.

Harriet Kingsolver knew Wanwadee Li well enough to consider a blanket offer of assistance foolhardy; he'd gotten her into enough unbelievably weird situations for a single lifetime. She considered the face on the screen and said nothing.

Wanwadee had painted the frown lines of his office dark and unusually broad for the occasion but there was genuine anxiety there too. And the frown deepened as the moments ticked by without a response from Harriet. Having practiced with a cat, Harriet could outwait him anytime.

At last he broke, as she'd known he would. "Harriet," he said, "you've worked with Crotonites. . . ."

"I've worked with Crotonites from Pssstwhit," she said, the world's name being a cross between a whistle and a spit. Admitting that committed her to nothing and it amused her to speak even that little of the language after so long.

It amused the Siamese cat in her lap as well. His Highness gave Harriet a cross-eyed stare and told her to mind her manners and watch her mouth.

"Pastwit," said Wanwadee, butchering the pronunciation the way most Erthumoi did. "Then I need you even more than I thought I did. Pastwit's sending us an ambassador."

Harriet leaned forward. "I beg your pardon?"

"You heard me. For some reason known only to themselves, the Crotonites of Pastwit have decided to send LostRoses a fully accredited ambassador."

As weird as usual. Tilting back in her chair, Harriet thought it over.

LostRoses had a population of five thousand Erthumoi, give or take a hundred. Its only exports were two kinds of spice and a leaf gall which, split and polished, yielded a gemstone that gave the planet its name. The moment galactic taste (or fashion) changed, LostRoses would become a ghost world.

Unless the Crotonites had suddenly acquired a taste for lostroses or for one of the two spices, their sending an ambassador made no sense whatsoever. Furthermore, given what she'd seen of the Crotonite temperament, a diplomatic Crotonite was a contradiction in terms.

Weird, but interesting, she concluded. She let Wanwadee stew a moment more, then she said, "I won't postpone my regular trade run for this. You've got me for three months, then I'm gone."

"Thanks, Harriet," he said, and but for the painted lines most of his frown smoothed away. "We meet him at St. Elsie's Field at ten."

"I'll be there."

Harriet flicked off the comunit and scratched His Highness behind the ears. "It's not Wanwadee Li who gets me into weird situations," she told him. "It's *me* that gets me into weird situations."

His Highness told her in no uncertain terms how many kinds of a fool she was. In perfect Siamese cat yowl-growl, she told him what she thought of his manners, his putative parentage, and his current sexual proclivities. He purred contentedly and rubbed his head against her chin.

Just as contentedly, Harriet said, "Well, we'll wing it."

When Harriet rolled onto the edge of St. Elsie's Field, the Crotonite ship was nowhere to be seen. Her guess was they'd landed, opened the lock, tossed out the ambassador (not much caring which end up), and taken off like the bats out of hell they somewhat resembled.

There was only one place anybody met at port and that was Sylvaine's Custom House—what passed on LostRoses for bar, inn, customs and immigration, and *Officio del Presidente*. She rolled on in.

Even before her chair climbed onto the smoother surface of the parquet flooring, she knew the ambassador had indeed arrived. She could hear him—hissing and spitting and spattering like overheated grease in a frying pan. Nothing could curse for a longer time without repeating itself *or* sound nastier in the process than a Crotonite.

Except perhaps a Siamese cat—Harriet was almost sorry His Highness had declined (with emphasis) to accompany her; the match-off would have been highly entertaining.

Sylvaine, bemused, stood peering over the edge of a huge assortment of unfamiliar containers, strangely wrapped packages, and odd-looking equipment. He glanced at Harriet long enough to give her a wave of welcome, then went back to his peering.

Good thing she'd come. He'd need help with all that baggage, and Harriet's chair had been modified from a cargo shifter. That was the one strength Wanwadee claimed—he did think ahead. That's why the population of LostRoses stuck him with the job of *el presidente* year after year.

From somewhere within the heap of baggage came the sound of boxes being opened, dug through,

rearranged, shut with an angry slam—and the constant
stream of Crotonite invective. Harriet whistled her chair
closer and listened with a smile to the familiar sound
of it.

"Slugs," said the voice. "May they crawl forever
on their faces. May their mouths fill with mud and their
noses with weeds. May their offspring fly forever lower
and lower until *their wings too* trail in the mud.
May—" The cursing broke off abruptly.

He couldn't have run out of steam this soon, Harriet
knew from experience. He must have been dropped off
earlier than Wanwadee had expected. Whatever the
case, she knew an opening when she saw one and took
advantage of the brief silence to introduce herself.

"May they eat dead food and choke," Harriet
offered in the same tongue. "May their fingers stink of
mildew and their wings rot of fungus. May the updrafts
smash them against the Torn Cliffs and the downdrafts
dash them into the Sumpwater Swamps."

She hadn't lost her touch. With a hiss of surprise,
the Crotonite shot up from behind a stack of crates to
scan the room with sharp eyes.

They were a vivid orange, those eyes—a color Harriet had not seen for some three years. She cut the
thought short.

When at last he was satisfied that Sylvaine's held no
other Crotonite, he turned the sharp eyes on Harriet—
and even his transparent breathing mask could not
obscure the look of startlement (or what Harriet had
always taken for one) on his birdlike face.

For her part, Harriet was equally startled: The Crotonite had no wings.

From where she sat, the scars at his shoulders looked
clean—as if the wings had been surgically removed.
She wondered what kind of disease or accident had
necessitated the amputation. The wings must have been
very badly damaged, or they'd have been left to him,

even useless, for the sake of esthetics. Wingspan was ninety percent of a Crotonite's pride.

She said, "I'm Harriet Kingsolver. May I be of some assistance?"

He'd regained his composure and, with it, his Crotonite arrogance. He eyed her from the treads of her chair to the top of her head, then he said acidly, "Can you fly?"

"Yes," said Harriet. She did not put the same question to him.

Again the look of startlement crossed his features, but this time there was something else as well, something that Harriet had never seen before and was unable to interpret. After a moment, he said something that she did not follow.

She shook her head, smiling, and said, in the Nevelse that was LostRoses's lingua franca, "Sorry. I only learned to curse in Crotoni—not to converse."

In Nevelse, he said, "You fly—in a mechanical contrivance."

His tone made it clear that airplanes didn't count. Harriet, of all people, could understand the distinction. She nodded.

"Slug," he said. It was the standard Crotonite insult for a nonflying species.

"Uninventive," she countered. "Get to know me and get personal. I promise you *I* will." She eyed the stumps of his wings just long enough to call his attention to the fact that she hadn't bothered with the most obvious choice of insults possible. "I await something worth my talents."

Again she drew from him an unidentifiable expression, this one unlike the previous one. If it was not actually admiration, it was at least neutral, because he jabbed a stubby finger at Sylvaine and said, "This crawler through mud wishes to pry into my private lug-

gage." In Crotoni, he added, "May he stick his fingers
into a fastgnaw hole and withdraw his hand fingerless."

"Sylvaine? What do you need to know?"

"If he's got any seeds, plants—the usual
contraband."

Harriet swung a hand to indicate the entire pile of
the Crotonite's belongings and said, "Have you got
anything alive in there—animal or vegetable?"

"No," said the Crotonite. "May his beak strike a
cliff's edge in the fog and shatter into a thousand
shards."

"He's clear," Harriet said to Sylvaine. "I vouch for
him. Now, how about a beer for me and a cup of glavsa
for the ambassador."

"Coming up," said Sylvaine.

"Oh! And, Sylvaine? Bring that busted chair, the
one with no seat. The ambassador will be more comfortable perching than sitting, I imagine."

Still no sign of Wanwadee Li. Harriet was not the
least bit surprised; Wanwadee Li ran on Wanwadee Li
time—which ran about forty-five minutes later than
standard. She rolled to the nearest table and gestured
at the chair Sylvaine provided.

Glaring, the ambassador wrapped sharp claws around
the upper rung of the broken chair and perched. She'd
guessed right—that brought him to the proper height
for the table.

Thoughtful as always, Sylvaine brought the glavsa in
a pipette mug; breathing mask or no, the ambassador
could sip his drink. Sylvaine put a beer in front of
Harriet and waved away payment. "I'll put it on Wanwadee's tab," he said. "It looks to me like official
government business."

He retreated behind the bar, leaving Harriet to handle
the Crotonite ambassador. Well, she'd just have to
make polite conversation until Wanwadee Li showed
up to make things formal.

"So," she said, lifting her beer in a toast to the newest comer to LostRoses. "Do you have a name or was your mother too appalled by your looks to claim you?"

His name was Wyss'huk—a whoosh and half a hiccup—and she and Wanwadee eventually got him and his belongings stowed in the Pssstwhit embassy, the Pssstwhit embassy being a hollow ceramic cube that Wanwadee had spent the afternoon forming.

"It had to be airtight—that's what held me up. I made it big, for the sake of prestige, but if he wants fancy, he'll have to extrude his own," Wanwadee said. "That was the only pattern I could find in the library that bore so much as a remote resemblance to Pastwit architecture." He gestured her into his own wood-frame home. "I should have asked you if you had any suggestions."

"I'd have given you the wrong ones, Wanwadee. You didn't tell me he was wingless."

Wanwadee gave an involuntary glance at Harriet's legs—then, visibly embarrassed, he turned away. "Drink, Harriet?" Before she could answer, he was halfway across the room to his private stock.

Harriet sighed. "You're being an idiot today, Wan," she said, softening it with a smile. "We both know my legs don't function. Your looking or not looking doesn't change that a bit. It's like being afraid to say, 'I see what you mean,' to a blind man."

"Sorry." He came back with a glass for each of them and a more normal demeanor. "It's been a long day, I don't understand a bit of this and, you're right, I'm being stupid." He downed his drink and poured himself a second. "I don't *mind* being *el presidente* most days—but that's only because, most days, being *el presidente* doesn't mean shit. Today I'm out of my league."

He pulled up a chair and sat heavily. "I hypered every authority I could think of for advice and all I got back, in some three hundred different ways, was 'Find out what they want!' We'll be getting some 'experts,' too, but lord only knows what they're 'expert' in."

"Then you don't know how he lost his wings?"

"Oh," he said, and he scowled. The painted lines across his forehead turned his face into a mask of anger. "That I can tell you—but you won't like it any more than I did. I don't blame him much for his mouth—I sure as hell wouldn't be all sweetness and light in his circumstances." Within the mask, his eyes were cold. "You'd better drink that drink. You'll probably need it."

Harriet raised first an eyebrow, then her glass. She took a sip to oblige him and then she said, "Tell me."

"Whooshuk was chosen as ambassador, so they amputated his wings."

"*What?*"

"Seems the Crotonites thought their ambassador would be able to understand us ground crawlers better if he were a ground crawler himself."

Harriet took in a long breath, looked down at the glass in her hands. "You were right," she said. "I hate it." She downed the drink in a gulp.

Harriet set the chair on automatic and let it find its own way home. She had things to think about—things she hadn't thought about for a long time. Here's your reward for being chosen as ambassador: We chop off your wings. What kind of mind did it take to think of that? She knew what it was like to be without wings. Wyss'huk would spend the rest of his life staring up into the sky—the way Harriet was staring into it even now.

The arrival beep from the chair put a momentary halt to her angry thoughts and brought her eyes back to earth. Taking the chair off automatic, she rolled to the storage shed. First things first—she'd see what condition her equipment was in. . . .

She hadn't looked at it for almost three years but she knew exactly where Majnoun had stowed it. The chair pinchers dropped the package delicately across her lap. Her hands hesitated over the careful wrappings. It would be in perfect condition; Majnoun had seen to that in the stowing.

He'd always assumed she'd use it again one day. That was before they'd learned that the regeneration techniques wouldn't work on her, of course. Still, Harriet suspected he'd have wrapped it just as lovingly had he known.

The thought made her smile—and her hands moved of themselves to begin unwrapping the package. Fiery oranges leapt out to greet her eye—the gaudiest bird on LostRoses. What a shame it hadn't graced the sky in so many years.

Well, Firehawk, she thought, it's time you hit the sky again.

Carefully, she rewrapped the package. Like a sun setting, she thought, then—but it'll be back up again tomorrow. She felt a fierce grin cross her face as she handed the package to the pinchers.

She was still grinning when she reached the house, still grinning when Majnoun answered her call. "I need a favor, Majnoun," she said.

"Name it!"

"I need you to adapt a hang-gliding harness to fit a Crotonite. He's not just smaller than a human—the torso-to-leg ratio's much different. The arms are stubbier. He's got only two fingers to each hand but I don't think that's a problem. To judge from the chest muscles and from the way he hauled crates this evening, he's got good upper body strength."

"He'd need it, to use those wings." Majnoun stared

out of the screen, suddenly puzzled. "His wings would get in the way, Harriet."

Harriet felt the grin fall away from her face. She shook her head. "No," she said. "This one doesn't have any wings."

"Oh!" His eyes widened. "Oh! So we're—"

"We're going to give him mine."

To her surprise, Harriet had no trouble coaxing Wyss'huk from the Pssstwhit embassy in the morning. His temperament hadn't improved but he did seem curious about the world he'd been sent to. Good enough.

When he took a momentary pause from cursing the weather, the lack of air pressure, the general quality of intelligence among the upper levels of Pssstwhit authority, and Harriet (perhaps only so she wouldn't feel left out), Harriet extruded a running board and said, "Hop on. I'll show you the best sight on LostRoses."

She might have extruded the sidesaddle but she wanted to make sure about that upper body strength before she launched her plan—or him.

Up close and clinging by her side, he said, "Why does Erthuma medicine not restore you the use of your legs?"

Harriet shrugged. "I'm the one in a million. For some reason, the regeneration techniques don't work on me." She swung the chair due west, aiming at the cliffs in the distance, and headed out for Fallaway Point. "Not that they've stopped trying. About once every six months, somebody shows up at the port with a new theory, I play guinea pig for a few days, and then they go away to revise their theory."

"May they catch the skin rot and be bled to death by their own colleagues," Wyss'huk said.

Harriet laughed. "There are times I'd've wished them the same—*especially* when it's blood samples they're after. But who knows? Maybe some day one of the theories will actually work in practice.''

"May they first be subject to their own experiments and those of all their colleagues.''

Harriet took her eyes briefly from the road. He showed no sign of strain from the ride. There was only the brightness of anger in his orange eyes. His silvery gray fur looked almost as soft as His Highness's, but the stumps of his wings were an unhealed angry pink. Surgically removed, she remembered. He's got less reason to like doctors than I have.

"May they spend one life as a worm and yet another as a snail,'' she agreed.

For a while, they were both silent as the chair sped through Hellup Woods. She did stop once to cut him a leaf gall but that led to no further conversation. If he showed that little interest in lostroses, Harriet decided, gemstones were hardly the reason for his presence on her world.

They emerged from the forest onto the hard-packed black volcanic sand of the beach below Fallaway Point. Harriet halted atop a small rise to inflate the treads for better traction and to scan the beach for the Only Birds. She turned to say something to Wyss'huk and found him staring up into the sky.

Her voice failed at the sight of his expression. Angry, yes, but more hungry than angry.

Without a word, she started down the gentle incline to the far end of the beach where she'd spotted the pickup crew. Wyss'huk did not take his eyes from the sky.

Well, she thought, in a moment he should have something to look at. The bright bits of color at the rim of the cliff sparkled, shifted.

Harriet braked the chair, flung up an arm and said, *"There!"* She didn't even know if he followed her point—she was too greedy of her own watching to take her eyes off them. The Only Birds soared from the top of the cliff—yellow, red, blue, purple. Every color of the rainbow, but for her orange.

She found herself grinning again, just from the pleasure of watching. Stupid of her to have denied herself that much for so long a time.

They swooped and soared—oh! the winds were with them today! The only birds on LostRoses. So beautiful . . .

And then they must have seen her, for they turned, almost in formation, and swept down the beach to display their colors in graceful dips directly above her head. Harriet found herself cheering and clapping and waving both arms in a wide sweep of approval.

The thermals over the black sand were glorious today. Isobel cut a figure eight in the air, the black "eyes" on her delta-wing twinkling against pure green—against the purer blue of the sky. Daffyd—navy blue with white stripes—crabbed to a second thermal and soared so high he might have been mistaken for a wisp of cloud. Winged in royal purple, Majnoun rode down a slope of air to duplicate Isobel's figure with a broader stroke.

Then he continued on downward. Twenty feet from Harriet's chair, he spilled air and touched down on the black sand in a dead stop. He didn't have to take so much as a single forward step to regain his balance.

Shaking her head in admiration, Harriet rolled toward him. "Pretty landing!" she said.

He looked up briefly from his postflight check to grin his exhilaration at her. "Thanks, Harriet. You picked a gorgeous day for this. The flying hasn't been this fine for months." He finished his check, folded his wings.

Harriet whistled commands and the spare pinchers reached out to take Majnoun's wings. Majnoun drew back protectively, then took in Harriet's smile, smiled himself, and let her take them. "Lift?" she said, extruding a second running board.

"Sure." Majnoun hopped on opposite the ambassador.

"Wyss'huk," Harriet said, "this is Majnoun. Majnoun, this is the guy I was telling you about."

Wyss'huk took his eyes from the sky only long enough to give Majnoun the once over and dismiss him. "Another slug," he said—but he said it in his own language, not in one Majnoun would likely understand.

Harriet supposed that was what passed for tact in a Crotonite. "No," she said. "You're a slug and I'm a slug but Majnoun's not—Majnoun *flies*."

She headed the chair toward the pickup crew. "What do you say, Majnoun? Can you cut the harness to the proper size?"

"No," he said.

Harriet was so surprised she hit the brake. "You *can't?* Why not?"

"Don't get riled, Harriet. I didn't mean that the way you took it. He can have the rig that Isobel outgrew—she's delighted with the thought of adding another bird to our flock." Majnoun laid a hand on the wrapped package that held Harriet's wings. "I meant I refuse to cut your Firehawk down for somebody else. You're going to want it someday. I just couldn't cut her down."

Nor could he look at Harriet as he said it. Harriet couldn't think what to say. Isobel gave them both a graceful way out with one of the clumsy landings for which she was infamous.

She came in crosswise to the beach, hit the ground running furiously—which was better than being dragged, Harriet had to admit—and finished up with a headlong sprawl into the surf, spattering all three of them with water.

Majnoun cursed and leapt off the running board to give rescue, needed or not.

Harriet laughed and turned to Wyss'huk. "We're the only birds on LostRoses—and Isobel's our goonybird. She's beautiful in the air but her takeoffs and landings are abysmal. The only person who ever made a worse landing was me. Luckily, Isobel never seems to hurt herself."

Majnoun had pulled Isobel, laughing and dripping, from the water, and the two of them gathered up her wings.

Above them flashed a delta-wing painted with clusters of lavender flowers that Lilac claimed were the flowers she'd been named after. "Isobel!" Lilac shouted down at the youngster standing hip deep in water. "Watch how it's done!"

Harriet expected to see another perfect landing, like Majnoun's—but Lilac was not the sort who cared about the expected.

Instead, she made a sweeping turn and skimmed away from the beach until she was far out over deep water. There she swept a second turn, to set a course that would land her in Harriet's lap if she kept coming. She didn't.

Still over deep water, Lilac dipped, spilled air, and—before Harriet's astonished eyes—dropped out of her harness, plunging feet first into sea. The flowery wings skimmed on without her, missing Harriet's chair by inches, to come to a gentle rest on the beach behind.

Harriet didn't manage to get her mouth closed until all three had come up to drip yet more water on her. Majnoun was still berating Lilac for her assorted sins: "Hotdogging, taking stupid chances . . ."

Lilac ignored him to grin at Harriet. "I had to do *something* to welcome you back." She turned her smile on Wyss'huk. "And something a little special for your special guest—ooops!" She darted after her wings, which had begun to scud away in the rising wind, snatched them up, and checked them over with infinite care.

Wyss'huk said, ''May the Raiser of Winds blow her wings to one who more deserves them.''

Harriet turned to him in surprise. His choice of curse was as unexpected as Lilac's landing had been. The only time she'd ever heard *that* one applied was to a Crotonite who did not, by the standards of his fellow Crotonites, take the proper care in preening his wings.

''What did he say?'' Majnoun asked.

''He thinks she was hotdogging, too. He thinks she risked her wings doing it.''

''Oh.'' Majnoun looked past Wyss'huk to where Lilac threw him a thumbs-up as she folded her wings, then he said to Wyss'huk, ''They're a lot sturdier than they look. She keeps them in good trim—and she doesn't usually take chances like that.''

The glance Majnoun gave Harriet was more than a little wistful. ''It is something of a special occasion, having you here again. Want to come up and watch us launch this time?''

Harriet turned to look at Wyss'huk. He said nothing but this time the hunger in his eyes was even stronger. She wondered if he could read the same hunger in her eyes. For him, she said, ''Yes. That's what we're here for.''

Majnoun and Wyss'huk still clinging to opposite sides of her chair, Harriet raced the pickup crew to the top of the cliff—and won.

''I'm getting a powergo like yours, Harriet,'' Lilac announced, as she leapt from the pickup cart.

''As long as you get it *voluntarily*,'' Harriet said, ''and not because of some stupid stunt.''

Lilac shook her head. ''It wasn't a stupid stunt. I worked it all out and I practiced until I knew I could get it right. If I hadn't been in the right position to cut loose safely, you'd have had to wait for some other flight to see it."

Harriet quirked an eyebrow. Lilac had been awaiting the question, of course, and delightedly launched into a flood of technical description.

When she was done, even Majnoun was nodding. "I take it all back," he said. "But Wyss'huk needn't take back *his* criticism. It *is* risky on your wings." His mouth pursed slightly, in thought, not in disapproval. "Perhaps we might manage a tether of sorts—you could guide the bird to safe landing. Let me think about it."

"Let's fly while you think," said Lilac. Isobel had already turned the pickup cart around and started back down to the beach. It was her turn to wait on the ground. Tomas was doing the preflight check on his vivid yellow wings.

Majnoun laughed. "Go ahead, Lilac. I've a few things to attend to here."

Lilac shrugged, stepped to the edge of the cliff, raised her delta-wing and stepped into the air, all in one smooth motion.

The wind tugged at Harriet, riffling her hair. All of it came back to her in a rush, almost as if she soared with Lilac. It was such a perfect day for flying, every muscle in her body—even those ghost muscles in her legs—remembered what to do. She could stand up, spread her wings, turn just *so*, and launch from where she sat. . . . Tomas stepped off the edge of the cliff and soared away.

"What do you say, Wyss'huk?" she said to the Crotonite.

It was a long time before he could tear his eyes away from Lilac's flight to look at her. His fingers gripped the arm of her chair so tightly she was afraid he might break something—either his fingers or the arm.

"I realize it wouldn't be the same," Harriet went on. "You'd have to learn an entirely different manner of flying but—" She didn't finish the sentence in words, but in a long look, out over the sea, to where Lilac and Tomas wove bright patterns in the air.

He followed her look. Lilac had caught a thermal— she rose and rose and rose, the color of her wings all but vanishing in the distance. Then Tomas found the same rising wind and rode it after her.

Wyss'huk turned abruptly back to Harriet. This time the expression on his face was pure fury. "May you brush through bugstickers and coat your wings with gum!"

Harriet recognized that one too, only because she'd once seen a Crotonite who'd done just that. Three months later, his fur was still tarry with the substance. Another of the Crotonites had confided to her that not only did it affect one's flight but it also stank, at least, to another Crotonite.

"Do you think I'd fly with artificial wings?" Wyss'-huk was working himself up to a full head of steam, this time in Nevelse. "You ground-crawling Erthumoi think you have a technological fix for everything! Use artificial devices to fly?" He raised a two-fingered hand, claws extended.

Involuntarily, Harriet drew back. The shift in position gave her a stark view of the scars on his shoulders. Where his wings should have been.

"Your wings," she said. "Did your people gnaw them off with their teeth?"

She knew perfectly well they hadn't. She'd seen Crotonite surgical instruments. But Wyss'huk was startled into a defensive response: "Stupid slug! They used surgical instruments—"

"Right," said Harriet. "If they can use *instruments*"—her inflection made the word nastier even than he had—"to drop you out of the sky, then you can use an instrument to get you back into the sky—*where you belong.*"

"Slug," he said again. "May you drop into a rip in the wind and be hurled against the PeopleKillers." That was a particularly rocky tor on Pssstwhit, whose crosswinds took a high toll of the nearby population every year.

Wyss'huk still hadn't answered her question though. Harriet listened to his further curses with half an ear. She was not about to give up. There was only one thing she'd ever given up on.

Once again the muscles in her body remembered. Stand, turn just so, and rise into the wind.

And then she was reaching for her wings and unwrapping them. "I had intended," she told the Crotonite, interrupting him somewhere in the midst of another ground-crawling metaphor, "to give these to you. Majnoun wouldn't let me." She nodded at Majnoun and grinned with anticipation. "Thanks, Majnoun. Could you give Isobel a call and ask her to stand by with the inflatable?"

Harriet had done the standard preflight check on Firehawk the night before but now she did it again. The familiarity of routine took the trembling from her fingers.

Majnoun looked up from his talker, the slightest of frowns across his face. "Harriet, are you *sure* you want to do this?"

It was the right question. She knew the answer. "I've never been *more* sure in my life. I can't land on the beach but I *can* use Lilac's drop into the water to land safely."

At her whistle, the chair's pinchers caught her gently at the waist and lifted her erect. She strapped into Firehawk's harness.

"All right," Majnoun said. "But you're out of practice, so I want you to make the first one an easy one. No fancy stuff, just a straight glide down to the water.''

Harriet nodded, unable to wipe the grin off her face even for such solemn instruction. Majnoun double-checked the harness, double-checked that Isobel already had the inflatable inflated and ready for action, then he grinned too. ''You figured out how to do the takeoff, I presume. Tell me what you need me to do.''

''Once I'm off, you can put the chair on automatic and hit B-6. It knows this route; it'll be waiting on the beach by the time I splash down. Now''—she spread Firehawk's wings over her in a glorious burst of flame ''—if you'll just pry Wyss'huk off the arm of my chair and stand back. . . .''

Wyss'huk had stepped from the running board. Harriet felt the wind and waited, realizing as she did that she hadn't heard a curse from Wyss'huk for some time. ''Run out of insults?'' she asked.

''I have nothing to say to a ground-crawling slug.''

Harriet laughed. There was her wind; she felt its rightness. She whistled for the pinchers to turn her just *so*. Yes! The wind filled her wings, tugging her to come away from her chair and soar.

''You stay here on the ground, Wyss'huk. May you enjoy your crawling,'' Harriet said. ''—But watch *this* slug *fly!*''

She whistled the pinchers' release. For a long moment nothing seemed to happen . . . and then Harriet was swept into the sky.

The feeling was one she'd had a thousand times before: It was freedom. As all her weight came to rest on the harness, she felt the simultaneous downward slip. Her hands adjusted of themselves, pulling the Firehawk's nose down the needed touch—and she shot forward, almost dizzy with the excitement.

She soared. A hundred feet later, she realized that the yell of triumph she could hear was coming from her own throat and, if she kept it up, she wouldn't be able to talk for a week. Even so, it took her a conscious effort to stop doing it.

When she had, she could hear from the cliff's edge behind her Majnoun's faint voice yelling, "Go! Go! Go!" into the wind.

There was another sound as well, a hissing, sputtering sound that carried much better than Majnoun's shouts could ever have. Harriet glided along, listening to the whisper of the wind in her wings and to Wyss'-huk's hissed instructions. She could make out every word, though she only understood one in a dozen. Wyss'huk was no longer cursing.

Harriet sailed, dreamlike, through the air, feeling for lift. The beach slid by below her. From the edge of the beach, Isobel waved and danced and shouted inaudibly.

The hiss behind her said, ". . . Short flight . . . lift to your right . . . *carefully,* child!"

She angled right, found the lift just as Wyss'huk had promised, and used it to lengthen her slope out over the sea. There she found the proper air to turn on and, remembering her promise to Majnoun, slid toward the surface of the water, aiming for a spot not far from where Isobel danced on the beach.

As she turned parallel to the cliff, she saw Majnoun in the air, gliding toward her. Her chair was speeding down the road. Wyss'huk was in the driver's seat but he wasn't driving—he was staring at her and hissing for all his worth.

It reminded Harriet of the noises her mother had taught her to make with the neck of a balloon. Ah! she thought, as she caught another rise that would put her closer still to Isobel, Wyss'huk's talking a kid through its first flight!

He couldn't very well talk her through this kind of a landing though, so she gave the approaching water her full concentration. Spill air, slow, spill air . . . She

was a leg length now from the surface of the sea and—
now!

Harriet hit the release on her harness and dropped
feet first. The water closed over her head. For a long
moment, she let herself arrow deeper. Even that was
not sobering. She reveled in the sudden shocking cool-
ness of the water. Then at last she raised her arms and
stroked toward the light.

She surfaced with a fling of her head to clear her
eyes and yet another involuntary shout of joy. The first
thing she saw was the sky, vast and inviting.

The second . . . Isobel, already paddling furiously
toward her. Then she saw Majnoun hit the beach, strip
out of *his* harness and run down to the water's edge.
She wondered, grinning, if he'd wait there or if he'd
just jump in. Then she spotted Firehawk's glorious
orange floating in the water a scant few yards away.
Harriet swam over to assure herself Firehawk hadn't
been damaged in the descent. Majnoun was right, she
needed some sort of tether to lessen the risk of damage
to her wings.

"Looks okay to me," said Isobel, from behind Harriet's shoulder, "but best we check it out on shore.
Give it a chance to dry."

Isobel caught the tip of Firehawk's nose and secured
it to the edge of the inflatable. Then she reached out her
hands for Harriet. "What's the best way to do this?"

"I pull my front half in, then you grab my legs and
pull them in after me."

Isobel got soaked a second time that day and the two
of them were laughing so hard they could barely paddle
back to the beach, where Majnoun waited, waist-deep
in the water, to carry Harriet back to shore.

Harriet was still laughing as Majnoun settled her into
her chair. He laid Firehawk, still dripping, across her
lap. "No damage," he said, "but still . . ."

"We'll work something out," Harriet agreed, and

added a nod to Wyss'huk, who was once again perched on the running board beside her.

Harriet had just enough vocabulary to put the question to the Crotonite in his own tongue: "What do you say, child? Will you let Majnoun teach you to fly—or do you want to crawl for the rest of your life?"

His orange eyes met hers, and they were as brilliant as Firehawk. "Let a human teach a Crotonite to fly . . ." He snarled the words, but Harriet knew they were not the scornful rejection they sounded—they were a yes.

Harriet grinned at Majnoun. "You're on, Majnoun. Let's get this slug in the air, too." To Wyss'huk, she added, "It's a *beautiful* day for flying."

"Yes," he said.

For all of Wyss'huk's cursing, Majnoun made him start easy, from ground school up. It was low, straight flight along a gentle incline while the Crotonite learned to fly with his hands instead of his missing wings, and while Majnoun made adjustments to both wings and harness to better suit the alien's physique.

But the Crotonite knew the wind and, once he'd gotten the trick to controlling his artificial wings, he was the quickest pupil Majnoun had ever taught.

"If the weather holds tomorrow, Wushock, I think you're ready to fly from the rim of Fallaway Point."

"Not today?"

The belligerence had been replaced by a quiet wistfulness that Harriet could detect even through the obstruction of the breathing mask and the flattened tonelessness of Wyss'huk's Nevelese.

"Not today," said Harriet, before Majnoun could respond. "Nightfall's coming and I want to get through the woods before dark. Furthermore, your breathing mask should need renewing soon. All this excitement is bound to have used up more than you'd planned for—"

Wyss'huk blinked at her, then made some sort of check, touching his equipment with claws alone. His eyes widened. "You're right, Ha'reet," he said in Nevelse. "We must start for the embassy soon."

He gave a last hungry look at the sky, then he said, "May the Raiser of Winds be happy tomorrow."

"I'll second that," said Majnoun.

To a chorus of good-byes, Harriet rolled off toward town, this time with Wyss'huk sidesaddle. Harriet was feeling the strain of the day's effort enough that she knew how tired Wyss'huk must be from the exertion of flying in such an unfamiliar fashion.

She was too happily tired to attempt to carry on a conversation. Wyss'huk, too, was silent all the way into town. Perhaps he was holding the day's joy quietly to his heart, as she was. She glanced once or twice to the side but could read nothing in his expression. Whether it was the fading light or her own ignorance she didn't know.

A few yards past St. Elsie's Field, His Highness shot from the undergrowth and yowled a greeting. Harriet slowed the chair and yowled back. A second later, His Highness was in Harriet's lap, sniffing furiously.

"Yes," said Harriet, "I flew."

But it was not Harriet, nor the smell of wind or sea, that interested His Highness. He stretched his neck and sniffed very hard in Wyss'huk's direction, his lips parting in the cat sneer that, Harriet thought, brought him a wider range of smells.

Wyss'huk stared back with equal fascination.

After a while, His Highness told Wyss'huk where to get off, what to sit on, and why he was not worth a wasted rat. Harriet told His Highness, in cat, that if he didn't shut his mouth she'd feed him to the recycler at the next house they passed. His Highness flicked an ear in her direction, decided she was lying, and told Wyss'-huk which orifice to insert what extremity into.

Wyss'huk said, "May the rot begin with your left toe and claim your body an inch at a time. May your ears and tail be last to succumb and may they drop from your bones with the putrid smell of a dying patpig. And may all your relatives be present to appreciate you to the last."

Harriet stared at him with admiration. His Highness purred and stepped delicately from Harriet's lap into Wyss'huk's. "I must remember that one," said Harriet. "That's *good!*" His Highness rubbed happily against the Crotonite's shoulder.

Wyss'huk only stared at the cat. In the dim light, his eyes were a baleful gold. His Highness glared back but continued to purr.

"I have never before seen eyes the color of sky," Wyss'huk told the cat in Nevelse. "Why should Raiser of Winds so favor a ground crawler?"

Oops, thought Harriet. "Wyss'huk, that's a pet. I don't know if you folks have a similar custom—it's a nonsapient species kept for company. He likes it if you rub him behind the ears."

"Not sapient? Are you sure? He curses like a sapient."

Harriet laughed. "He does at that. But considering the fights he gets into, if he's sapient, he's still an idiot."

"Like humans and Crotonites," Wyss'huk observed. He was, very delicately, scratching His Highness behind the ears with his claw tips.

"Very like," Harriet agreed. She braked to a stop in front of the Pssstwhit embassy and patted her lap to coax His Highness back into it.

Neither His Highness nor Wyss'huk seemed to take notice. After a long while, Wyss'huk spoke again—so softly that it seemed a part of His Highness's purr. "You speak a little of my language and you understand more than you speak. Do you understand the word *pippest?*''

"No, sorry."

"Translated literally into Nevelse, it would be . . . 'changer.' It means a person who has made a profound change in one's life, specifically a change for the better. You are *pippest* to me."

Harriet raised her eyebrows. "And you to me, Wyss'huk. I wouldn't have flown again if it hadn't been for you. You made me see the possibility—and made me stubborn enough to act on it."

He was silent for a long moment. His Highness's purr deepened as Wyss'huk's fingers found a preferred spot. Then he said, "I did not think it possible for an Erthuma and a Crotonite to be *pippest* to each other."

"I don't see why not, Wyss'huk. I think we've got a good thing going here and we ought to keep it up."

He made a ticking sound that she'd always suspected meant pleasure to a Crotonite. "Are you aware that phrase is untranslatable in Crotoni—'why not'? You Erthumoi leave open possibilities my people do not. I am only now beginning to understand its use. With a 'shrug,' am I right?"

"You're right. Quite often with a shrug—and a smile."

"Then perhaps we two might even become friends." His shrug was exaggerated and, given the beak, he couldn't manage the smile, but Harriet knew it was there all the same. "Even though a friendship between a Crotonite and an Erthuma is unthinkable—why not?"

"Why not, indeed," agreed Harriet. "And, if we run into problems, we'll wing it."

Then she knew that sound from a Crotonite meant pleasure. " 'Wing it'! Yes! I had never thought about the phrase." Liking the sound as much as Harriet did, His Highness thudded Wyss'huk in the chest.

"I would like," Wyss'huk said, "to give you something in return for what you've given me."

"I told you, Wyss'huk. You're *pippest* to me too. But if you really feel the need—you could satisfy my curiosity."

"What are you curious about? Unless it's a taboo subject—*even* if it's a taboo subject, I'll try."

"Why would Pssstwhit send an embassy to a backwater world like LostRoses? It's completely incomprehensible to me and I've been trying to figure out a reason ever since I heard you were coming." She met his eyes. "If that's some kind of state secret, forget I asked. I wouldn't want to cause trouble for you with your own people."

There was surprise in the bright orange eyes. "Oh, but . . . you don't know anything about our factions, then. Ha'reet, if Pssstwhit hadn't sent an ambassador, then Stiss might have. And Stiss might have claimed to speak for Pssstwhit. Pssstwhit could not allow that. Does this make sense to you?"

Harriet couldn't help it; she giggled. "Yes, I'm afraid so. It makes at least as much sense as some of the things Erthumoi do. You're here to 'establish a presence.' The way His Highness sleeps in the middle of my bed to let me know the territory is his, not mine."

"Are you sure His Highness isn't sapient?"

"Not anymore," Harriet said, with a smile. "Thanks, Wyss'huk. As silly as their reasons were, I'm glad Pssstwhit sent you here."

"So am I."

He coaxed His Highness back into Harriet's lap and stepped from the sidesaddle to the embassy grounds. Still, he made no move to enter the embassy. His Highness, having been moved against his wishes, told Wyss'huk several unprintable and impossible and unquestionably unpleasant things he could do with himself and with simple items found in any home.

Harriet told His Highness which of his rival toms she'd prefer having a midnight fling with. That settled him contentedly in her lap.

"Is that the limit of your curiosity, Ha'reet?"

"Oh, no, Wyss'huk. Just the beginning. Tomorrow you can start teaching me how to speak your language without cursing. If we're to be friends, I'll need to know."

"Yes," he said. "We'll begin tomorrow with the names of the winds. Why not?"

The weather had turned gray. It was just as well, Harriet thought, as she loaded her plane with goods for the settlers outback. She'd have hated to make her trading rounds knowing that everybody was flying without her. It was a selfish thought but she was pleased by it, if only because she'd missed so many years of flying.

Besides, the flyers had promised to take Wyss'huk hunting for lostroses 'the first day of bad weather,' and she thought he should probably have some idea of what life on LostRoses was like in general. Next trip, she'd probably take him along trading for the experience.

He'd regretfully declined this one. Some embassy to-do or other, he hadn't said what. He'd just kept ticking away, so Harriet knew whatever the situation it would keep him amused, probably until she got back.

Last but not least, she'd whistled up His Highness and taken him to stay at Sylvaine's Custom House as usual. As usual, His Highness was *not* amused and told her—and Sylvaine—his objections at length. Harriet rubbed his ears and told him she'd be back in two weeks.

She'd just finished her preflight check on the plane and was loading herself and her chair when a figure dashed across the field toward her, waving its arms and yelling, "Wait, Harriet!"

It was Wanwadee Li, forehead hastily but broadly painted. He clung to the cargo hold door, panting. "I'm glad I caught you. I need your help."

"No, you don't. I warned you, Wanwadee. I have work to do."

"You don't understand! We're getting another Crotonite ambassador—this time from some planet called Stiss!"

That should keep Wyss'huk ticking all right. Harriet laughed, too. "I've got supplies to deliver. *You* teach the ambassador from Stiss to fly." And still laughing, she closed the cargo hatch, narrowly missing his fingers, rolled forward to the cockpit, and took off into the sky.

THE REINVENTION OF WAR

GEORGE ALEC EFFINGER

ON THE UNCLAIMED PLANET OF POREA, ON one of the continents in the northern hemisphere, there was a nation that called itself Yempena. The population of Yempena consisted of eight hundred thousand primitive anthropoids and one snake.

The snake's name was Black Sphere, and it-she was a fugitive from Naxian justice. Black Sphere had come to Porea in a small scout ship and decided the world was isolated enough to make a decent hiding place. Then it-she set about becoming a fearsome Serpent Goddess to the semisavage anthropoids. The indigenous creatures called the Naxian Yersoth, goddess of victory.

Its-her duties as goddess amused Black Sphere, who had fled from one Naxian world confederacy to another. It-she had a peculiar turn of mind that too often caused it-her to run afoul of both the Naxian legal codes as well as some of the agreements governing trade among the Six Races. The galaxy had become civilized in the interests of interspecies peace, but Black Sphere had managed to attain a rare status within it: It-she was an outlaw.

It was dawn, and the orange red sun of Porea, which the Yempenese called Ksul, had just climbed above the rock-rimmed western horizon and was already heating up the still air. Black Sphere was comfortable in this continent's temperate climate, although it-she had to wear a breathing apparatus strapped to its-her sinuous body. Black Sphere had painted the mask and tank in a bold red-and-black striped pattern. The Yempenese thought it was Yersoth's battle dress.

There was indeed a battle taking place on this tree-less, dusty plain. Black Sphere had organized an army from the adult population of Yempena, and had led it across the undefended border of the neighboring nation of Daglawa. There had never before been a war between Yempena and Daglawa, because both countries had more than enough territory and resources to support their populations.

Black Sphere had thought long and hard to find something that would rouse its-her followers to martial fury. Finally it-she revealed that before blessing Yempena with its-her presence, Yersoth had dwelt in Daglawa. The brutish Daglawans had enjoyed its-her patronage until Yersoth was raped by Jind, the Daglawan god of the underworld. Vowing revenge, Yersoth fled to Yempena, where the somewhat stupid inhabitants were glad to pledge their lives to it-her. After all, Yersoth was the goddess of victory, and they thought they couldn't lose.

Black Sphere emerged from its-her scout ship, which it-she had set up as a command post well protected by the Yempenese forces. Not far away, the foot soldiers were huffing on the embers of their camp fires and preparing their meager breakfasts, while the cavalry troopers were tending to their green, chitin-clad mounts.

There were twenty-four thousand infantry and four thousand cavalry, and each soldier had sworn an oath to defend Yersoth's honor with his life if need be. Across the plain to the east was the camp of the Dagla-wans, a mere fifteen thousand foot troops and one thou-sand cavalry, hastily assembled, poorly armed, and badly trained. Black Sphere's forces had easily routed the defenders at every meeting until a bat-winged Crotonite had shown up to rally the Daglawans.

Two Yempenese males waited outside the scout ship for Black Sphere. One was tall, well-muscled, dressed in leather helmet, tunic, and skirt; the other was much smaller and wore only a tattered blue garment wrapped around his waist.

The small anthropoid squatted in the dust and peered up at the soldier. "Here comes the snake, General," he said. "She likes to sleep late. If she awoke with the army, you could've been at those Daglawans two hours ago."

The general frowned.. "If you weren't her pet, Daocan, you'd be flayed alive for speaking of the goddess that way."

Daocan grinned, showing his huge, crooked teeth. "But I am her pet. It means I can say what I think, and I don't have to worry about Daglawan spears and arrows, either."

"I greet you, General Xinseus," said Black Sphere through a battered Erthuma-made simultrans machine. The device translated its-her words into the rough, guttural language of the Yempenese, but still managed to keep a trace of the Naxian's sibilance.

The general gave a little grunt as he dropped to his knees and pressed his forehead to the ground. "I thank and praise you, O Gracious Holy One," he said.

"Yes, of course," said Black Sphere. It-she turned to Daocan. "No obeisance, my pet? No terror of a goddess's displeasure?"

"Mighty Yersoth," said Daocan, "it is terror of your displeasure that prevents me from making obeisance. You see my scrawny, twisted limbs. They make even the act of worship into a mockery. As a goddess, you must know that you have my absolute adoration, and I know that you are the most magnanimous of deities, so that you will once more grace me with your forgiveness.''

Behind its-her red-and-black striped breathing mask, Black Sphere smiled. It-she was not fooled by Daocan's labored eloquence. It-she knew the little anthropoid was always testing the limits of his liberty. That meant, of course, that eventually Daocan would make one test too many.

"Goddess," said General Xinseus, his face still in the dust, "I must meet with my subordinates and give them the battle plan. Will you guarantee victory again today?"

"You may rise, General," said Black Sphere distractedly. "Yes, I guarantee victory. Your losses today will be minimal. Tell your brave soldiers that the ultimate conquest of Daglawa is within reach."

The general stood before the goddess of victory with his head humbly bowed. "I thank you for choosing me to be the instrument of your vengeance, O Gracious One."

"Now go, General." The Naxian watched as Xinseus hurried away toward his tent, where his subordinates were waiting for the news.

"He is certainly earnest and devout," said Daocan thoughtfully. "But don't you find him just a little stupid?"

Black Sphere gave the long hissing sound that was its-her laugh. "To me, my pet, you are all stupid. Dying in this war is stupid, yet you are all eager for it every morning."

"Mighty Yersoth, I am glad to be your pet because I am not eager to die in this war. Besides, we did not have war until you arrived in Yempena and taught it to us."

Black Sphere's slitted eyes narrowed. It-she considered that Daocan might just have gone too far, but then it-she wriggled briefly and forgot the stunted creature's words. Instead, the Naxian turned and gazed toward the Daglawan camp, where her opposite number, the Crotonite, was preparing his own army. The day's entertainment would begin soon.

Xinseus shouted orders to subordinate officers as he made his way through the camp, and Black Sphere watched with growing excitement as the army began to form itself into companies. There was no such thing as warfare among the six starfaring races, so the Naxian's great enthusiasm for what it-she'd instigated on Porea amounted to cultural perversion. Of course, Black Sphere was not interested enough in warfare to take an active role that might endanger it-herself, but it-she never tired of watching the terrified, screaming anthropoids hurl themselves against each other in bloody combat. Black Sphere felt that it-she had discovered a long-neglected vice, one that was more deliciously addictive than any other.

Xinseus led the Yempenese army on the back of a *nahl*, one of the green, spindle-legged creatures. He rode at the head of a cavalry wedge made up of fifteen hundred mounted anthropoids armed with clubs and stone-tipped spears. Xinseus's wedge came up on the right, and there was another cavalry unit on the left. Between them were three well-spaced phalanxes of spear-carrying infantry with ranks of archers behind, and a reserve of infantry and cavalry in the rear.

There was little shouting as the army surged slowly across the plain toward the Daglawan encampment. As one unit after another passed abreast of the Naxian's scout ship, a cry went up that Black Sphere assumed was something like "Hail Yersoth!" It-she turned and saw that the enemy was also moving. The Daglawan general had put five thousand foot soldiers in front as a screen, with the remaining ten thousand split into two flanks and the small cavalry unit pulled off to the right. Slowly, slowly the two armies drew nearer.

"Look, Mighty Yersoth," said Daocan, pointing. "There is Xinseus, your noble general."

"Yes," it-she said, "he has my blessings."

"He risks his own life at the head of our army. The Daglawan general hides in the rear with his bodyguards."

"The Daglawans are cowards, like their god," said Black Sphere.

"You must hate Jind, the lord of the Daglawan underworld," said Daocan with a hint of slyness in his voice. "Still, you tell me that although there are six different races of gods, you never make war among yourselves. Why do you not?"

The Naxian was making itself-herself comfortable in the pavilion its-her priest-slaves had set up. It-she was beginning to get annoyed with Daocan's questions. "We have found other and better ways to settle our disputes than physical violence. We are superior in that way to the mortal races who worship us."

"Ah, I see, Mighty Yersoth. Then why can't you teach us those ways? Why must our people die in this war?"

Black Sphere turned its-her yellow eyes away from Xinseus's advancing cavalry wedge, and stared at Daocan for a moment. "Because your people could not comprehend them."

Daocan nodded. "What you say is true, of course. Still, I wonder. You have a terrible grievance against Jind, and you teach me that the gods do not make war, but have other ways of settling such matters. And these ways dictate that my country and the Daglawans must slaughter each other? How will that make up for what Jind did to you? How will that restore your honor and punish him?"

For an instant, Black Sphere came close to murdering Daocan, but then it-she realized that the filthy anthropoid was probably the most intelligent of all his countrymen. That made him a possible threat to the Naxian, but for the moment it-she let its-her anger go. "My honor will be restored," it-she said, "and Jind will be punished in ways that you cannot comprehend."

Daocan considered all that for a moment. "This is what you mean by having faith, isn't it?" he said.

Black Sphere nodded. "Religion is even more difficult than war," it-she said.

The two opposing forces had drawn nearer, and now Xinseus stabbed the sky with his spear and urged his *nahl* to top speed. Behind him, the remainder of the Yempenese cavalry wedge raced toward the Daglawan front ranks. The air was shattered by battle cries and screams of rage and fear. The second Yempenese cavalry wedge on the left followed Xinseus's lead, and in a moment the two units ran into the Daglawan infantry, cutting through the terrified soldiers with little resistance. A quarter of the Daglawans fell at the first pass.

The small Daglawan cavalry had had little training, and hadn't yet mastered the art of handling weapons while thundering along at top speed. Black Sphere said nothing, but its-her yellow eyes narrowed in pleasure as it-she watched the enemy riders swing their clubs weakly, sometimes even falling from their *nahls* to the ground, where they were trampled and killed by the Yempenese cavalry.

While Xinseus reformed the right wedge after it had passed completely through the Daglawan force, the left wedge decimated the Daglawan cavalry. At the same time, the Yempenese infantry phalanxes began running up to take advantage of the disorder their mounted comrades had created.

"Ah," said Black Sphere with satisfaction.

"As you promised, Mighty Yersoth," said Daocan, "I already foresee victory."

"If Xinseus does not complete the annihilation of the Daglawans today, then it will be a small matter to put off until tomorrow. We will take our supper tomorrow night in the capital city of Daglawa.''

"And then you will wreak your just vengeance. What will you do?''

Black Sphere let out a long, sibilant sound. ''I will do what I please. I have made no plans yet. I will wait to see what piques my fancy.''

A sly look passed across Daocan's face. ''They must be trembling in Daglawa now. O Goddess, might I ask a favor?''

"You may ask, creature,'' it-she said. ''I guarantee nothing.''

Daocan paused a moment in thought. ''When we get to Daglawa,'' he said at last, ''may I have a house? Just a house. I do not have a house in Yempena. It would be fitting for the pet of the mighty goddess Yersoth to have a house of his own.''

Black Sphere hissed. ''Yes, you may have a house,'' it-she said. ''Now, what is happening?''

Both of the Yempenese cavalry wedges had reformed in the rear of the Daglawans, attacking the reserves and slowly stabbing and clubbing their way nearer to the center, where the Daglawan general stood surrounded by his bodyguards. At the same time, the Yempenese infantry and archers were destroying the fighting capability of the Daglawan front lines.

The fighting proceeded all morning with the eventual outcome never in doubt. By the time Ksul had reached its zenith, the battle was over. The parched plain was littered with the corpses of the Daglawans, and with the celebrating Yempenese, maddened by victory and engaged now in looting and dismembering their dead enemies. Black Sphere thought it was the most horribly fascinating sight it-she had ever beheld. ''Look at the anthropoids,'' the Naxian said softly, ''and understand the behavior of the Erthumoi.''

Much later, as the bloated ball of Ksul sunk purple

red toward the eastern horizon, General Xinseus led a throng of Yempenese warriors toward Black Sphere's pavilion. It-she had retired to the scout ship, and only Daocan and two of the priest-slaves waited in the pavilion to receive the crowd. Black Sphere's pet squatted next to the tent pole where his leg was chained. Xinseus stood before his soldiers and led them in a solemn prayer of thanksgiving.

"Gracious Goddess of Victory," cried the general, "we thank you for showing us the ways of war. We thank you for giving us the means to crush our enemies and to protect your honor and our homes, now and in the future. Now that we have studied these bloody arts, we will fear no nation as long as you look with favor on our armed sons. Mighty Yersoth, accept our thanks and our love and our worship."

There was a moment of silence, and then the assembled warriors began chanting "Yersoth! Yersoth!" Black Sphere could hear them from within the scout ship. It-she was sorry that the Yempenese had made such quick work of the Daglawans. Perhaps another war could be instigated soon with another of the neighboring countries.

"Yersoth! Yersoth! Yersoth!" The chanting didn't go away; if anything, it got louder and more enthusiastic. After a few minutes, Black Sphere thought it might be entertaining to go out and be publicly adored by these anthropoids.

The Naxian put on its-her breathing apparatus again and cycled through the air lock. When it-she appeared, another booming cheer went up. After a lifetime as an outlaw, being chased from one Naxian colony world to another, Black Sphere rather enjoyed playing the role of beloved goddess—even though its-her worshipers were little more than hairy primates who had been given the gift of speech. It-she had no illusions about these creatures—there were tens of thousands of years of development between them and even the least advanced of the Erthumoi. Still, these Yempenese were its-her people, and it-she felt generous toward them. It-she made its-her way from the scout ship to the pavilion.

"Yersoth! Yersoth! Yersoth!" chanted the anthropoids. Even the burly Xinseus was joining in enthusiastically. Black Sphere couldn't help but notice, however, that the one anthropoid who was not participating was Daocan, its-her pet.

"My people!" it-she cried as loudly as the Erthuma simultrans device could project. "I thank you for the honor you do me!"

"We thank you for the favor you've shown us, Mighty Yersoth," said General Xinseus.

"Gracious goddess," said a soldier who'd evidently been wounded in the battle.

Black Sphere extended one of its-her stubby fringed flippers toward the bloody creature. "My son," it-she said.

"My son," muttered Daocan in a low voice. Black Sphere glanced at him but said nothing more.

"Many of my comrades fell in the struggle against the heathen Daglawans," said the wounded man. "I myself felt the bite of their spears. Yet I know that none of my mates would regret his death, just as I don't regret my hurts, because we have learned for all time how to protect our wives and families. Our homes are secure now through eternity because of what you've taught us. Centuries from now, all this will be myth and legend, and our descendants will wonder at the truth of it. I feel privileged to have seen these events with my own eyes."

"Mighty Goddess, don't you think this has gone on long enough?" said Daocan sourly. He was sitting in one corner of the pavilion, with his left leg chained to the tent pole.

"What do you mean, my pet?" asked the Naxian, a threat audible in its-her tone.

"I just mean that many of these men are weary or wounded. Perhaps the celebration should be continued tomorrow."

Black Sphere flicked its-her yellow eyes at him. "What difference does it make to you, who did none of the fighting?"

Daocan only shrugged.

Black Sphere stretched sinuously on its-her couch. "My children," it-she said, "Daocan has made a good point. We have fought a great battle today, and many of you require rest and time to bind your wounds. In the morning I will receive your General Xinseus, and at that time I will give him my instructions for the future. Tonight I will ponder our choice of actions. Either we will press on to reduce the capital city of the Daglawans to rubble, or we will show mercy to their shattered army and return to our own country. Sleep well with the knowledge that I bless you for your courage and devotion."

"Yersoth!" shouted the Yempenese army again and again. At last, though, the weary soldiers turned away from the Naxian's pavilion and went back to their scattered campsites.

"Now," said Black Sphere in a voice that came through the simultrans unit in low and ominous tones, "I will deal with you."

"Deal with me, O Gracious Goddess?" said Daocan with a crooked smile. "I have done nothing—"

Black Sphere ignored him. It-she turned to two of the priest-slaves. "Unchain this one. Take him beyond the farthest camp fire, where his cries will be heard by no one, and beat him severely. Do not let him die. Then bring him back to me."

"Yes, Goddess," said the priest-slaves, their faces

empty of emotion. Daocan said nothing as they removed the chain from his leg and led him away.

Black Sphere turned to the remaining priest-slaves in the pavilion. "I choose to be alone for a time," it-she said. "I expect to receive news from other deities tonight, and that is not a matter for mortal ears."

The anthropoids bowed low and backed away from Black Sphere's couch.

A short while later, after Black Sphere returned to its-her scout ship, it-she received a message on the ship's hyperspace radio. "Naxian," came the harsh voice, "will you receive me now? Shall I appear in chains like a defeated chieftain?"

Black Sphere frowned. Besides the actual battle, the only true entertainment it-she had on this forsaken world of Porea was her secret meetings with the Crotonite. Yet it-she had always hated and mistrusted the bat-winged race—well, to be fair, it-she had always hated *all* of the other starfaring races. And it-she didn't get along with other Naxians that well, either.

"Come along, then, Katua," it-she said, speaking into the old Erthuma simultrans. "Be careful that you're not seen. You're supposed to be Jind, the Daglawan god of the underworld. It would be difficult to explain your presence in my sacred temple."

Katua made an unusual sound; Black Sphere wondered if he was laughing. "It would not be hard to devise a likely story for these anthropoids, Naxian. You worry too much."

"You can leave this planet whenever you wish, Katua. I'm a fugitive hiding here. I like being the goddess of victory. I don't want anything to happen to make my life more difficult than it has to be."

"As you wish—Goddess!" And he made that same unsettling sound again.

Black Sphere relaxed in its-her scout ship, thoroughly pleased with the day's events. The invasion of

Daglawa was proceeding without significant hindrance. Despite what it-she had said to the Yempenese, it-she had no intention of leaving the neighboring anthropoids in peace. Black Sphere entertained itself-herself with daydreams of leading its-her wild army on a great crusade of conquest, moving from one benighted, uncivilized nation to the next until it-she had subjugated the entire world of Porea. With its-her vastly superior knowledge of science and military tactics, the Naxian would be the sole dictator of this promising world within a few years. All that stood in its-her way, as Black Sphere saw it, was Katua, the Crotonite. But surely Katua had no designs on Porea. There were plenty of other worlds better suited to an outlaw Crotonite's schemes.

An acrid scent alarm alerted Black Sphere that someone was attempting to gain entry to the scout ship. It-she checked the security monitors and saw Katua, invisible within his ominous, matte-black EVA suit. The Naxian enabled the air lock, and listened as Katua clanked up the metal catwalk to its-her nestlike command pit.

"You are a worthy opponent, Naxian," said the bat-winged creature. His voice was distorted first by his suit's speaker, then by the simultrans unit.

"Be comfortable, Crotonite," said Black Sphere, well aware that there was a complete lack of furniture suitable to Katua's size and shape.

It was impossible to see Katua's face within his helmet, but Black Sphere shared the remarkable ability of the Naxians to gauge the mental and emotional state of any intelligent creature. It-she knew that the Crotonite was in a very good mood, almost exuberant, despite the horrible losses his army had suffered.

"I did not allow my army to pursue yours," Black Sphere said. "I was experimenting with gallantry and mercy."

Katua nodded. "I tried that once. I suppose my army is grateful. My soldiers are regrouping and dressing their wounds this evening. I will meet with my general later and discuss strategy for tomorrow's battle."

Black Sphere was startled. "Tomorrow?" it-she said. "Surely your forces are completely destroyed. Surely you've come here to discuss the surrender of your cities."

The Crotonite made the laughing sound again. "Yes," he said, "there will be a battle tomorrow. I have two secret weapons that I believe will turn things in favor of Daglawa."

"But we outnumber you—"

"You outnumber us, yes. But, Naxian, our own races have put aside war for so many centuries that we've forgotten some of the important lessons. For one thing, the battle does not always go to the largest army."

Black Sphere was becoming annoyed again. "I understand that. You think you have secret weapons that will make up for your disastrous losses today."

"Yes."

"Then why didn't you use them this morning and prevent the destruction of your army?"

Katua didn't reply, but a few small changes in the way he tilted his head and held his body told Black Sphere that the Crotonite hadn't used the weapons on purpose. He had enjoyed watching the slaughter as much as it-she had.

"They are only mud-lickers," the Crotonite said, aware of the Naxian's empathic ability. "I am the god of the Daglawans, but they mean as little to me as the Yempenese must mean to you. They are but ground-crawling savages, and their lives are an affront to my sensibilities. All that can be said about them is that their deaths are somewhat amusing."

They sat and stared at each other for a while longer.

Then Black Sphere hissed and made an attempt to honor the established interspecies etiquette. "I do not have appropriate food to offer you," it-she said.

"I have brought some," said Katua. Black Sphere knew that Crotonites preferred to eat only other flying creatures, and usually only those they had caught themselves. The Naxian wondered what kind of thing Katua had captured; it-she hadn't seen many winged animals in the sky over the dusty plains of western Daglawa.

Black Sphere prepared its-her own food, which it-she took from the scout ship's stores. The Naxian was fastidious in its-her diet, and wouldn't eat anything native to Porea. When the ship ran low of supplies, Black Sphere would travel on to the nearest Naxian world confederacy to restock. Whether it-she returned to Porea or roamed on to another unclaimed world would depend on its-her whim at the time.

When they'd both consumed their meals, they sat across from each other in silence. Finally the Crotonite spoke. "Well, Naxian," he said, "we have paid our minimal respect to the social laws that govern our races in this galaxy. I may leave now; neither one of us need pretend any longer that we enjoy each other's company."

Black Sphere hissed. "Leave, then, Katua, and do your best to ready your few straggling survivors. I warn you, though: My followers hate Jind worse than they fear him, and if you get in the way tomorrow, you may find yourself killed by stone-tipped spears. What an unseemly end for a representative of one of the Six Races."

Katua laughed. "Look to your own safety in the morning," he said. Black Sphere did not rise as he found his way back to the air lock.

As night fell and the first stars appeared in Porea's sky, Black Sphere's priest-slaves returned with Daocan, her pet. He had been carefully and thoroughly beaten according to its-her orders, and the priest-slaves took him to Yersoth's pavilion and chained his leg to the tent pole again.

Black Sphere watched on its-her remote monitor and wondered whether it-she should order food and water for its-her pet. It-she decided against it. It would make it-her look weak, when it-she wanted to demonstrate that although Yersoth was a just goddess, it-she was also too harsh to fool with. Daocan's refreshing cynicism had struck a little too close to home, and Black Sphere definitely didn't want any of the other anthropoids getting the idea that they could take such liberties.

The evening grew cooler, and Black Sphere watched Daocan begin to suffer miserably from hunger, thirst, and the severe beating. The Naxian's yellow eyes stared unblinking at the monitor until darkness made the anthropoid's form indistinguishable. Then Black Sphere dug it-herself deeper into its-her nest pit, wriggled sinuously, and slowly, deliciously, surrendered to sleep.

In the morning, it-she arose and came out of the scout ship into the red, dusty light of Ksul. Both General Xinseus and Daocan were waiting for it-her as before.

"I have spoken to Jind," said Black Sphere, "and he neither apologized nor sued for peace. It was in my heart to let the Daglawans flee back to their homes, but they spurn my generosity and mock my strength. I am saddened, but nothing remains now but to exterminate their force to the last man. We must make certain that the peace of Yempena is never again threatened by these renegades."

General Xinseus looked grim. "I am saddened as well, O Great Goddess. The Daglawans were in times past our brothers. Our nations can gain more by peaceful trade than by armed raiding."

Black Sphere stared. "Yes, peaceful trade," it-she

said distractedly. It-she was gazing toward the horizon, where a long line of Daglawan infantry was approaching. "Behold, General Xinseus," it-she said.

He turned and faced the enemy spearmen. "They've changed tactics," he said. "Instead of each company running madly on its own into battle, they're marching in disciplined order, as you taught us. Who could have made this change in their battle plan?"

"Jind," said Black Sphere. "He said he had two secret weapons to use against us."

Xinseus glanced around his camp, where his subordinates were getting the companies ready to meet the Daglawans. "If that is his idea of a secret weapon," he said, "our archers will quickly change his mind."

"Look there, Mighty Yersoth!" cried Daocan. His thin body was covered with wounds and terrible bruises. He looked too weak to stand, and so he knelt beside his goddess.

"What is it?" asked the Naxian.

"Their cavalry," said Daocan.

"It is nothing," said Xinseus. "Our cavalry is five times as great. We'll chase them off the field, as we did yesterday."

"But look!" insisted Daocan. "They ride their *nahls* on strange saddles. They stand and wield their clubs!"

"How can they stand?" asked Xinseus, his expression troubled.

"Stirrups," muttered Black Sphere. "The damned bat has given them stirrups. Where would he have learned about them? Crotonites fly, they don't ride beasts of burden."

"Stirrups? What are they, O Goddess?" asked the general.

Black Sphere's eyes became angry slits. "I've seen them used on other worlds," it-she said. Its-her voice seethed with fury, even through the translating device. "But only the Erthumoi and the Locrians ever travel on the backs of dumb beasts, and there are no Erthumoi or Locrians here. I would know if there were." It-she wriggled, more of a spasm of rage than anything else. "With stirrups, the Daglawan riders will be able to strike hard with their clubs and spears without the danger of falling off their mounts. Our cavalry is best used only to chase fleeing foot soldiers. Now their cavalry is more than a match for ours—our riders cannot fight without being knocked to the ground. Our numerical superiority means nothing now. And their new discipline—"

"You need not worry, Mighty Yersoth," said Xinseus. "We will own the battlefield today, as we did yesterday, despite their new equipment. After all, how can they defeat the goddess of victory?" He hurried toward his own saddled *nahl*.

"Ha!" laughed Daocan.

Black Sphere turned slowly to regard it-her pet anthropoid. "Do you need another lesson in respect, Daocan?" it-she asked.

"Perhaps it is you who needs a lesson," said Daocan.

The Naxian's yellow eyes did not blink. "What do you mean, little one?"

"The Crotonite came to me last night while I cowered in the cold."

Black Sphere read the anthropoid's mood and feelings, and felt the beginning of fear in it-herself. Daocan was filled with triumph. "You mean you spoke with Jind, god of the underworld?"

Daocan smiled slyly. "There is no god of the underworld here. He is a Crotonite. He explained to me what that means. He also told me about Naxians. And Erthumoi."

Black Sphere was silent for many seconds. "Why did he tell you all this?" it-she said at last.

Daocan looked out over the battlefield. "We made a trade."

"What did you give him?"

"The stirrups," said Daocan quietly. "Thank you for telling me their name. I did not know what to call them."

"Where then did you learn of stirrups, my pet?" The Naxian's words were deceptively quiet.

"It was an idea, an inspiration," said Daocan proudly. "While I watched the battle yesterday, I thought the cavalry riders would be much more effective if they could brace themselves when they swung their clubs. They cannot stand on the ground, so I devised a way for them to stand upon something else. There was not enough time to fashion the stirrups as I imagined them, so the Daglawan cavalry is making do today with looped lengths of rope fastened to their saddles. Soon, though, their artisans and saddle makers will add their own improvements to my invention."

"*Your* invention—!" Black Sphere was furious. It was clear that it-she had terribly underestimated Daocan's native intelligence—and his hunger for revenge. "Then that is the Crotonite's second secret weapon," it-she said.

"No," said the anthropoid, "only his first. The marching in ranks he copied from the Yempenese. He still has a second secret weapon about which you know nothing."

There was another long pause. The fierce clamor of the battlefield echoed in the Naxian's head. "What is the second secret weapon, then?" it-she said.

Daocan grinned. "He sent a message to his people. He asked for help. They told him that a party of Naxians would arrive soon to make certain you don't interfere on Porea any longer. And there will be some Erthumoi, too, to make certain the Crotonites don't interfere. He gave this to me in trade for the stirrups.

The Daglawans worked all night to outfit their cavalry with the looped ropes, and the riders may still be getting used to them, but it seems to me that their cavalry is finding the stirrups a great advantage.''

Black Sphere watched as the newly equipped Daglawan cavalry soldiers rode back and forth across the battlefield, creating havoc wherever they went. It-she stood in thought for a moment, then turned toward its-her scout ship. There was plenty of time to get cleanly away from Porea, and plenty of space in the galaxy to make another beginning.

WOODCRAFT

POUL ANDERSON

AT FIRST THE AIRCRAFT SHONE ABOVE THE SEA
so much like a star that Laurice Windfell felt something
catch at her throat. Venafer is beautiful in the morning
and evening skies of Ather, but on Venafer itself there
is never a glimpse of the sister planet, nor of anything
in the heavens other than a vague solar disk when
clouds thin to an overcast. She had been here too long.
Suddenly the wish for home, cool winds across green
hills, the snow peak of Mt. Orden afloat above the
northern horizon—and afterward a ship, outwardness,
space, space—became almost unendurably sharp.

In due course, she told herself. Right now I have a
job to finish. A promise to redeem.

Recognizing the approaching object for what it was,
she turned and trotted off the headland toward the landing strip. At her back, the ocean murmured against
cliffs. Surf rarely boomed loud on this moonless world,
though the orbit around Florasol was small enough that
the sun raised considerable tides. The water glimmered
yellowish green close in, darkened to purple farther out.
A storm yonder hulked black and lightning-streaked,
but overhead and eastward stretched silver gray blank-
ness. Before her, forest grew to the shoreline, a wall
of great boles, vines, brakes, foliage in hues of russet
and umber, brilliant blossoms, shadowful depths. It
dwarfed the clearing where the Naxian compound

stood. The multitudinous smells of it lay heavy in the heat and damp.

Thick serpentine bodies, as long as hers or longer, were writhing from the huts. Glabrous hides sheened in a variety of colors; the New Hallan colonists were from many different ancestral regions, alike only in their faith and hopes. Several still clutched tools or instruments in extruded pseudohands. Excitement can spread with explosive speed and force among beings that sense emotions directly. Not that it wasn't justified. Laurice's own eagerness had driven her onto the promontory to stare southwestward, once the curt acknowledgment came that help was on its way.

She reached the strip. It lay bare, soil baked bricklike. A hangar of wood and thatch gaped empty. The camp's flyer had borne casualties away to medical care or eventual cremation, after quickly leaving off the uninjured here. Impatient, she squinted up. "C'mon, move it," she muttered. "What're you dawdling for?" A drop of sweat got past her brows, into an eye. It stung. She spoke a picturesque oath.

Parabola arrived and joined her. The botanist had thought to bring a simultrans. It rendered rustles, hisses, purrs into Merse, unnecessary for her but doubtless needed with the newcomer. "That is an exceedingly cautious pilot, honored one."

Laurice replied in her language, which the Naxian understood though unable to pronounce it intelligibly. "Well, I suppose this area is new to him, and he doesn't want the airs to play some trick that catches him off guard. I've learned to fly warily myself." She begrudged the admission, and knew that Parabola felt that she did.

However, fairness compelled. She mustn't lose her temper, her judgment, when she had Copperhue to save. The fact was that Venafer remained an abiding place of mysteries, and within some of them were death traps.

A whole planet, after all, she thought. (How often had she thought the same, here and elsewhere?) Not the global hell of jungle and swamp that most people imagined; no, as diverse as Ather. But dear Ather was well-nigh another Old Earth, renewed and again virginal. Erthumoi soon made it theirs, and in its turn it claimed them for itself. Throughout the centuries that followed, few ever cared to set foot on Venafer, and none to make a home there. A handful of scientists; two enterprises kept small by difficulty as well as by the danger their growth would pose—scant wonder that most of it was still *mundus incognitus*. The explorations that she hitherto went on had been to worlds of other suns, equally strange but more attractive. Until now.

"Hs-s-s, he descends!" Parabola exclaimed. It-she laid its-her blunt-snouted head on Laurice's shoulder, an oddly mothering gesture. Glancing about, the Erthuma looked into big eyes that were not really onyx, being so warm. "Take heart, honored one. Our waiting time has been less than it seemed; observe your chrono. Surely Copperhue lives and you will find it-him soon enough."

Could any Erthuma have been quite that sympathetic, in quite that way? "May it be, may it be," Laurice half prayed. "For your sakes too, and mainly."

Parabola withdrew a few centimeters. "It-his loss would indeed strike a blow deep into us." The simultrans failed to convey a gravity at which Laurice could well guess. "It-he is more than a symbol, the hero who won for us our home. It-he has become a leader, in ways that I fear we cannot fully explain to your kind. Yet we, like you, would grieve most over the passing of a friend."

Side by side, surrounded now by the rest, they gazed back aloft. The teardrop shape had ceased to hover and was bound slowly down. Landing gear made contact. Through the silence that fell, the nearby screech of a leatherwing and the distant roar of a deimosauroid sounded as insolently loud as the wild blossoms were gaudy.

Laurice advanced to meet the pilot. He opened a hatch and sprang to the ground. For a moment they stood confronted.

He was tall, lean, dark, aquiline of features—handsome, she thought, and imagined herself as he saw her. Rejuvenated just a few years ago, her medium-sized body was not yet as full-figured as usual; but she believed maturity showed on her face, hazel eyed and tawny skinned within its coif of auburn hair, strong in the cheekbones and, she'd repeatedly heard, sensuous in the lips. Except for Uldor Enarsson, with whom intimate involvement would be unwise, she'd been months alone among Naxians. . . . They could tell what she felt. It didn't matter to them. Nevertheless her cheeks heated and a quite irrational irritation stabbed at the newcomer.

Besides, his expression was less than cordial. "Greeting," she said formally. "My name is Laurice Windfell."

"I know, milady," he replied with the same stiffness and a Westland accent. "I'm Kristan Arinberg, the relief guide you demanded."

She forced a smile. "Requested, if you please. Though rather urgently, I grant." Their handclasp was brief.

"Your tone when you called was as peremptory as I've ever heard," he said meanwhile.

"A life is at stake," she snapped. "I have an outfit ready to go. Let me fetch it and we'll be on our way. We haven't too damned much daylight left."

He matched his stride to hers. Was he curious about this outpost? "I brought my own stuff, of course."

"Is it suitable for such an excursion?"

He flushed. "I've made a career on Venafer. How long have you been on it?"

"About a year." She meant an Atheran year, naturally, but that was close to the standard Erthuma period. "However, I'm here because of my experience on several different planets. We'll take what I've packed. In flight I'll inspect yours and rearrange it if need be."

He bit his lip. That was tactless, Laurice realized, especially when I did ask for knowledgeable help. A scion of an Atheran House isn't used to being talked to like this. Why, no decent person would be so brusque with a client or even a patronless.

Unless it was necessary. Oh, Copperhue—

Trying for conversation, she inquired, "Have you any information about our wounded?"

"No," said Kristan. "They hadn't reached Forholt Station when I left."

She had expected as much. Her group's aircraft was capacious but slow, his the exact opposite. "I only know several Naxians and one Erthuma are hurt enough to require hospitalization, at least overnight," he added, perhaps also seeking peace. "How badly?"

"Uldor Enarsson worst. Not to the point of mortal danger. They gave him first aid in camp, and then I went along when our flyer picked them up and did some more for him on the way back here. But I'm afraid he'll be out of action for weeks at best, and we may have to retire him from the project, return him to Ather. Chaos take it!" burst from her.

"A Windfell client, isn't he?"

"Yes, though actually he's spent decades on Venafer, independently researching and exploring."

"I know. He did excellent work before he . . . joined you."

With an effort, she ignored that last. "My worry goes beyond a patron's obligation. He was, is, a comrade—an equal, as far as I'm concerned. And damn near indispensable. Without his information and skills, unless we can find a replacement, our progress will slow to a crawl."

"Suitable for snakes." She glared. "Sorry, that was rude, wasn't it?" He didn't sound overly apologetic. "I am upset. This business yanked me from my own research, at a critical point, too. Nobody else happened to be available and qualified. But naturally, if a sentient life is in danger, I should help out." He paused. "Assuming you absolutely must have someone like me."

"It improves the odds significantly."

They entered the compound. She saw the surprise on him. He must have been too little interested, or too resentful, to learn more about this undertaking than the fact of its existence. True, the Naxians didn't want publicity; they went about their business as quietly as possible.

A stockade, erected to keep animals out and serve as a windbreak during storms, enclosed a dozen buildings. Some were living quarters, some for storage or utility, one a laboratory. All were cylindrical in shape, built of rocks cemented and chinked with hard-dried mud, roofed with logs and sod. Chimneys showed that several contained fireplaces. Doors and fittings were wood, supplemented by sauroid leather; window frames held glass, unclear, obviously made by amateurs from local sand.

"Good wisdom!" Kristan blurted. "How much labor went into this?"

"Quite a lot," Laurice replied. "Less will in future. We were learning as we worked."

"But . . . when you could simply have assembled ready-made shelters? They're available, you know, developed for Venaferan conditions."

"I know. We all knew. Weren't you aware that a

main objective of ours is to find what we can do with native resources?''

She had meant it amicably. He tensed. ''Yes,'' he said, ''I suppose that will expedite their takeover, once they're breeding in earnest. Until they're ready to start mines and factories and—'' He broke off. ''How does your adobe withstand the kind of rainfall you get?''

She respected the intelligence that asked a question not merely valid but directed away from a quarrel they could ill afford. What age is he? she wondered. If he's had more rejuvenations than my single one— ''The Naxians experimented under Uldor's direction, before I arrived. They found that the soil hereabouts needs only a little gravel added and a few hours kept dry, to set like concrete. You noticed the surface of our airstrip, didn't you?''

Again she had said the wrong thing. His nostrils flared. ''Yes. When you've logged off the woods, this whole region will be sterile.''

''We don't intend to.''

''Perhaps *you* don't. Those who come after you—''

''Here we are.'' She led him into the hut that was hers. He peered around, but in the gloom saw little of her personal things before she had taken up her pack. They were few anyway: pictures of her kinfolk and the Windfell estates; a player and numerous cartridges of books, shows, music; a sketch pad and assorted pencils; a flute; a letter to a friend afar, half composed on paper. The rest was equipment.

Emerging, the Erthumoi found the Naxians had likewise returned. ''Not many,'' Kristan remarked.

''Most are in the field, investigating,'' Laurice told him. ''These are busy with lab studies or chores.''

''What were you yourself doing before the, uh, incident?''

''I was taking a party of canoeists along the Harmony River. Teaching them how. Our work is still mostly exploratory, research and development, but we're beginning to assume an instructional function as well. When it's turned into the main job, I can leave."

He smiled. How attractive he became, all at once. "Then you received the call about an emergency, and the flyer took you off and brought you to that scene. What about your—pardon me—tenderfeet?"

"I left them on an islet in midstream. They'll be all right for a few days, if air transport is preempted that long. I can even hope they'll learn something by themselves."

Renewed bitterness tightened his mouth. "The better to occupy this mainland later, eh?" he muttered.

Parabola and Bluefire approached. "Are you certain you do not wish any of us to accompany you, honored one?" the botanist asked.

"Thank you, no," Laurice replied. "We must move fast. Given the knowledge of my new companion, no harm should threaten me, and the two of us can conduct the rescue operation."

"We are most grateful, benevolent one," said Bluefire to Kristan.

"I was assigned the duty," he answered.

"Come," said Laurice. She walked away fast. The Naxians were sensing the man's hostility still more keenly than she heard it in his voice. Surely they were hurt by it. Let her take it out of their range of perception.

Silent, the Erthumoi proceeded back to the flyer, stowed her backpack, and settled down side by side at the front. "Do you have the coordinates?" she asked.

"The autopilot has them. Up in the foothills of the Sawtooth, right? We are not entirely moonbeam-distilling academics at Forholt, whatever you suppose." His fingers stabbed the control board. Power whirred.

I'm feeding his resentment, she understood. And I should know better. I've led expeditions, haven't I?

We've gotten off on the wrong foot, Kristan Arinberg
and I. He began it— Stop that, Windfell. Your child-
hood is fifty years behind you. Isn't it?

"Apologies," she said. "No offense meant. I'm
anxious, you see, tired, overwrought."

The aircraft lifted. "Then shouldn't you rest before
we go, or send somebody else?" His tone had
smoothed. "That would have to be a Naxian, I imagine, but I—" He hesitated. "I have nothing against
Naxians as such."

She shook her head. "I dare not delay. Copperhue
can come to grief at any instant. It-he was on New
Halla till lately and has had time to learn virtually nothing about wilderness survival. Besides, under the circumstances, I think I'm the only person of any species
on this planet who could find it-him."

If that can be done at all, she thought. The trail is
already cold.

They gained altitude and bore east. The ocean, the
curving shoreline slipped from view. Below them
reached another sea, ruddy brown, the crowns of trees
in their millions, from horizon to horizon and beyond.
Wind made great slow billows over it. Here and there
gleamed a lake or the meandering thread of a river. A
marsh passed through vision, nearly hidden by antlike
forms, browsing animals that in reality were huge.
Often a flock of winged creatures, thousands strong,
scudded above the forest. Far ahead, cloud banks towered beneath the opalescent sky. Air-conditioning made
the cabin blessedly cool.

"Well—" In almost Naxian wise, Laurice felt how
Kristan tried to veil skepticism. "This, uh, Copperhue,
I gather he—it-he's important?"

"Why, yes," she answered, surprised. "I thought
you'd remember. It was a sensation, twenty-odd years
ago. How it-he led us to those black holes about to
collide, at risk of its-his life, such a scientific prize that

my House was glad to award it-him the island it-he asked for.''

"Oh, *that* one? Of course. I'd forgotten the name, that's all. Ather may be just a quick flit away, but we on Venafer, we're preoccupied—isolated. Hardly anybody there seems to appreciate what we're doing." In haste, doubtless to avoid a suspicion that he was whimpering: "I know full well that you were involved too, milady. It's . . . an honor to meet you." With a kind of desperate frankness: "I wish it could have been under happier conditions."

That made it hard to keep anger fueled. The pain of her loss yonder had long since faded away; the pride of achievement endured. "I hope we can improve them, then. Tell me about your work." Always a good conversational gambit.

"Regionalist." He chuckled, a deep and pleasant sound. "The United Universities Planetary Institute doesn't like that for a title, and carries me as a geologist." Seriously: "But when we're so grotesquely understaffed, each of us has to be a bit of everything, from chemist to naturalist, and try to understand a domain as a whole. I've specialized in hill country on this continent, though well south of here. That's why the chief decided I'd be the best to accompany your search."

"I see. For my part—" Never mind. Mention of her activities might upset him afresh. "I'm grateful. Any life is important, but Copperhue means especially much to me, after what we went through together in space, and our correspondence and meetings since then. Its-his people are even more in your debt. They revere it-him on New Halla. Its-his words, its-his leadership may make all the difference in what happens during the next few centuries. It-he came to the mainland to learn for itself-himself, in hands-on detail, what we're accomplishing and how."

Kristan's fists had doubled on his knees. She'd touched a nerve regardless. He stared straight outward. "I daresay it was it-he who persuaded you to join the project."

"Yes. However, I was interested from the beginning."

"I should have thought one like you, who's been in many wildernesses, would care about them."

"I do! Can't you see—" No, she mustn't say more. "What I'd learned has applications on Venafer. For instance, those hogans at our base were made at my suggestion and under my direction. The whole idea is not to destroy the natural environment but to fit into it."

"As if you could do that without causing an upheaval's worth of changes." Kristan drew breath. "Look, I don't want a fight. I really don't. But may I ask that you study some history? Pioneers, voortrekkers, they normally do your minimalist, economical sort of thing. They haven't the means to do more. But after them come the farmers, the miners, the cities, the factories— and that's the end of anything you could call nature."

"We've kept Ather green." Mostly.

"Domesticated," he snorted. "Manicured. What old growth and wildlife remain are in carefully managed reserves. Anyway, the case is entirely different on Venafer, and you know it."

At the aircraft's speed, they were already beyond the coastal plain. Ground rose in swells and ridges, still densely overgrown but with lighter-hued foliage and frequent shrubby openings. Rainclouds shrouded the Sawtooths themselves and spilled westward beneath the high permanent overcast.

After a silence too filled with the thrum and whine of their passage, Kristan said, "I must confess the problem today isn't clear to me. All I was told was that a camp had been attacked by predators, several persons were hurt, including the Erthuma leader, and one was missing. Your Naxian friend, it turns out. Doesn't it-he have its-his radio bracelet on?''

Radio collar, for one of them. Laurice quenched the correction. ''No, but that wasn't due to carelessness. The trouble was unforeseen—unforeseeable. The Naxians were familiar only with New Halla, an island, and getting some acquaintance with part of the continental seaboard. Uldor had worked in the highlands, and deemed the time ripe to start exploring and experimenting there. In many respects, he said, they might prove to be the best site for the first mainland colony.''

Kristan scowled. She hurried on: ''Copperhue went along to observe. The Naxian leaders need to know how these efforts are conducted. Uldor's party was conveyed to a suitable spot and left to itself. The first couple of days went to settling in. Then everybody relaxed last night, before commencing their studies. They held a party to celebrate. Perfectly sober—Old Truth believers don't use recreational drugs of any kind, and Uldor might have a single well-watered shot of whiskey if he's feeling expansive. They saw no need to post a watcher when they went to sleep, but did. In short, they took every precaution.

''But a little before daybreak, a pack of silent-running large carnivores entered the camp. As dark as the night was and as fast as they moved, the watcher doesn't seem to have been aware of anything till they were almost on it-him, and then probably only through its-his emotional sense. We don't know; it-he barely had time to cry out before being torn apart. The creatures ran wild, blood-frenzied. Uldor and a couple of others had kept loaded firearms handy, and shot several, two fatally, but fangs slashed them nevertheless. After a horrible battle in the dark, the beasts retreated and our people called the base. We evacuated them—but you know the rest.''

"No, I don't," Kristan said. "What sort of beasts? You say dead ones were available to look at."

"Lycosauroids. I asked Forholt for data, and they identified them from my transmission and were amazed. None had ever been seen this far north. Why should Uldor provide against them? Getting struck by lightning seemed much more probable."

"Hm." Kristan's expression turned thoughtful. He rubbed his chin. "Did some extraordinary set of chances take a single pack hundreds of kilometers from its hunting grounds? Or is this an early sign of an ecological fluctuation? The ceratodon herds do seem to be declining in the southern range, and that's the principal lyco prey. . . ."

Laurice sighed. "Your science can wait. No, I take that back. It can well be a first-chop practical question. Another deadly stunt pulled by a world never really meant for us."

But just homelike enough to draw us into its snares, she thought. If Naxian and Venaferan and Erthuma life didn't happen to be biochemically similar, able to provide nourishment of sorts for each other, none of us would have dreamed of any such ventures here as ours.

Kristan's face congealed. "They could have left it alone, in peace."

Laurice shook her head. "You know how the Old Truth people have needed a place of their own. Discriminated against on the Naxian worlds, even persecuted, for centuries—though their standards of honesty, industry, all-around decency put most of our race to shame—"

"I didn't begrudge them an island," he retorted. "Not too furiously. Venafer can spare it, if we don't mind losing a few fascinating species. But now they propose to move onto the continents. And not only onto land claimed by your House. I checked a map before setting off. This new territory they were investigating belongs to the Seaholms. What secret deal have they struck with the Head of the Seaholms? What with other Houses?''

''Nothing big, I'd guess. Need I remind you how nominal those claims are? Every Atheran company that ever tried to exploit anything has gone broke, except for Evenstar Minerals and Exotic Animal Products; and they're tiny, barely paying their way.''

''Which is as it should be. No, milady, you don't need to read me a lesson in the elementary economics of an inhospitable environment at the bottom of a middling-deep gravity well. After thirty years in the field, I'm reasonably familiar with the situation.''

She tried to smother offense by the inward admission that he could justifiably have taken her words as patronizing, an insult. . . . Thirty years? How many rejuvenations had he been through? What had occupied him before he embarked on this career? Marriage, children, grandchildren? A wife today? Or was he, at least during these past decades, wedded to Venafer? Surely you'd have to love not only your science, to devote so much to it, but also the planet itself, its discomforts, dangers, treacheries, its wild beauties and the overwhelming richness of life-forms that it mothered.

She wrestled pride to the ground. ''I'm sorry. If I've annoyed you again, please believe me, it wasn't intended. On a visit home, I had to try explaining things over and over to people who knew practically nothing and cared less about the subject till suddenly they heard they were getting non-Erthuma next-door neighbors. I guess it became a habit.''

His smile seemed forced, he kept his eyes aimed at the ruggedness rising ahead, but he spoke levelly. ''Suppose we get back to the problem at hand. What's become of this Copperhue?''

Queer, how thinking about that came as a relief. ''The Naxians remove their transceivers when safely on the base or in camp. You can well imagine a collar around the body is a nuisance, not like a bracelet on the wrist. Most were unarmed, and when the beasts attacked, naturally they fled every which way. Trees in the immediate vicinity aren't climbable, mingled thornbark and flexy. When the attack was repulsed and first light came, those who could made their way back. Searchers quickly found the injured, and three more dead, and brought them in. Except for Copperhue. It-he was gone. Some comrades who were able beat the bush—within a narrow radius, as difficult as that was— and when we arrived in our flyer, we scanned from above before returning. Not a trace.

"I wanted to stay and commence hunting on the ground, but that would have been crazy by myself. Also, Uldor and a couple of the Naxians urgently needed further attention, which I was best able to give. So I called Forholt, and . . . you were good enough to come help."

He smiled anew, but sourly. Did he take that for sarcasm? she wondered. Blaze! This is like juggling a case of fulgurite.

The smile faded. "Could the reason that Copperhue didn't show up be that it-he's dead?" he asked rather quietly.

She swallowed. "That's what we're going to find out."

"Can we?"

"We can give it a damn good try." Laurice arranged her words with care before she uttered them: "I expect you consider it a gross waste of your time. You aren't necessarily unsympathetic, but why drag you into the mess? Well, I need a partner, and it has to be someone who knows that kind of region. I've gained a certain familiarity with the lowlands—*these* lowlands, I mean—but not the hills. Uldor had some, which is why he led that expedition, but Uldor's disabled. So, you."

"If you're such a stranger to the area, what can you hope to do?"

"I have my ideas. You'll see."

He was silent a while before he said, "Look, I've never been in these parts myself. The lycos would have caught me off balance too. I can't guarantee nothing else will."

Blast, she thought, he infuriates me, and then turns right around and charms. I wish he'd make up his mind. "Another reason not to hare off alone. Uh, I was going to check your gear."

"I thought you meant to heed the voice of experience."

I've flicked him again. To chaos with it. "This mission is special. You've never had anybody lost, have you? Not with their bracelets."

"Did you ever, on your expeditions elsewhere?"

Is he implying incompetence? "Natives, a couple of times. And I don't understand how your bunch imagines it can learn much about wildlife without old-fashioned tracking and stalking."

She unharnessed and wriggled into the rear of the flyer. Cramped, she carried out her inspection slowly, unconscious at first of thinking aloud: "—Clothes serviceable, but one change is ample, we won't be gone long. . . . Rifle, by all means. I'll leave my pistol but keep my machete. If those critters are still loping around, I'd as soon we didn't become part of the ecology. . . . Rations, yes, we can't take time to live off the country. . . . Cookware, no, unnecessary weight, we'll eat cold food. . . . Tent? M-m, more weight and bulk, but goes up faster than making a shelter. We'll give it a try. . . ."

She returned to her seat. The aircraft slanted downward. "Rather high-handed, aren't you?" Kristan said. "Be warned, in case I have doubts about your judgment, we'll follow mine."

"Oh?" Beneath the frostiness, dismay. There had to be a boss. It was a bad oversight of hers, not to have made clear at the outset who that would be. Haste and anxiety were a poor excuse. "I reserve my right to disagree. But we can't squabble now. I trust you'll listen to reason."

"The same for you!"

The landscape on which they descended reached enormous heights and depths, forested except where steeps were eroded to the bare rock. Rivers foamed down gorges. Mists eddied in the hollows and along the intricately folded flanks of hills that in many lands would have been called mountains. Clouds drifted low and murky above. From the west, where lightning danced, Laurice heard thunder come rolling. Wind hissed. The aircraft quivered within it.

On a horizontal shoulder halfway up a hillside, woods ringed a glade where a spring bubbled, Uldor's campsite. Perforce Laurice admired Kristan's skill as he landed. Nothing grew underneath save scattered low shrubs—no equivalent of grasses had evolved on Venafer—but air ramped wildly in the narrow space, while around it the big trees were covered with thorns and the lesser ones lashed about like whips. When Laurice climbed out, the wind struck at her, almost cold. The smells on it recalled musk, vinegar, cloves, and things for which she lacked names. Through them wove storm's ozone.

Kristan followed and stared about, astonished. He ignored strewn supplies and equipment, left behind at the hasty evacuation. What caught his attention was the camp itself, thatch tipis and a rough stone fireplace grill. "Not even tents?" he blurted.

"I told you, a large part of our project is to find out what can be done with local resources," she flung back. "This is my design. Perfectly adequate. Now go unload our packs and batten down the vehicle. We'll set off as soon as I've found the trail."

"Have you brought a chemosensor, or what?"

"I wish I had, but we've got nothing adapted for this kind of work, and I doubt they do at Forholt either. I did bring my eyes and my wits."

He grimaced but yielded. She walked to and fro, peering downward. Presently she went on all fours to examine leaves, twigs, soil. Altogether engaged, she forgot time and him.

Emerging at last, she saw him considering a stone in his hand, and joined him. "Well, have you found anything?" he asked. His intonation said that he didn't believe so and that the lengthy wait had exasperated him.

She nodded. "It took a while because those amateur searchers ruined a lot of spoor, but I've figured out what must have happened and which way it-he set off. Let's saddle up and go."

"Really? I'm afraid you'll have to convince me. This is dangerous terrain, not for us to head into blindly."

"Huh? You expect me to teach you right now what it took me years to learn?"

"No, if it is in fact an art, not a hunch. But you'll show me you know what you're doing or we'll flit straight back."

"We will? Listen, you—" Laurice gulped acridness. Whether or not she went along, this son of a spewbelly had the power to wreck her chances. "Very well. Kindly pay close attention. That's what tracking is mainly about."

She led him to a chosen spot, hunkered down, and pointed. "Traces often last a considerable spell. Years, under certain conditions." Or geological eras if they happen to fossilize. "But they generally weather fast, at a rate that also depends on the type of ground, the depth of the impression, et cetera, et cetera. So I took care to get area weather records from the satellite for the past several days before we left base. Observe. The

wind has strewn leaves and dust and other debris, but
I've uncovered a trail—shallow, wavery depression,
can you make it out? I can't identify many Venaferan
animals by their prints, not yet, but no mistaking a
Naxian's. Now these little pockmarks were made by
rain—a shower, not a downpour—and the last time any
fell was four days ago. Therefore the track is older,
and no use to us. Except that at this point and a later
moment, as you can tell by the sharpness of the impres-
sions, a bounding four-legged creature crossed it. The
pattern of the prints indicates the gait. A big beast,
clearly a lyco. The claw marks are faint, but if you lie
prone and squint your eye just over the surface, you
can identify them, and they're pointed downhill. So
that's the direction the pack fled in. Which is obvious
from the mangled brush and dried flecks of blood farther on, but I've illustrated the principle. Finding where
Copperhue went was a process of elimination."

"I get the idea." Did she hear respect? "You
needn't continue. I'll follow your lead."

Gladly, she bounced to her feet and made for the
packs. "Practicing due caution," he added.

"Sure. You said something about the terrain."

"Mm-hm. I've conducted my own examination. The
rocks lying around are friable. The reddish dirt is
another clue. Considerable iron in the region, and
Fusillus ferruvorus has been at work. That's a microbe
that gets its energy by oxidizing iron. The result is
crumbly formations, easily leached. Be extra careful on
steep grades. And even on a level surface, you might
fall into a sinkhole hidden by deadfall or whatever."

"I see. Uldor never mentioned that bug. Is it confined to a few areas, so he hadn't encountered it? Well,
I definitely need you with me." We need one another.

They donned their packs. "It's pretty clear about
Copperhue," Laurice said. "It-he fled into the woods,
uphill as it chanced. One lyco pursued, but only a short

ways, because the growth hindered it more than a Naxian, and the killing seemed easier back in the glade. The noise behind Copperhue and, yes, the ravenousness that it-he sensed, those made it-him move as fast as possible for its-his race, which is quite fast, and keep going for some distance. Philosophers can panic too. Finally it-he—after calming down and resting, I assume—must have tried to return. Where else was there to go? But in dense woods, an inexperienced person can get completely lost within less than a kilometer and wander farther and farther astray. It's especially easy on Venafer, where you have no definite shadows or heavenly bodies or anything to steer by. I only hope it-he soon realized the sensible thing was to settle down and wait to be found. And hope it-he survives the wait.''

They entered the forest. For some meters the going wasn't bad. Laurice wove among hooklike thorns; arms before her face, she parted withes, passed through, released them slowly enough for Kristan to intercept before they slapped him. Then the trail, hitherto clear to a practiced eye, went into the thicket that had baffled the lycosauroid. No, not a coppice, more like a wall, too wide to go around and have any likelihood of finding the track again on the other side. It was duck-walk or hands and knees, machete, long pauses to search for the next broken twig, bruised sapling, disarrayed tuft marking where fear had gone. Gloom and rank odors closed in. Sweat runneled over skin, hung in clothes and reeked, grew sticky under the gathering chill. Cries, croaks, whistles jeered from unseen mouths.

Kristan cursed. Briefly, Laurice marveled at his vocabulary. She'd have to remember some of those phrases. He stopped with an abruptness suggesting that he had remembered her presence. Looking back, she saw how he struggled. ''I was afraid of that,'' she sighed. "Your tent poles are catching on everything. Get rid of them. Might as well discard the entire roll."

"Trashguts, no!" he snarled. The black hair lay plastered to his brow. "It's the best— Have you any idea what it costs? How wretchedly short of funds we always are?"

"Try programming your computers to give a flying fart about a sentient life." No, wrong approach. She made an effort to speak mildly. "It could cost us hours we haven't got. Leave it. We can retrieve it later."

"Well—well, my sleeping bag's waterproof. Is yours?" He lessened his burden.

When they won free of the brake, progress wasn't much faster. Already at this slightly higher altitude, trees grew farther apart and underbrush became sparse. That, though, meant stretches of bare dirt or exposed rock where it could take minutes to make sure of the traces. Wind moaned louder, leaves soughed, clouds raced low and swart overhead.

"You'd think the snake would backtrack himself," Kristan grumbled once.

Laurice told herself not to resent the word he used. She'd been guilty of it too, now and then in the past. "It's all I can do to find how it-he went," she reminded him. "Do you expect that a stranger to wilderness could?"

"N-no. You're right. Stupid question. I'm tired, brain going numb. How do you keep fresh?"

She must laugh. "And fragrant? After enough running around in woods, you learn ways to save your strength. No, *you* don't; your body does."

"It's remarkable how you handle yourself. I wouldn't expect that experience on one planet would be useful on another."

"Oh, there are countless differences, of course, but the principles are pretty general and the techniques pretty adaptable. When I mentioned that to Copperhue, it gave it-him the idea of persuading me to join this team for some years.''

His manner iced up. She'd put him in mind of his opposition to the whole undertaking.

The traces angled off. Copperhue had evidently noticed that it-he had gone above the camp, and sought to turn downhill. Unfortunately, on this irregular ground that was not a simple either-or proposition. A check against the flyer's radio beacon showed that the general direction of the lurching path was almost at right angles to what might have helped. After a while the descent sharpened. Here creep and erosion had thinned soil, so that trees stood three or four meters apart and gnarly knorrig was commoner than thornbark. In between were gray trident bushes, dirt littered with windblown detritus, boulders, and bedrock.

"It-he must have known by now this was the wrong way." Kristan's voice came hoarse.

"Certainly," Laurice agreed. "I suspect, though, it-he was fire-thirsty, in random search for a streamlet or a puddle or anything." They had emptied their canteens along the way, and refilled them at a pool she had found and the Naxian had not.

The man glanced aloft into roiling, hooting gloom. "No dearth of water by nightfall."

"Which isn't long off. Damn, oh, damn!"

"We have lights. I can keep going if you can."

She did not so much reach decision as feel it thrust upon her. "No. In rain and the Venaferan dark, they'd be useless. We'd better hole up, get some rest, proceed after dawn."

Once more, as often during the past hours, they shouted their throats sore. No response. No response. Laurice's vision strained ahead through the early dusk. Beyond the nearest trees, woodland merged into a single blackness. She could still perceive how rapidly the slope rose yonder, and recalled from her aerial view that on its other side the ridge gave on a canyon which Copperhue would surely not enter.

It-he can't be far. We arrived late, and had to find the signs and read them, but I swear they show it-him slowing down, closer and closer to exhaustion. Maybe we've less than a klick to go. But in exactly what direction? The cursed wind blows our cries back onto us. Oh, dear kind Copperhue, thirsting, hungering, shivering, alone, alone.

"Too bad we had to leave the tent behind," Kristan said. "No matter how sturdy our bags, if I know hill weather, we'd be glad of a roof."

At least he doesn't blame me, he admits it was necessary. "We can arrange that," Laurice told him, "provided we hurry. Will you hop to my orders?"

He sketched a salute. In the haggard, grimy, stubbly countenance, how boyish his grin flashed.

With her machete she chopped down a slim flexy and lopped off its boughs. Propping an end in a forked knorrig, she leaned the larger branches against the pole and wove the lesser ones between to make a framework. He had gathered withes, deadfall still leafy, whatever small stuff he could find. Together, she directing, they heaped and plaited it over the lattice. "Got to pitch the roof just right," she explained, "but this will keep us snug."

"Yes, and I notice how the ground slopes," he replied. "We won't get runoff. Good job!"

Tired or no, he possessed a quick intelligence. "It's an ancient device, primeval," she said. Unable to resist showing off a bit: "Ordinarily I'd pile a circle of stones outside the entrance and bank a fire there, to reflect heat inside, but we haven't time, it'd probably drown anyway, and our sleeping bags will serve. Hoy, pass that vine *over* the thatch, or it'll blow loose during the night."

The first drops flew heavy, cold, and stinging.

"After you," he said with a bow. She crawled into the narrow space. Best avoid possible misunderstandings and undress in the dark. By feel she arranged her things, got out of her stinking clothes, slid into the bedding. Never mind a bath, toothbrush, all ordinary amenities. "Your turn," she called.

He took her hint and also left his light in his pack. Often, inevitably, groping and twisting about, he bumped her. She grew acutely aware of it and commanded herself to think like an adult. That didn't quite work.

Rain roared, wind brawled, branches creaked. Where did Copperhue huddle? It-he'd never been taught how to make a shelter, a fire drill, snares for small game, or—or anything—

She heard a slight metallic pop. By contact rather than sight she knew Kristan lay raised on an elbow. "I've broken out rations," he said. "You may not be hungry, but I'm starved."

"Hoo! How could I have forgotten? Let me at it."

"Have a spoon— Excuse me, I was searching for your hand."

She barely suppressed a giggle. "That isn't where it grows. Here. Thank you."

They shared hardtack and meat paste. "This does beat lying in the open, no matter how well wrapped up," he murmured. Quickly: "If only we had your friend by us. We'll find him tomorrow. We will."

Alive, let us hope, said neither of them.

"How did you acquire all this woodcraft?" he asked. "I'd heard of you—who hasn't?—but always associated you with spacefaring."

"One spacefares to someplace," she answered. "From time to time I get bored with being a daughter of House Windfell and go explore. My preference is for more or less Atherlike worlds, not so thoroughly Atherlike that they're overrun by Erthumoi."

"I don't believe you ever get bored, milady. No proper House raises its children to be idlers."

No, Arinberg didn't make a playboy of you, did it?

Though her muscles ached, she wasn't sleepy yet. Talking kept thought of Copperhue at bay. "Well, early on I observed some aborigines in action, and got interested. Back home I ransacked the databases and found they did similar things on Old Earth in primitive times. I decided such a bag of tricks would be handy as well as instructive. No better way to really learn about a given wilderness; and you get a flexibility you don't have if you always depend on manufactured stuff. Frankly, I'm surprised you never developed anything similar, you people studying Venafer."

"We've been . . . understaffed, overworked, and without natives to provide an object lesson. Nobody can think of everything. I'll have proposals to make at Forholt Station."

"Give me an acknowledgment line," she laughed. "And the Naxians. They're smart, they've already worked out a lot of variants adapted to this planet."

She heard the reluctance: "I have to credit them with brains, courage, determination. If they'd chosen any other planet, I'd cheer them on."

"This was their only possibility, you know. All else habitable for them that's been discovered is claimed by some nation among the Six Races, or has natives."

"Yes, yes. Well, if they keep themselves to that island you Windfells gave them—it can support a reasonable population. But no, they won't control their numbers, they've begun breeding like vermin."

The bitterness in his tone caused her to forgive his language. Could she somehow ease him? "Numbers are exploding everywhere, among all the Six. Fill available habitat. A law of life."

"Nonsense. Natural species keep within bounds. Oh, some have population cycles, but when they get to be too many, nature cuts them back. Against high-tech sentients, she's helpless. And the Six aren't vegetables or dumb brutes. Nor ignorant primitives anymore. They have no excuse for destroying their worlds.''

She frowned into the darkness. "If I remember rightly, from time to time in history a nation has managed to stay in balance for a while. But these days—I wonder if the speculations of the Odenko school may not be right. You've heard? They think a basic instinct is at work. With robots proliferating at the rate they are, organic beings are driven to try to match them. We rationalize in different ways, but the truth is that we're in the grip of an aroused life force.''

"Yes. I've met the idea. Rather farfetched speculation, but conceivably right. Still, we could have spared Venafer. A unique biosphere, billions of years of evolution, countless revelations waiting for us—gone, wasted, wiped out before we know a thousandth of the questions we should have asked it.''

"Come, now. Look at Ather. Very little left that's primeval, true. Like you, I'd have loved to've been among those who found and explored it in its original state. But the essentials were conserved. Modified, yes, but conserved. Erthumoi and their imported species didn't replace Atheran life, they joined it, became part of it, and in many ways the planet is more wonderful today than it was before.''

"That's a matter of taste." Kristan hesitated. "Don't get me wrong, please. Sentients also have a right to exist, and nonsentient life also works changes on the environment. But some changes are disasters." His voice harshened. "You know quite well that the sort of new symbiosis you picture for Ather is impossible for Venafer. Industrial civilization on any sizable scale cannot coexist with nature here. Even agriculture can't. Your House meant well, but when you failed to make a law that the snakes—the Naxians—must stay confined to their one island, you sentenced this world to death. What harm had it ever done you?"

Memory rose in Laurice, as vivid as if she sat again by her father, hearing him explain to his council the implications that a few scientists had discreetly brought to his attention. "We should perhaps have studied the situation more before we made our agreement," he had said in his grave manner. "It turns out that Venafer is perpetually on the brink of catastrophe. Florasol was cooler gigayears ago, when the first life developed there, and evolution kept pace with the slow warming, but today the planet is at the inner edge of the habitability zone. Nothing maintains liquid water temperatures except the worldwide forests. Vegetation from outside can't replace them; nothing else known to us takes up carbon with the same efficiency. At that, the forests barely maintain the composition. If Venafer loses any significant fraction of them—"

Runaway greenhouse. Increased atmospheric carbon dioxide trapping more solar energy. Rising temperatures evaporating more water, whose vapor is itself a powerful greenhouse gas. Drought, fire, dieback, desert spreading and spreading, while the heat mounts. As the life that renewed them vanishes, oxygen and nitrogen are again locked in minerals. The oceans boil. Water molecules go on high, where ultraviolet splits them asunder; the hydrogen escapes into space, the oxygen is soon imprisoned in the rocks. When at last an equilibrium is reached, it prevails over a searing hell, it is the peace of the graveyard or the slag heap.

"Didn't you foresee?" Kristan cried. "Didn't you care?"

Laurice echoed her father's words: "We had pledged our honor." Then: "Remember what a tremendous service Copperhue had done, not just for Windfell or Ather or the Erthumoi, but all the Six Races. If the

Pythons had kept a monopoly of what we've learned since—''

She felt him shift about in his bag, but he spoke more quietly. "I suppose so. At least, maybe that has a certain amount of truth. Nevertheless, a large and fertile island, where that cult can live as it chooses, was quite generous payment. Couldn't they restrict themselves to it?"

"That was discussed, behind the scenes," she admitted. "Some of the Naxian leaders said it would be fair. Unfortunately, it would be unenforceable. New generations in particular are bound to ignore or disown any such prohibition."

"Not if you forbid," he said starkly. "You've got the weapons."

"To attack unarmed civilians? No! Besides, our fellow Houses wouldn't allow it. They have property on Venafer too."

"You could all have joined together on the policy."

She shook her head, hair rustling across fabric. "Are you really that innocent? Often the Houses can't agree on the time of day. They might conceivably have formed a cartel for the purpose, but cartels are always unstable. You see, for several of them, a Naxian population expanding over the planet means a growing market—for capital goods, services, everything—which pays them out of its own production. Venafer will finally become profitable."

"At the price of its life."

"They don't extrapolate that the effects can be radical for at least five centuries."

"You'll still be alive, milady. Most of those concerned will be, to see what they've done. Do you look forward?"

"Extinction won't happen. They aren't that foolish. Including the Naxians. Haven't you seen the proposals?" Maybe not, she thought. This whole matter is obscure, a minor item, buried under an avalanche of more exciting news. And nobody has made any definite announcement about it. Because no decision has thus far crystallized.

"Oh, yes. Grandiose schemes. Increase the planet's albedo to compensate, for instance by orbiting a cloud of reflective particles around it. Or cut down the sunlight with a giant reflector at the L2 point—use part of the excess energy to power a station-keeping motor— or—never mind. No doubt it can be done, if the gains are sufficiently tempting. At any rate, the engineering part of it can be done. But none of Venafer's own life can survive so drastic a change, you know. There'll be nothing but cities, machines, and drab genetically tailored plantations. A corpse with worms and fungi feasting on it, a corpse that greed murdered."

A world that you loved, she thought.

Wind and rain sang around the shelter. She heard their mighty rushing through the trees and across the heights. From somewhere resounded a call, some wild creature. It was like a trumpet in the night. Yes, marvels, mysteries, and nobody knew what insights to gain or what profits of knowledge and inspiration to forgo forever.

Almost, she told him more. But no, she dare not, she mustn't, she knew him too little and what she had seen of him bordered on the fanatical. One flame, unguarded, can kindle a forest.

"This has become a head-butting contest," she said. "Later, if you want, we can argue. But right now I'm exhausted, and we've work to do in the morning. Good night."

He growled and rolled over, his back to her. The rainfall grew louder. She lay staving off anger, fear, despair until she blundered into an uneasy sleep.

She had set her brain to wake at earliest clear light. In these latitudes at this time of year, nights were short.

She sprang to consciousness, gasped, and sat up. Kristan's eyes were already open. They widened—in appreciation, she felt fleetingly—but he put an arm across them before she could cross hers over her breasts. "Do you want to dress first or shall I?" he mumbled. Laughter broke from her of its own accord and shook her to full alertness.

The rain had ended a couple of hours ago, easing her worst dread. When she emerged, she found mist a-smoke over the ground and among the trees. The cold didn't belong on the Venafer of popular imagination. A whole world, though, a whole congregation of miracles like none other in the universe— How was Copperhue? She sped to the last signs she had found yesterday.

"I'll fix breakfast," offered Kristan at her back. She nodded absently, her mind concentrated on brush, dead leaves, mud. It was not easy to trace the spoor farther; the rain had obliterated much. In vague wise she noticed him gather deadwood, use a lighter to start a fire, make a grill of green sticks on which to heat food in its containers. Well, naturally he'd have elementary skills.

He brought her a serving, together with one for himself. She glanced up from her crouch. He didn't look as though he had slept well either, but if he could smile, so could she. "Here." She lifted a branchful of crimson berries she had cut off a chance-encountered bush. "Redballs for sweetener."

"Have you eaten any?" he exclaimed.

"Not yet. I meant to share— What's wrong?"

"Whew! That's not proper redball, it's a highland species, closely related but poisonous to us. Those little yellow dots on the leaves identify it. You'd have been one sick girl."

"Thanks." You *are* necessary, damn you. And you are trying to be friendly again, damn you. And I think

you're succeeding—and why, damn you, when your
rage has good reason? Laurice took the opened container, set it down, scooped from it with her right hand
and a spoon while her left hand turned debris over.

"Can you really still pick up signs?" he asked
wonderingly.

"Yes. Tracks in the dirt don't all slump away under
rain. Many collect water before silt starts to fill them
and are temporarily more visible than before. Leaves
blow onto others and protect them. Bent twigs and such
don't disappear overnight. The problem does get extra
complicated. I find plenty of breaks in the trail. Just
the same, I'm getting an approximate direction. Once
this flinking fog lifts I'll have better clues. Copperhue
wouldn't move purely at random, you see. No animal
does. Whether or not it-he had much consciousness left,
the body itself would tend to follow the least strenuous
course. If we look ahead and study the contours—a-a-
ah!'' A breeze made rags of the gray. Dripping trees,
begemmed shrubs, wetly gleaming boulders hove into
sight.

Having gulped their rations, swallowed some milk,
and separated to do what else was required of them,
the hunters moved onward. Laurice led the way,
slowly, often pausing to cast about or for eyes and
fingers to probe, yet with a confidence that waxed and
tingled in her. Up the slope they climbed, topped the
ridge, and gazed across vastness.

The air had cleared, though it remained bleak, and
heaven was featureless, colorless, save where the
unseen sun brightened it a little, low above eastern bul-
warks. Ground slanted downward, begrown with
bushes and dwarf trees well apart, otherwise ruddy
bare, to a narrow ledge. Underneath this a talus slope
plunged into unseen depths. The far side of the gorge
reared a kilometer beyond. Its course zigzagged north

and south, a barrier between distant plain and distant mountains.

"Look!" Laurice shouted. "The trail, straight and clear!" Runoff had gouged the slight hollowing unmistakably deeper, every turn to and fro. No normal track left by a Naxian, wavery as the footprints of an Erthuma staggering at the end of his endurance, it pointed to her goal.

Kristan caught her arm. "Easy," he warned. "Remember what kind of soil and rock we've got hereabouts. You could lose your footing at best, touch off a small landslide at worst."

"Copperhue didn't." Still, she placed her boots warily, one, two, one, two, on the way down.

The long reddish body lay coiled in a clump of scrub. Laurice fell to her knees, crushing branches, to cast arms about the cable of muscles. "Copperhue, Copperhue, *s-s-siya-a*, shipmate, here I am, how are you, comrade, comrade?"

Cheek against skin, she felt not the wonted warmth but a faint incessant shuddering. Otherwise the Naxian barely stirred. Glazed eyes turned toward her and drooped again. The least of sibilations reached her ears.

She scrambled erect. "Hypothermia," she heard her voice say; it rang within her skull. "Extreme. Fatal, I think, unless we act fast."

"No clothes, none?" Kristan asked incredulously. He must be half stunned by the sight.

"Naxians seldom wear any," she rapped. "Not too practical when you move on your belly. And they aren't reptiles, you know. Nor mammals, but they are warmblooded, with thermostats better than ours. The windchill factor throughout this night overloaded its-his, though. You or I would be dead. It-he's dying."

"I know, I know all that. But—"

"We haven't got a thermal unit, or any of your fancy gear. There is one simple treatment. Quick! Untie your sleeping bag. Open it fully, spread it out.'' Laurice released her backpack, dropped it, squatted to pluck at the fastenings of her own bedroll.

He followed suit while he asked, ''What do you have in mind?''

''Warming him, of course. Putting him between our sacks and ourselves.'' She glanced about, saw a spot that wasn't truly level but was not so canted that they would roll off, and brought her bag there. Returning, she said, ''It'll take both of us to carry him. Naxians are massier than you'd think.''

Kristan had the strength to be gentle as he hauled the limp form up and draped the larger part across his shoulders. Laurice took the head end. Grunting with effort, they bore Copperhue over and laid it-him down on the cloth, stretched out. Their burden was passive. Kristan fetched his bedding and put it above. ''Now what?'' he inquired.

''Clothes off,'' Laurice directed. He gaped. ''Strip, I said! To chaos with modesty.'' She ripped at her garments.

He removed his more slowly, eyes at first locked on her. Then, doubtless realizing how he stared, he swiveled his head away. A moment later he turned his back while he completed the task. She was already between the bags. When he must face her again, he tried to cover himself with one hand. Though big, it wasn't quite enough.

Laurice couldn't help herself. Laughter pealed. ''Oh, fout, don't be that embarrassed!'' she called. ''I'd feel slighted if you did not react. C'mon, join the party.''

Still fiery cheeked, he obeyed. They snuggled close on either side of Copperhue. That put their upper arms in contact across the Naxian while glance met glance over its-his head. The chill made them shiver too. Then as heat flowed from them, replenishing itself within, and the victim's blood began to respond, they felt a growing voluptuous comfort.

"Another useful trick," he murmured. "I must tell my associates. We do take our field equipment too much for granted." Smiling: "I'm afraid I'll never practice this again with so attractive a partner."

Well, well, Laurice thought. Getting over the shyness, are we? Not but what present circumstances don't encourage that. Actually, I could imagine far worse partners myself, and you're too modest if you take your field equipment for granted. "Thank you, kind sir. We'll be here a fairish while. May as well relax and enjoy it, now that we know it's working."

"It does feel good, saving a life. Uh, that sounds smug, doesn't it? Wasn't meant that way."

"Of course not, my earnest friend. Though I admit to a touch of smugness in me, and consider it well earned. Relax, I said. Let me tell you funny stories or something. Unless they'll make your face hurt."

"Do you really find me such a sobersides?" He pondered. "Yes, you'd be bound to. At Forholt I'm known as 'Free-Fall' Arinberg."

"Why?"

"Oh, I've played various pranks, I've composed a few ballads, that sort of thing."

"Free— Wait a minute! Do you mean you're the creator of 'Free-Fall Fumble'?"

"Well, uh, why, I didn't think you—"

"Ha! I've helped sing it scores of times, when the party got good and drunk. My, my. Let me shake that bawdy hand of yours." This clasp lingered. "Tell me about yourself. Unsuspected depths and all."

"I'd rather listen to you reminisce. You've had a far more colorful life than I."

"Colorful is as colorful does. Ordinary folk don't dedicate themselves to a wild and often dangerous world. What got you interested?"

Piece by hesitant piece, his biography emerged. He was older than she was, though only by four decades, less than she had guessed. His manner had misled her, she decided; and, to be sure, his latest rejuvenation predated hers. He'd done geology on several planets and moons, but mostly he'd taught at the University of Ilis, till his marriage broke up. His sole one, it had lasted some fifty years, unusually long these days; Laurice's parents were extraordinary. That fact, and everything else about him, caused her to suppose that if it had been left to him, he'd be married yet. As it was, seeking a new life, he joined a son of his, likewise a scientist, on Venafer, and gradually discovered that here was the meaning to his existence that he had sought. Since he didn't mention any women except as colleagues, despite some questions that she flattered herself were shrewd, he probably had only casual liaisons; and thus, while amiable and popular among his fellows, he must bear an inward loneliness such as she had known all too often.

Rare among men, he genuinely disliked speaking in the first person singular, and wanted to hear about her. Well, she did have quite a lot of stories, and did not mind shining in his eyes.

Copperhue writhed a little. It-he raised its-his head, stared about, let it sink again but whispered words that were plain to Laurice. "Everything is well," she replied in Merse. "Be at ease. We'll soon take you home."

"To New Halla?" Kristan asked.

"Well, first to our base on the coast, of course," Laurice answered. "From there, we can call for further transportation if need be, but I don't think we'll have to. A couple of days' rest ought to set Copperhue in fine fettle."

"But what shall he do? The upland project's spoiled, isn't it?"

"Not permanently. First it-he can join another group, maybe my river cruise—"

"S-s-s." She heard. "I would enjoy that, your company, darling comrade." She patted the big bald pate.

"Meanwhile somebody can talk with Uldor at Forholt," she continued. "If he's up to it, and I bet he will be, perhaps we can arrange audiovisual transmissions, so a new expedition here keeps the benefit of his advice. I can lead it, once my canoeists are finished, if nobody better is available. And I doubt anybody will be better, considering what I've learned from you."

His visage stiffened. He withdrew the hand that had been touching hers. "A detail or two, nothing more."

"But they point me toward what else I should watch out for and get educated about," she said eagerly. "In fact, while we wait here—"

The dark head shook. "No."

"What?"

"No. I will not lend any more help to the . . . the wrecking of this planet."

Oh, wisdom, she said in her bosom, I've punched that button again, just when we were beginning to understand one another. "Listen, you've complained about shortages of funds and manpower. Well, you can have more, if your group will cooperate with ours. We're not prospectors or timber cruisers or anything like that, you know. We're scientists too."

"For what purpose?" he flared. "Pure knowledge? No, you're preparing the way for colonists." He drew breath. "This incident—I, we at Forholt, we'd only been peripherally conscious of your activities. I see now that we didn't want to think about the snakes, and told ourselves we'd get them stopped later, sometime when we weren't so busy. Well, this incident has awakened me to what an immediate menace they are. The time to halt them is *now*, before you gain too much momentum, too many investors in your damned projects. I'll be going back to Ather, Milady Windfell, and campaign. It will take years, I know, hard work, harder bargaining, but I and those who are with me will fight you every millimeter of the way.''

"Speak softly," Copperhue hissed. "He is indeed enraged, although he regrets that he is.''

And he might actually, eventually succeed, Laurice thought. Besides the conservationists, quite a few people are uneasy about the Naxians, for various reasons and unreasons. I don't want to believe Kristan would deliberately appeal to xenophobia, but he'd find himself with political allies who'd welcome a chance to cultivate it.

"I'm sorry you feel like that," she ventured.

His wrath collapsed. For an instant he looked strangely vulnerable. "The same for you, milady. I wish I could persuade you.''

"Or I you? We're both honest. That's something. Well, we aren't at any crisis point, remember. We'll have time to think and study and debate. Nothing has been definitely decided yet, nor can it for years to come, and nothing irrevocable will happen for years after that. Maybe, when we've learned more, your scenarios will dissolve like nightmares.''

Grimness took him. "Or yours like daydreams. Those schemes to change the sunlight itself, can you swear they'd work? We aren't gods; we ruin much more than we create. Why, the sheer mass of dead organic matter, as native life goes extinct—how well have you modeled the chemistry of that? How might it affect your agriculture? How sure are you of anything?''

Hardly at all, she refrained from confessing. Except—but I may not tell you that. May I, Copperhue?

"Let's not argue." She sighed. "Let's only share warmth.''

"Agreed." But his voice was cold, and he fell silent,

lying motionless alongside the serpent shape between them. An hour crept by.

At last, at last: "I believe I am recovered." Copperhue sounded like it. "Thanks to your kindness, honored ones."

"Splendid," Laurice replied dully. "Uh, Dr. Arinberg, our patient is cured. I suppose, though, you noticed it-he's cut and bruised—thorns, rocks—and weakened, in poor shape to travel cross country. Can we do an airlift?"

"I've been thinking about that." Kristan remained distant, impersonal. "I can fetch the flyer. Whether or not a safe landing is possible in this vicinity, I don't know. If necessary, I can hover and lower a cable with a loop, but that could be tricky. Let me look around."

She wondered how defiant the openness was with which he left the covers and dressed. While she dressed he set off down the slope.

A wind had arisen as the air warmed. It boomed, slewed about, shook boughs, sent dust devils awhirl. Yes, Laurice thought, he's right. A hoist on a flapping line out of a bucking vehicle has its risks. But if he lands and the ground slips from under—

His tall form had borne right and left, stopping to examine outcrops and dig boot heel into gravel, till he reached the ledge above the canyon. She saw him glance at his bracelet, and well-nigh read his mind. Guided by the radio beacon, he could make most of his return distance on that bare strip instead of struggling through the forest. The smile that tugged her lips was half sad. She didn't want him for an enemy.

The rock broke beneath his feet. He flailed air, then pitched downward out of sight.

Laurice screamed and bounded forward. "Hold, wait, be careful," Copperhue sibilated at her back. Whoa! she told herself amidst the hammers of her pulse. No use two of us going over. If the stone betrayed him, how easily it could fool me.

Slowed to a gliding walk, she sought Kristan's footprints and took that exact route until it approached the verge. There she hunkered down, peered at the rock and rubble ahead, piecemeal made sure of where it had crumbled and where it might crumble and where it seemed reasonably safe. Cracks meant water seepage, which occasionally froze and expanded; but you must also shun bands and blotches of soft iron oxide—

Prone as a Naxian, she thrust her head over the edge and squinted. Talus littered a slant into remote mistful depths. Kristan sprawled on its darkness, come to precarious rest after sliding some four meters. His face, turned skyward, was a mask of blood, and he did not stir; but the brilliant red stream out of his right thigh showed a heart still beating.

A sharp edge cut a major vessel, she knew. He's exsanguinating. If he doesn't get help fast, he's dead. Eternally. We couldn't bring him to revival before the cerebrum cells that make him human decayed beyond restoration.

Pebbles gritted under a heavy slither. Copperhue had joined her. "You should have stayed," she said automatically.

"One can summon up one's ultimate reserves when one must," it-he responded. "I believe I can assist you to recover our comrade."

It-he says "comrade," after listening to Kristan. The thought flickered past and was gone. Laurice weighed her chances. Did the Naxian overestimate its-his strength? Well, if so, but if she took care, she needn't perish, though Kristan certainly would. Trapped on an unclimbable hillside, she could relay a radio message through the flyer to base, and a rescue party would arrive. Unless, of course, her efforts triggered a slide.

Then she'd lie chopped to flitches, smashed to pulp, buried beyond finding.

No time for worries. Glancing about, she saw the bush Copperhue plainly was counting on. It grew within centimeters of the edge, but inspection showed thick roots that must go deep, and above them a bonsai twisting that decades or centuries of wind must have wrought. Probably it could withstand a few hundred kilos' worth of stress.

A dash back to fetch cords or straps would take too long. Cutting a stick, she put it between her teeth. She pulled off her shirt, slashed it in two, knotted the halves together at the bottoms and one sleeve around Copperhue's neck. The other sleeve she took in her hand, with a bight to secure her grip. Copperhue curled its-his tail around the lower stem of the bush. Laurice sat down and went over the side on her rear end.

Shards rattled, slid, slashed at pants and boots. The Naxian strained backward, easing her descent, paying out its-his length bit by bit until at last it-he was stretched taut. The scree must be cruelly painful against its-his skin, but she heard no murmur.

At the end of her line she lay side by side with Kristan. She dared not kneel, but by cautious use of palm and elbow she could support herself well enough to work on him. Her sheath knife slid forth. Best single tool the mind of man has yet hit on, she thought, not for the first time. She ripped the trouser leg, exposed the wound, cut a cloth strip, made a tourniquet with the stick and tightened it. The lethal flow ceased.

Sweat beaded his face under the blood, he felt clammy and his breathing was shallow, yes, he was in shock. Got to get him upstairs quick. Slip her improvised hawser under his back, below the arms, and secure it. "All right, Copperhue, haul away!"

Could it-he? If not, she'd yell for help and try to keep Kristan alive where they were. Whether she could or not was a crapshoot. It was just about as uncertain whether his weight, as he was drawn higher, would start a rockslip fatal to her.

Somehow it didn't. Somehow, from somewhere, Copperhue got the power to haul him aloft, undo the line and cast it down, raise her in turn. She went backside under, keeping her bare torso above the flinders that would have lacerated it. The tough material of her trousers didn't give way, but she'd be seating herself gingerly for the next couple of days.

Pulled to the ledge, she lay briefly, heaving air in and out of her lungs, before she clambered to her feet. Copperhue was almost as limp as Kristan. "I can drag him the rest of the way by myself," she mumbled. "Can you make it? You've got to."

"I . . . can . . . since you . . . wish—" her friend whispered. "And then?"

"Why, then—" Laughter shrilled. "We apply naked bodies to him, you and I."

Once between the covers, both Erthumoi unclad and Copperhue on his other side, Laurice sent her message. The relayed voice from Forholt Station sounded faint but crisp out of the bracelet: "We'll dispatch our ambulance immediately. It should reach you in about an hour. Can you manage that long?"

"I'd better, hadn't I?" she retorted.

She could not simply lie waiting by the man. From time to time she must tend him, massage, loosen the tourniquet and tighten it anew. The blood that ran out made a gluey mess, but some went into the injured limb to keep the flesh alive. Of course, if gangrene set in, a surgeon could amputate, and at a clinic on Ather they could regenerate what was lost. However, she didn't want him subjected to that.

Strong and healthy, he responded well. Before the medics appeared, his eyes had fluttered open to hers.

Laurice must needs admire the adroitness of the res-

cuers. The ambulance hovered high and lowered a platform which had thrusters to stabilize it against the
wind. A man started to work on Kristan while they
lifted him. "You did fine, milady," he said. "This
shot's the only added thing he needs to put him out of
danger. Thanks. We're pretty fond of ol' Free-Fall."

Aboard the vehicle it was possible to wash, receive
treatment for injuries, and don fresh clothes. Laurice
hadn't minded the masculine looks she received—to the
extent that she noticed them—but how good to settle
down warmly swaddled and fall asleep by Copperhue.
Neither woke till they landed at Forholt. The director
greeted them courteously and offered overnight accom-
modations, that they be well rested before they were
flown back to their base. They accepted, and emerged
from bed only for dinner. Nonetheless, at the meal
Laurice enjoyed telling the staff what had happened.
Nobody mentioned the dispute.

As they returned to their quarters, Copperhue asked,
"Can we visit honored Kristan Arinberg in the
morning?"

"I'm sure we can," she said. "I mean to."

"With some privacy."

"Hm?" She caught the implication. A thrill shot
through her. "Well, we'll see what the conditions are."

Dawn brought rain, the quick, silvery rain of southern Ebland, filled with odors of growth and joyful animal cries. Laurice and Copperhue took covered paths
between buildings to sickbay. Windows stood open on
that wet wild air. As it happened, Kristan lay alone.
The injured Naxians had been returned to New Halla
and Uldor Enarsson was getting physical therapy. His
prognosis was excellent, the doctor had said.

The least bit grudgingly? Uldor would be able to
resume his work with the settlers.

The callers entered a space of misty lights and empty
beds. Kristan was propped up reading a printbook. She

glimpsed the title when he laid it aside. *Rusa Irmansdaughter's Saga,* from pioneer times on Ather; why, that was a favorite of hers. He was pale from the blood loss but wholly alert and his hail rang clear. "Milady! Comrade!"

She took a chair beside him. Copperhue coiled opposite, head raised. The usual remarks passed to and fro.

"It seems I owe you my life," he said then, awkwardly.

"As I owe you mine," Copperhue replied. It-he had borrowed a simultrans. "Yours would not have been imperiled had you not come after me."

Laurice made a flinging gesture. "Spung the sentiments!" she scoffed. "We all three clowned our way through a string of bollixes that should never have been in the first place. Because we were ignorant, right?"

"It couldn't be helped," Kristan said. "We have to learn as we go. I . . . learned a great deal from you."

"And I from you, though in either case it's been a lot less than it could or should be. If we shared—" She didn't finish, but waited for him.

His smile was wistful. "You know why that's impossible."

"Is it? We, the Naxians and I, are more than willing. It's your choice."

"No, I'm merely one man."

"A free man. Furthermore, an influential one. You think you can generate some fierce political opposition to us. I suspect you're right. Well, you can work for us with the same force, if you will."

"I'm sorry." He sighed. "After these past days, genuinely sorry. But you know I can't." His gaze went beyond her, to the rain and the hidden rain forest. "If you, if you'd understand why this world matters, what it means—"

"We do," Laurice said most softly. "We hope to preserve it."

He blinked.

"I don't want to press you while you're convalescent," she went on, "except that, well, certain information may give you a new viewpoint. Not that I expect to make an instant convert of you. But we've gotten to know you a bit, Copperhue and I. So if you'll hear us and respect our confidence—because we must first have your pledge to keep a secret for some years—"

"Let me think." He looked at her, and at it-him, and down at his hands, and again out the window. Presently he nodded. "I trust you that much," he said.

"And we trust you," Copperhue told them both.

It was enough. Sensing the man's feelings, the Naxian knew he would abide by his word.

Laurice's heart thuttered. "The reason for secrecy is precisely to protect Venafer," she began. "There *are* people and interests who stand to profit in a big way from its . . . transformation, the thing you dread. Given advance warning, they could forestall us. For instance, by logging off or burning off the forests on their holdings, they could tip the balance beyond recovery. That'd leave no alternative to proceeding full speed and building industries that can afford to make screens against the sun."

"The slimeguts," Kristan rasped.

"In their minds, they are not evil," Copperhue said. "They see their plans as beneficial."

"Doing well by doing good," Laurice added with a grin.

"Many among my people take the same prospect as a given," Copperhue continued. "Under present circumstances, they would look upon the industrialists as liberators. For without them, what else is there? That we remain confined to our original territory, either breeding ourselves into poverty or else surrendering the freedom and sacredness of family life to dictatorship—

compulsory sterilization and infanticide. Neither outcome would be stable. Either means unrest, subversion,
revolution, ultimate war.''

''At the same time,'' Laurice joined in, ''the industrial approach has too many uncertainties of its own.
You were right when you claimed we can't predict the
effects. Our computer models are inadequate.''

''The entrepreneurs are attempting to refine them,''
Copperhue conceded. ''But most of the leadership on
New Halla is deeply dubious. Can any model of an
entire world be complete? Chaos lurks in the very equa-
tions. No matter how carefully we prepared, we would
risk ending, in a thousand years or less, with a planet
uninhabitable and unsalvageable. Where then could we
go?''

Kristan glanced from it-him to her as if in appeal.
''Why've I never heard of this?'' he wondered.

''It's been discussed, argued, wrangled over,'' said
Laurice, ''but not in any large official way. After all,
the colony is new, still small, not important to anybody
but itself, except potentially. And you've been too busy
with your work, you and your colleagues, to follow
debates that are mostly in an alien language and an
alien society.''

Thought drew his brows together. ''Well, actually,
what you've spelled out isn't startling,'' he murmured.
''I've heard the same notions explored to some extent—
in conversations among us here at Forholt, for instance.
The trouble has been, the only choices seem to be
exactly those you've named. Either New Halla becomes
a kind of big concentration camp, or Venafer becomes
a shell with machines on it, or everything ends in disas-
ter.'' He sat straight. ''Have you another possibility?
What is your secret?'' He sank back onto the pillows.

''This.'' Laurice leaned nearer him. ''It's something
we're working on, mind you, a hope, a dream. Maybe
it'll prove unfeasible. We ought to know in another five

or ten years, at least well enough to make it public. As I said, if the opposition gets wind of it too soon, they can spoil its chances, figuring us for impractical obstructionists who should be swept off the scene before we brew real trouble. But once it's announced, with ample scientific evidence that it is worth investigating further, they'll have to stay their hands. Social pressure will see to that.'' She paused. ''I like to think their own consciences will.''

''We Naxians have not sensed those we have met as being more wicked than is inevitable among mortal creatures,'' Copperhue remarked.

''The idea is,'' Laurice said into Kristan's intentness, ''that the colonists will in the course of time settle all Venafer, but living in the forests, *with* the forests.''

''As hunters, you mean?'' he asked, astounded.

''No, no. Not most of them. We can't force them into a stone age, nor would we if we could. Literacy, medicine, transport, communication, labor-saving machinery, everything that a civilized life demands, they'll have. But can't they have it from nature? Houses, not the crude shelters our expeditions are using, real houses, but made from wood that gets replanted, or maybe from trees that are kept alive. Food, fiber, chemicals, not from agriculture or factories but from cropping wildlife and vegetation. And cash crops taken out of the forests, to sell on Ather so they can import the manufactured stuff they want—''

''Although,'' Copperhue added pensively, ''I think that as such a way of life develops, it will find new roads, new directions and desires, until we have become indeed children of our world. It is an ideal that accords well with the Old Truth.''

''It isn't simple, of course,'' Laurice said. ''Anything but. None of us can foresee a hundredth of the problems, the ramifications, the future it might bring about. We're just trying to learn enough about the planet to see whether it's possible. We believe the answer will be yes."

Kristan stared before him. "The forests tamed," he breathed. "No more wilderness."

"But still Venafer," Laurice answered. "And did you imagine, if everybody left this world and never came back, it would stay the same always?"

"No," he agreed. "Nothing is forever."

"We'd be bringing something altogether new into being," she said. "No way to tell what shapes it will take. But I'll bet 'tamed' is the wrong word. 'Evolving' might be better."

Slowly, he nodded.

"I'm acting as a consultant for the first several years," she finished. "Then it's deep space again for me. You, though, if you stay—if you decide to help— you ought to have an interesting few centuries ahead of you. A lot of challenge, a lot of fun."

Once more he was silent, until he said, "I must think this over. Think hard." The fading voice told her that she and Copperhue should depart and let him rest.

She smiled. "Certainly."

He looked at her. "Will you help me think?" he asked. "Can we meet some more?"

"Try and stop me," she said, and left him with the shared promise.

About the Authors

Poul Anderson

One of the most versatile writers in the history of the genre, Poul Anderson is equally adept at hard and soft science fiction, high fantasy, and sword and sorcery. He is also one of the most honored writers, having won seven Hugo Awards and three Nebula Awards for such wonderful stories as "No Truce with Kings," "The Queen of Air and Darkness," "Goat Song," and "The Saturn Game." His many novels include such masterworks as *Brain Wave* (1954), *The High Crusade* (1960), *Tau Zero* (1970), *The King of Ys* (1986), and *The Boat of a Million Years* (1990).

Hal Clement

"Hal Clement" is the name used for the science fiction books and stories written by the gifted Harry Clement Stubbs. A science teacher from Massachusetts, with several degrees from Harvard, he has always brought a strong measure of serious scientific extrapolation to his fiction, which includes such notable novels as *Needle* (1950), *Mission of Gravity* (1954), *Nitrogen Fix* (1980), and *Still River* (1987), among other important works produced in his over forty year career in science fiction.

George Alec Effinger

George Alec Effinger became a full-time writer in 1971 and has since developed a sizable audience for his frequently humorous, sometimes surreal stories that take typical science fiction conventions and turn them on their heads. Notable novels and story collections include *What Entropy Means to Me* (1972), *Irrational Numbers* (1976), *The Wolves of Memory* (1981), *The Bird of Time* (1985), and the very impressive *When Gravity Fails* (1986). His Maureen Birnbaum stories constitute what is perhaps the funniest series in the field.

Karen Haber

A fast-rising new science fiction writer, Karen Haber's well-crafted stories have appeared in such diverse venues as *The Magazine of Fantasy and Science Fiction*, *The Further Adventures of Batman*, and *Isaac Asimov's Science Fiction Magazine*. Two volumes of her brilliant new series of novels, *Mutant Season* (1990) and *Mutant Prime* (1991), have appeared to date. A talented editor as well as author, she coedits the important *Universe* series of original science fiction anthologies with her husband, Robert Silverberg.

Janet Kagan

Janet Kagan's first novel was the bestselling *Uhura's Song* (1985), which many enthusiasts feel is one of the very best *Star Trek* novels ever written. She followed this with *Hellspark* (1987), a fascinating hard sf tale based on linguistics. Her excellent short fiction has appeared in *Pulphouse*, *Analog*, and especially *Isaac Asimov's Science Fiction Magazine*, where her story "The Loch Moose Monster" won for Best Novelette in that magazine's Reader's Choice Awards for 1989. In 1990 she won the *Asimov's* Reader's Choice Award once again for Best Novelette with "Getting the Bugs Out." Both award-winning stories (as well as "The Return of the Kangaroo Rex," the second-place winner in the 1989 *Asimov's* Reader's Choice Novelette category and "The Flowering Inferno," the third-place winner in the same category for 1990) will be part of her latest novel, *Mirabile*, to be published in Fall 1991.

Allen Steele

Perhaps the fastest rising young star of hard science fiction, Allen Steele's first novel, *Orbital Decay*, was acclaimed as one of the best books of 1989 and has been favorably compared to the best work of Robert A. Heinlein. He followed this success with *Clarke County, Space* in 1990 and *Lunar Descent* in 1991. A former journalist, his short fiction has appeared in *Isaac Asimov's Science Fiction Magazine*, and the anthology *What Might Have Been?* vol. 3: *Alternate Wars*. Mr. Steele was nominated for the John W. Campbell Award for best new writer in 1989/90.

Harry Turtledove

Harry Turtledove combines excellent writing skills with his extensive knowledge of ancient history in such novels as his four-part historical fantasy series (*The Misplaced Legion, An Emperor for the Legion, The Legion of Videssos,* and *Swords of the Legion,* all published in 1987), which received widespread critical acclaim, as did his novels *Agent of Byzantium* (1987), *Noninterference* (1988), and *A Different Flesh* (1989). In addition, he is known as an *Analog*-style writer of hard sf short stories. His latest books include *A World of Difference* (1990) and *Krispos Rising* (1991).

Lawrence Watt-Evans

Lawrence Watt-Evans is equally at home with science fiction, fantasy, and horror writing. Since the publication of his first novel, *The Lure of the Basilisk*, in 1980, he has produced some fifteen books, including the bestselling *The Misenchanted Sword* (1985), *Denner's Wreck* (1988), *Nightside City* (1989), and the excellent horror novel *The Nightmare People*. His short story, ''Why I Left Harry's All-Night Hamburgers,'' was nominated for a Nebula and won the Hugo Award in 1988.